PAPER MOON

A Novel

Rehana Munir

HarperCollins *Publishers* India

First published in India by
HarperCollins *Publishers* in 2019
A-75, Sector 57, Noida, Uttar Pradesh 201301, India
www.harpercollins.co.in

2 4 6 8 10 9 7 5 3 1

P-ISBN: 978-93-5357-400-0
E-ISBN: 978-93-5357-401-7

Typeset in 10.5/14 Warnock Pro at
Manipal Technologies Limited, Manipal

Printed and bound in India by
Manipal Technologies Limited, Manipal

*With deep gratitude to the late poet and professor,
Eunice de Souza.*

For Kausar, who makes things possible.

CHAPTER ONE

The rainy July afternoon demanded sleep, and the professor wasn't helping matters. Fiza looked out of the covered terrace classroom and saw the famed St. Xavier's College quadrangle transformed into a hazy watercolour, all blurred lines and dripping corners. The Indo-Gothic architecture made for a nice anachronism in a city that was fast giving itself over to haphazard newness. The lecture was interminable – political satire in Dryden's 1681 biblical poem *Absalom and Achitophel* – and all she could think about was getting into a semi-dry compartment at Churchgate station. Would the 1.13 p.m. slow train to Andheri from Platform 1 be a reasonable hope? But even the thought was squelchy. And there was one more thing to do before the college day ended. Something that she didn't let her thoughts drift towards for fear of it taking over.

When the electric bell sounded after fifty wasted minutes, Fiza finally allowed herself the luxury of excitement. Down the stairs, past the reference library and further down, turning left for the lending library. It was, as was usual for that time of day, empty. Nothing more than a stray studious sort finding comfort in musty aisles. But, generally speaking, the lending

1

library was less a place for the wise than the wayward. Dim lighting. Hidden corners. Friendly chairs. Sleepy librarian. If you were labouring over an assignment or cramming before an exam, the solemn reference library was your hangout. *This* was a hideout for hurried embraces and long-drawn sighs.

'You're late,' a voice softly accused from the poetry aisle. Fiza moved quietly in the direction of the war poets, towards a tall figure wearing too much aftershave. Clasping his wristwatch with the glow-in-the-dark markings, she countered, 'What, by a minute?' 'By a heartbeat,' he whispered. Fiza rolled her eyes in her usual manner – romantic declarations were a strict no-no, unless they were wry or ironic, and this one was decidedly cheesy. He knew this about her and used it to get under her skin. It was all he was allowed to get under. And it had been what, two months since they'd been 'borrowing books'? He slid the Wilfred Owen he had picked up back into its slot between Kipling and Sassoon.

A sudden shuffle of feet from the next aisle made Fiza and Dhruv look up. Fiza's French teacher, the charming Ms Mirza, cast a glance at the two. 'Bonjour, comment ça va?' she asked breezily. 'Ça va très bien,' Fiza blurted out, glad of the six-inch distance from the wearer of the aftershave. Having exhausted her French, and her powers of repressing a blush, Fiza moved to the next aisle – Elizabethan Drama – followed by her lanky Romeo. 'God, did you empty the bottle out?' she complained when they were out of the mademoiselle's earshot. 'And I can *still* smell the smoke on your shirt.' 'And on my breath?' he said, grabbing her close under the watchful gaze of Marlowe's *Faustus*.

That library scene of 1996 replayed itself with slight and dramatic variations over the next five years. Stolen kisses in the chapel and bad Chinese in the canteen. Showdowns in the woods and making up in the arches. Romance flowed out of the gargoyles on the roof and broadcast itself in the multimedia room. Scratched itself onto desks and scrambled itself in the hostel mess. The days were packed with little pleasures and exaggerated pains straight out of an ancient manual of young love, recast with debutant actors.

This charmed life was contained within the few kilometres in and around St. Xavier's College, Bombay, where Fiza Khalid and Dhruv Banerjee went through time like it was in endless supply. An Arts degree made few demands on them, and so they escaped as many lectures as they could, while avoiding the dreaded blacklist. Matinee shows at Sterling cinema and peanut-crunching evenings at Marine Drive. Nawabi chicken pizza at Intermission Restaurant in Metro cinema and blazing afternoons at Azad Maidan.

Dhruv had always been serious about his cricket and so Fiza joined him at the ground for the odd match or net session. She liked seeing him in his muddied whites, smiling proudly at her from a distance. She had once seen him struggle against Anjuman-i-Islam's famed bowling in a tournament decider and said earnestly in private, 'Perhaps you could look at moving your feet a bit more?' Dhruv had laughed derisively. 'Riiight. Anything else, coach? Grip okay?' 'Ass,' she'd said and walked off. He'd taken on the advice, though, he admitted in a soft moment. After the cricket, there was pav bhaji at Khao Gully. And that bizarre neembu paani, blitzed with ice, chaat masala and industrial amounts of sugar.

At Strand Book House at Fort, the old Mr Shanbhag presided over affairs, a smiling angel in a business suit. Famous for his remaindered books sold at studently prices, he found good profits in big volumes, and everybody won. Always on a tight budget, Fiza had developed a nose for libraries, sniffing her way around yellowing books. At Strand, she could never afford much more than the Great Artist series, ₹25 per ragged copy, which she would pore over for days. Renoir and van Gogh, Rembrandt and Monet – a buffet of artistic appetizers that left her hungry for more. For the main course, there were the trusty pavement bookstalls at Fort with their dog-eared treats.

Fiza had picked up most of her college texts here, from Shakespeare's sonnets to G.V. Desani's *All About H. Hatterr*. And Dhruv had gifted her innumerable books off the street, too. In the early days, he tried to impress her with Schopenhauer and Naipaul. When the relationship had reached a level of comfort, Harry Potter and Tintin made an appearance. When comfort had turned to confidence, he'd advanced to science fiction. She protested but he persisted. The books remained untouched.

Now there was one bookshelf on her wall that was filled with books gifted by Dhruv. The inscriptions told the story of their romance. From short, scratchy addressals to flowing tributes. From 'Fiza' to 'Fizzy' to 'Fez'. On their second Valentine's Day together, he'd gifted her a sentimental greeting card and a giant pink teddy bear, just to get a rise out of her. Those last two she'd done away with. But the little flower that accompanied them, she had kept quietly pressed between the pages of Vikram Seth's *The Golden Gate*. The last thing she'd want to be accused of was sentimentality. Especially by Dhruv.

Most weekdays, Fiza would return home from college and walk straight into the kitchen of her mosaic-tiled Bandra flat. She'd make two cups of adrak chai and knock at her mother's door through which strains of music and smoke would invariably be sneaking out. Growing up, Fiza had been in awe of Noor, the way she owned any room she walked into. She'd spent twenty-five years singing jazz and the blues, till the heavy smoking had taken its toll. In her glory days, she could slip from Nina Simone to Farida Khanum in one gulp of single malt. It's what Fiza's father had fallen for when he'd first met Noor.

Years ago, in one of her rare forthcoming moments, Noor had told Fiza all about those heady first days with him. It all began at the Royal Bombay Yacht Club, a short distance from the Gateway of India, at a mutual friend's engagement. Noor had agonized over which sari she should wear that evening. Struggling to find hotel gigs, she would spend every spare rupee on records and often find herself without presentable clothes for the performances that did spring up.

'It was a deep purple and gold Benarasi I'd swiped from your nani. But when I got up, the pallu got caught in a nail between two wooden seats of the second-class compartment. My heart stopped. But I could do nothing. Bharti had warned me about reaching late – even said she'd pay for my cab, but it was my socialist phase, don't ask. She had boasted to all of Mahesh's friends about my singing,' Noor recalled with remarkable clarity.

'So then?' Fiza asked, horrified. She tried to soak it all in – the room, the people, even the smell of the flowers. There was so little she knew about her father; she couldn't afford to miss any detail.

'It was too late to do anything. So I walked straight to the bar, leaving the ripped pallu trailing, gulped down a whisky and grabbed the microphone.'

'*And*?' Fiza asked with widening eyes and quickened breath.

'And I don't remember much else. That glass somehow kept refilling itself and the mike stayed in my hand. The last thing I remember that night is your father driving me back home in his white Fiat.'

'Did he...?'

'Take advantage of my drunkenness?' Noor asked with mock horror. Fiza wouldn't dare ask something so coarse, but her mother somehow had a knack for doing the heavy lifting in any conversation.

'Well?'

'No, he didn't. He brought me home, waited to see the light come on in the corner window and left. Bharti later told me how they'd alternated whisky with glasses of water all evening – explains why I didn't fall flat on my face.'

'Not too bad, then.'

'Uff, it was horrible. She said I refused to leave the stage. That I'd upstaged her at her own engagement. I don't think she's forgiven me for that yet.'

'Bharti Aunty is too sweet. She'd never hold a grudge like that.'

'Fizu, you think all the world is sweetness and light. Just because you are.'

This is where Fiza would tune out of any conversation – the point at which she was complimented. To her, it always seemed like a terrible mistake, an undeserved grace. Noor steered the conversation back to safety.

'How's the aftershave boy?' Noor had picked up on exactly the thing that bothered Fiza about Dhruv. She often made jokes about the trail of musk he left in his wake whenever he visited. She even examined the books he gifted Fiza, passing wry comments about the choice of author and title, which struck Fiza as being exceptionally canny. Why did she have to share so much with her mother? It made her feel like a pale imitation of the real thing.

'Dhruv is good. He's sent in his university applications.'

'Hmm. So then? Long-distance romance? Chat on the computer?' Noor asked playfully. ICQ, the Internet chat application, was becoming a lifeline for young far-flung lovers, hanging by a temperamental TCP/IP account.

'We'll see. He'll visit. Plus, it's just a two-year programme.'

'I still don't see why you can't apply, too.'

'Just because he is?'

'No, because you're smart. And with your record, you'll get in easily.'

Fiza didn't have a response. Her mother was right, but she just didn't have it in her to make the big push. The form and the loans. The GRE monster, with maths for fangs. It was all too daunting. Dreams were for other people. She was content with reality. After all, it hadn't been too bad for her, despite the early setbacks. Her mother had copped the blows, and now they had a system – a system of containment.

Like most people who spent their days together, soul-searching conversations between the pair were few. Noor seemed to have spent her vast enthusiasm for life on her singing career. The days of live performances long behind her, she conducted a radio show for AIR FM Rainbow – golden oldies and evergreen classics. Fiza tuned into the

show religiously when her mother first took over from the
ancient RJ who had famously collapsed at the console one
evening. 'He was playing "*What a Wonderful World*"! It
played on loop five times before someone noticed and called
in,' Noor would repeat with glee every time the story came
up. In the early days, Fiza even rang in with requests. But
then she lost interest. She could see how it killed Noor to
sit in a dark studio, speaking to the void, peddling other
people's voices. But the options for singers past their prime
were few.

Both she and Noor were grateful to the job for keeping the
home afloat, if not Noor's ambitions. They were comfortable,
too, in their home. It had belonged to Noor's parents, who'd
died within a year of each other when Fiza was just two –
one of heart disease and the other of heartache. Noor's older
brother, Faraz, was settled in Sydney, married to the aloof heir
of a pharmaceutical empire. He had left home when he was
just a teenager, and Fiza had never met her cousins, Emma
and Nicole, both of whom were doctors. Cursory greetings
around birthdays and Christmas were the slender threads
that connected the distant families.

Fiza had spent plenty of time trying to piece together the
days that Noor would rarely speak about. Thoughts of her
father would come charging into her brain like an occupying
army at the most inconvenient of times. All she knew was that
he'd left a few months after she'd been born, unable to cope
with her mother's post-partum depression. Noor's closest
friends – Bharti and her husband Mahesh – were the only
link between Noor and the outside world those days. Too
cut up to even eat or sleep, Noor's violent episodes would
often end with smashed plates and broken records. It was

Bombay of the early 1980s, and the upheavals in the mind and body of a new mother weren't deemed science-worthy. The options for medication were few, considering she was breastfeeding. It came down to yoga and meditation, and inevitably, homeopathy. Noor even tried some of the much-touted little pills. She still asked friends to get her some when they visited their homeopaths. She said she treated them as guilt-free alcoholic dessert.

Fiza simply couldn't wrap her head around her father, Iqbal. The great walkout followed by radio silence, a metaphor that fitted the situation all too well. All Noor would say on the subject was: 'He had other plans for his life.' When asked why he chose to have a wife and child instead of pursuing those plans, Noor replied, 'You were my choice, not his.'

The words echoed in Fiza's head like some kind of Greek chorus of doom. Choice or not, there she was. And what of duty? Of feeling? Whenever she probed further, she ran the risk of opening the Pandora's box of Noor's mind. And she'd learnt early not to unsettle the delicate balance of her relationship with her mother. There were hidden depths there, which Fiza wasn't sure she was strong enough to deal with. On good days, Noor was an artiste in exile, looking at life telescopically, wryly. On bad days, she was a soul trapped in limbo, bitter about her fate. The key, for Fiza, was to stay rooted in *real* things. In sharing cups of chai and making grocery lists. Logistics, she found, could help keep the demons of her mother's past at bay.

Now she switched on the TV and ran through the channels, finally settling on one. A third of the movie had already played, but they'd watched it a few times earlier. The good old Shop Around the Corner, run by feisty bookseller Kathleen Kelly. A well-loved store that she had inherited from her mother, but was threatened by Joe Fox, heir to a cut-throat book empire. Meg Ryan's Elizabeth Bennet vs Tom Hanks's Fitzwilliam Darcy. Mother and daughter settled into the sagging couch, comforted by a make-believe world where the heroine wins even when she loses.

The much-feared Y2K, with its promise of digital doom, was ending in a whimper. Fiza was at a New Year's Eve party with Dhruv and his family at their glittering farmhouse in Alibaug, Sting blaring out of the fancy speakers.

> *Turn the clock to zero, sister*
> *You'll never know how much I missed her*
> *I'm starting up a brand new day*

'So it's decided?' asked Deb Banerjee, a few minutes before midnight. 'About?' wondered Dhruv disingenuously. His father held Fiza's hand, filled with liquor-fuelled love. He'd run an advertising agency successfully for years. He even spoke like ad copy, in short, goal-oriented sentences.

Fiza smiled weakly. In their five years together, they'd never had 'the discussion'. Dhruv sometimes hinted at their married life together, but Fiza always brought the conversation back to the here and now. Dhruv's mother chimed in, 'I say, have a small engagement ceremony before you leave. Just family and close friends at Tolly Club. You kids decide the rest. Take your time.'

Dhruv looked expectantly at the clock. Why had the year slowed down to a crawl right at the home stretch? And this was the first time that his mother had actually suggested a venue. The elite Calcutta club where his uncles played golf, while his aunts chatted about Tagore and tussars over ham sandwiches and shandy.

He wished they would stop and would ordinarily have asked them to. But this wasn't exactly the time for a confrontation. In fact, was there any need for one? He loved her, she loved him. The families were supportive. By early next year, he'd have left for New York, in time for the spring semester. Even if the funding didn't come through, his parents would pitch in. And if he had this part of his life sorted, the rest would fall into place. A good solid couple of years in the Big Apple: writing, thinking, living. Some work assignments while there. And, eventually, a lead into a paper or magazine, using his father's excellent contacts.

The uncooperative clock finally struck twelve. All around, people hugged and kissed exaggeratedly under sprawling trees twinkling with fairy lights. Dhruv and Fiza held each other for a moment, his intended kiss turning into a peck. As usual, she'd swiftly turned her head away at the last moment to forestall any public display of affection. But he was determined not to let the moment slip.

'It's the Space Odyssey year, Fez. Finally.'

'Yes. Happy Year of Kubrick.'

'Will you marry me?'

'Good one, Skywalker,' she laughed, exhausting her science fiction repertoire with the Star Wars reference.

'No, really.'

'No, really what?'

'Will you?'

Fiza suddenly felt like she'd walked through the looking-glass into an alternate reality, and yet, what was troubling her was that the question was all too real. *Would* she marry him? She. Him. Marry. Something didn't fit.

'I don't think this is the time or place ...' Fiza replied limply.

'What? It's perfect. Anyone else would even find it romantic.'

'It's kind of ... sweet ... but ...' she trailed off.

'Kind of sweet? I'm not offering you lemonade, Fez. Even for you, this is a bit cold.'

'I'm *not* cold!'

'Okay. You're the picture of warmth and tenderness. So, will you?' Dhruv persisted. A bejewelled friend of his mother's caught hold of his arm. 'You two love birds are so MFEO!' she chirped and flew off.

'Excuse me. I'm going and getting another drink,' Fiza said, looking to escape the inescapable moment.

'Classy move.'

'Why're you being so mean?'

'I just proposed marriage and you're going to refill your glass. I don't mean we announce it right this minute, of course. But is it something you're interested in at all?' Dhruv asked with rapidly growing insecurity about Fiza's reply.

'Can't we discuss this when we're alone? This is *so* not the place—'

'Fez, it's never the right place or time for you. You're even turning me into this – this...'

'Go on. Unfeeling robot?'

'This unenthusiastic ... settler. You settle for everything. And you want me to settle, too. And every time I reach for something more, something fantastic, something romantic – New York, marriage, whatever – you dismiss it with laughter.'

'And yet you choose to propose to me,' Fiza shot back.

'I love you. And I thought we'd reached a point where the relationship could actually go somewhere.'

'*Go* somewhere? Like it's public transport?' She had read that phrase somewhere, but was in no mood to cite sources.

'Very good, Fez. Your snarkiness quotient is rising by the minute. All I'm saying is, it's a good time to do this.'

'Why? Because you're going off to NYU? I'm at university, too. How come *that* isn't a landmark?' Fiza said with a defiance that only Dhruv provoked in her.

'You know that's different. Stop stalling. Answer the question.'

'So if I say no to your proposal, it's because I'm cold and unfeeling? How about I'm not ready, huh?'

'That's just a cop out. You're never ready for anything. Too scared to apply to universities abroad, to ask your mom a question about your father, to say yes to me.'

'Okay. I have an answer,' she said, riled by the cruel reference to her parents.

'I'm all ears.'

'No! Because you're *not* the centre of my universe, Dhruv. And I get the feeling that if we were to end up together, you'd expect to be.'

'Is it too much to expect? You're the centre of mine.'

'No, Dhruv. *You're* at the centre of your universe. I'm welcome so long as I fit in with the plan. *Your* plan. Engagement. University. Marriage. Move abroad. Kids. Home. Dog.'

'Sounds about right to me.'

'That's the problem. I have one plan at the moment. I want to refill my drink. And the rest is up in the air.'

Fiza walked off, leaving Dhruv more confused than disappointed. How could she not want those things? She left wondering how he could assume she would.

And just like that, the relationship unravelled. Ripped out of the comforting daily routine of college, it came apart at the slightest tug. Fiza spent the days after the proposal in deep introspection about the relationship. Dhruv, meanwhile, was already checking out of it, partly due to the embarrassment of rejection and partly given the prospect of starting a new life in New York. If he couldn't have it all with Fiza, he didn't want it at all. Finally, it was an email that did it.

Fez,

I think enough time has passed since that New Year's fiasco. It's time to put things behind us and move on. It's clear we see things differently. And it will only get worse once I leave. So it's best that we end this here. Let's not make a mess.

I'm over the whole proposal bit; so don't stress about it. I guess we should keep some distance till I leave. Just a couple of months to go. Let's avoid unnecessary chats or meetings. It will only complicate things.

I wish you well.

Dhruv

It hurt Fiza deeply that this message was delivered electronically, in language that would do Hemingway proud. After all those inscriptions and dedications that documented their time together, the least she had expected was a thoughtful, handwritten letter.

CHAPTER TWO

Life hasn't really begun yet, thought Fiza one still afternoon on the bus to the Kalina University campus. And yet, here was this ending – so final. So surprisingly hurtful. She really did love him. But was she simply too afraid to get into the mess of real life? But who defined 'real life'? To Dhruv, the future was to be invented. She, on the other hand, thought of the future as something to respond to. In this, she admired Dhruv; he was so sure of what he wanted. Always chasing after something. Shaping the world to fit his size.

The MA was a natural progression after her BA. It allowed Fiza another couple of years in the safety of books. There would be time to find a way into the outside world, but she was in no hurry to get there. She had already begun contributing to household expenses, writing short pieces for websites and magazines, and taking up editing jobs. She sometimes tutored students in English language and literature. It wasn't much, but it pointed to future options.

After the decorative pillars and echoing corridors of her college, the university campus was a letdown, with dreary government-style buildings dotting an unkempt forest. But it wasn't the facilities that made students lose their enthusiasm;

it was the faculty. The English department professors ranged from the criminally dull to the hopelessly inept. Luckily, a bunch of German exchange students livened up proceedings with their enthusiasm for theatre. One quiet afternoon, the towering David from Hamburg peeped into Fiza's classroom. Her first impression was: Hugh Grant, only taller and younger. She was disappointed to find out that he lodged on campus with his charming wife. Twenty-two years old and already married! If this was a new European trend, she heartily disapproved.

The Germans were running auditions for a play, a Shakespearean parody put together in an attempt to beat the campus blues. Fiza would never have considered it, but David was adamant she read for the lead role: they were desperate to find someone who'd carry off the English dialogue, and that was one skill she couldn't say she didn't have. So, every afternoon after lectures, she'd meet the theatre bunch in a disused classroom. It rid her of the awful feeling of stagnation that the campus – and her life at that moment – evoked.

After rehearsals one Friday afternoon, Fiza was lucky to catch the double-decker bus just pulling up at the stop. Settling into the much-vied-for first seat on the upper tier, she plunged into *Catch-22*, prescribed for her American Literature class. Luckily for Joseph Heller, the novel was being taught by visiting faculty. Earlier, in a rare talkative moment in class, she'd said out loud, 'There's so much pathos in the character of the chaplain. He's a man of faith, struggling with doubt. That's so difficult.' Mrs Ghosh, the live-wire guest lecturer, had launched into a spirited discussion based on that comment. She had that special teacherly talent for spinning wisdom out of seeming banalities.

Fiza got off the bus and headed straight to the coconut seller, Ismail, who conducted business from the streetlamp outside her building. As he beheaded a coconut with practised ease, she noticed he'd given his hair a fresh coat of jet-black dye. Fiza had always admired his confidence, his cheerfulness. Looking at the world through one good eye, Ismail found himself equal to it.

Up in her flat, she found her mother's room empty, and a sticky note on the fridge: 'At Bharti's for dinner. Maria's made cutlets for you. XX'. Fiza headed straight for the prawn cutlets, but was waylaid by the ringing phone.

'Hello?'

'Hello. Is that Fiza Khalid?'

'Yes. May I know who's speaking?'

'D.K. Batliwala.'

'Sorry, do I...?'

'No, but I'm a friend of Iqbal's. Your father.'

Fiza instinctively raised her guard.

'I would have asked to speak to Noor, but your father insisted that you heard it first.'

'Hear what?' Fiza uttered, with a calmness she didn't feel.

'Iqbal is ... gone. He had been ill for a while, and he was prepared for it. The end was painless. Everything happened according to his wishes. I'm so sorry.'

Her mother's words flashed quickly through her mind: 'He had other plans for his life.' Even death was a planned affair.

'I'm sorry, this must be very sudden and difficult—' the voice continued tentatively.

'Thank you for informing me, but I'm not sure what I can do about any of this,' Fiza cut in.

'His body has been donated to cancer research, as per his wishes. He didn't want any ceremony or memorial.'

That was precious information about her father. He was a man who had no wish for ritual or mourning. He *was*.

'Can we meet sometime soon? There's an important matter concerning your father. When would you be free to meet? Are you still at Little Flower?'

The ease with which the stranger just mentioned her building's name discomfited Fiza even further. Pulling out her voice from somewhere dark and deep, she murmured, 'I'm sorry. I need to speak to my mother before we can—'

'Yes, of course. I understand. Please let Noor know D.K. called. Will you take down my number, please?'

Fiza distractedly pulled an electricity bill, still in its envelope, from the centre table. *Have to pay this soon*, she made a mental note. Her mind was pretending that things were okay, that there was no need to panic. The phone pen was missing, so she fished out a kajal pencil from her bag, robotically writing the number she heard on the other end of the line.

'You can call any time between ten and six on a weekday, beta. I'll wait for your call. And once again, I'm sorry to give you this news.'

Fiza put the receiver down and gazed blankly at her living room. Everything seemed slightly altered, vaguely menacing. She considered calling her mother at Bharti Aunty's, but found the thought to be absurd. Giving her mother information about her father – this was not how it worked. She walked to her room and got into bed, unsure whether her limbs and faculties were still at her command. Fiza didn't know how much time had passed before her mother walked into the dark room, wondering why the food in the kitchen had remained untouched.

'Fizu, all okay? Are you ill, beta?' she asked, turning on the light.

Fiza hadn't noticed, but her face was wet with tears. She would later wonder what the tears meant. Pain or anger? Regret or disappointment? At that moment, all she felt was an intense estrangement from her own life and body. It was like losing a loved one in a dream.

'What is it, Fiza? Something to do with Dhruv? Beta, you can still work it out. Nothing's really final—'

'I received a phone call from someone called D.K.,' Fiza began.

'D.K.? D.K. Batliwala? Iqbal's friend?'

'Yes.'

'What does he want all of a sudden?' Noor asked belligerently.

'I don't know yet.'

'He called for you?'

'Yes. Though he mentioned you, too.'

'*And*? Fizu what's with the suspense?'

'He said … he said my father was dead.'

Noor sank into Fiza's bed and clutched her daughter's foot in a desperate gesture. 'What?' she whispered.

'Cancer, I think. Or that's what his body is donated to. Research. There was no ceremony. He didn't want rituals.' The words were coming out scrambled. She didn't want to leave a single detail out. Didn't want to leave anything in.

Taking both of Fiza's feet in her hands, Noor said, 'I'm so sorry, Fizu, but he never once said he wanted to meet or to include you…'

For the first time since she had heard the news, it occurred to Fiza that it would be painful for her mother to hear it. Seeing her mother hurt, voice choking with unidentifiable emotions, Fiza snapped out of her stupor.

'I know,' she said, still unable to move.

'Did D.K. leave a number?' Noor asked, not sure what else she needed to hear.

'Yes. He said there's something he wanted to discuss with me...'

'Oh. I hope Iqbal hasn't left any debt ...' she said with characteristic caution.

'No, it didn't sound like that,' Fiza replied, unused to hearing her mother say her father's name.

'What did it sound like?'

'I'm not sure.'

'I should call Bharti,' Noor said and walked out.

Fiza was relieved to see her mother leave the room. This was not a scene they had rehearsed even in their thoughts. And yet, it had always been a looming possibility. The initial shock was already giving way to deep melancholy.

It was 10 a.m. and Fiza was dialling the number she had jotted down the previous evening.

'Hello, is this Mr Batliwala?'

'Hello, Fiza? And you can call me D.K. Everybody does.'

His voice sounded friendly today, even cheerful. She wondered how long it had been since her father's death.

'If it is convenient, I can pick you up from your home today at twelve.'

'I can meet you at your office or wherever directly—' Fiza replied stiffly.

'No, that's all right. I'll be passing that way anyway. So I'll see you downstairs. How is Noor? How did she deal with the news?'

Fiza was still uncomfortable sharing private details with this near-stranger. 'She's okay. Yes, I'll see you at twelve.'

'Okay. And please carry some ID proof, if you can. It will help to get things started. Bye, then.'

So this *was* about legalities. Could it be that her father had been in financial trouble, like her mother had feared? But the conversation with D.K. was far too pleasant for that to be the case. Inheritance was out of the question. He hadn't even bothered to say hello in two decades. Fiza put her voter's ID and passport in her bag and waited for noon.

A new thought entered Fiza's mind for the first time since hearing the difficult news the previous evening: should she email Dhruv? They hadn't spoken since he had left the previous month, and she wasn't sure this was the best ice-breaker. The thought of Kavya, her college friend, crossed her mind, but this news was too sudden to spring on her, and completely without foreshadowing. Fiza didn't yet have the language to deal with the situation. There was just no template for this kind of thing.

D.K. was promptly at her gate at twelve, waiting in his grey Hyundai Accent. He opened the front door for her and greeted her warmly – like she were the daughter of a close friend. He looked distinguished and agreeable, something in his manner suggesting compassion.

'So ... you're studying?'

'Yes. I'm at Bombay University, doing an MA.'

'Oh. Good, good. What are you studying?'

'English literature.'

'Ah, that's wonderful. Iqbal used to worry you would be one of those MBA types. But he hoped you'd be a book-lover. He was banking on it, almost,' he carried on familiarly.

Fiza was part bewildered and part resentful. Her father had conducted casual conversations about her, speculating about her interests while never once reaching out to her in over twenty years.

D.K. sensed her discomfort and changed the topic. 'Is Noor well?'

'Yes, thanks. She's a bit—'

'I can imagine. But she's a strong woman. And she's raised you well.'

There it was again. Him speaking about her like he knew her. Knew what it had been like for Noor.

They were soon pulling over at an old commercial complex in Prabhadevi. Up in his wood-panelled office, D.K. got straight to the point.

'Fiza, this is going to come as a bit of a surprise to you – over and above the shock of Iqbal's...'

On high alert, Fiza gave nothing away with her expressions.

'Your father was a complex man. Too much reading and thinking. He was a perfectionist. If he didn't think he could do something well, he just gave it up and never looked back. He knew that was his biggest problem, and still...'

Fiza took a sip of the water placed before her, pretending this was a story she was hearing about strangers.

'He built a good life for himself. Even did well. But he was disturbed by – by what happened with Noor and you. He knew he had behaved...' D.K. looked up awkwardly, leaving the sentence trailing. 'But he was also sure that he was not capable of making amends.'

'He chose not to,' Fiza said, shaking off her superficial composure.

'Yes, you're entitled to your response. Anyway, I'm not here to fight a case for him, beta. At this point, all I'll say is he was a great friend of mine and leave it at that.'

'You asked me to carry an ID,' Fiza said, eager to escape the oppressive situation.

'Yes. But before that, I'd like you to listen very carefully. Your father was not a rich man. But he was wise with his money. And he had put away enough to fulfil a dream. He wanted to spend his retirement running a bookshop in Bombay. He loved Bombay till the end, even though he left,' D.K. said in a voice he was trying hard to keep steady.

At this point, Fiza experienced a swell of emotion even greater than when she had heard about his passing. *My father wanted to run a bookshop*, she recited in her head. This was something she found to be immeasurably sad and sweet.

'But he was a practical man. When he was diagnosed with cancer four years ago, he began to put all his finances together and even wrote a will. He left money for his brother and some of his other relatives in Bangalore, but he also put away a sum for the bookshop he had always wanted.'

Fiza was trying to keep up. She was used to piecing together her father's life using hard-won information gathered over years – a Frankenstein created out of scraps of her mother's memories. Now, here was a flood of facts she wasn't prepared for. He had lived in Bangalore. She had an uncle. Perhaps cousins. She tried not to let them settle in her brain.

'And you are the sole inheritor of that sum in his will.'

D.K. waited for the import of this statement to sink in, but all he got from Fiza was a silence imploring him to go on.

'Did you – should I … go over what I just said?'

'I'm sorry. Did you just say he's left me money to set up a bookshop?' Fiza stuttered.

'Yes. You've got it, then,' he smiled. 'Which is why I was relieved when you said you were studying literature.'

'And what if I weren't?'

'His wishes are just a suggestion. The money is yours, beta. Do what you like.'

'This is all too much. All together,' Fiza said after an uncomfortable pause.

'I know. And I'm sorry this news had to be delivered to you in this way. But now you need to decide if you want to...'

'Set up a bookshop with the money my father has left me,' she said slowly, as if repeating a line in a foreign tongue.

'That's right. If you like.'

Fiza lowered her face and held it in her hands. She was neither in control of the thoughts in her head, nor of the expressions on her face. And her hands had gone very cold.

CHAPTER THREE

When Fiza returned home, Noor was sitting on the chequered couch in the living room, which was unusual for her. She had always hated that bit of furniture, but felt duty-bound to keep it in the flat after her parents had died. Her father had built the couch when she was a teenager. In the early days of her romance with Iqbal, she would lie on it, phone wire twisting in her fingers as they chatted about Herbie Hancock's music and the trouble with Marxism. Now she was looking up at her daughter, waiting for news that she was sure wouldn't be good.

'So?' Noor asked even before Fiza could shut the door.

'Ma, can I have some water first, please?' Fiza responded with a hint of irritation. She walked up to the kitchen, poured out a glass of water from the jug and beat out two ice cubes noisily from a tray in the freezer. Then she walked straight into her room with the cold glass, needing the refuge.

'You have me worried, Fizu. This D.K. is very chaalu. He seems sweet and all, but he's very business-minded ...' Noor said, following her in.

'He's left me money to start a bookshop.'

Noor took a moment to let the information sink in. 'D.K.?'

'No, Ma. Not him. That would make no sense.'

'*Iqbal* left you money? Which bookshop? Why?'

Fiza hadn't yet arranged these thoughts in her head and so she wasn't able to present them neatly to her mother. For once, this was not about protecting Noor. In fact, it had nothing to do with her mother, if she had to break it down to its core. This was a development entirely to do with Fiza, and the implications of the fact were slowly beginning to form in her head.

'He ... Iqbal ... left me a sum in his will. He had wanted to open a bookshop in Bombay. But his illness took over. So he willed me the money. And that's all I know so far.'

Noor wore a confused look, veering towards incredulity. What was this bookshop business? Was this Iqbal's final scam? Years of practice had made Fiza a pro at decoding her mother's words, expressions and thoughts. She knew how to turn confusion to calmness. But at this moment, she didn't feel it was her duty to do so.

'What about his *real* family?' Noor asked coldly.

'I don't know. D.K. said something about his brother and others inheriting something. But they have nothing to do with this.'

'What does Salim think about this money being left to you? The brothers never got along,' she said in a voice hardening with remembered hate.

Fiza thought it best to ride this wave of her mother's bitterness and try not to let it interfere with how she felt about all of it. In her usual style, she broke it down in her head. Dead father. Saved money. Bookshop dream. No, this sounded too mechanical. *My departed father, with whom I had no contact my whole life, has bequeathed me a sum of money that he wished would go into setting up a bookshop.* Now here was a useful sentence, comforting in its remoteness. This she could work with.

Noor had left for her room unsatisfied with her inquisition. *If music blares out soon, things will be all right; if not, there will be trouble,* Fiza thought to herself.

She needed to speak to someone who had a clearer view of things. Fiza switched on her PC and modem, and waited for the floral chat icon to turn from yellow to green. It would be the middle of the night in NYC, but she hoped Dhruv would be up, surfing the net at those famous American speeds.

And there he was.

'Dhruv,' she typed gingerly. They hadn't spoken since that last, terse email.

A few moments of silence. Then an unexpected surge.

Dhruv: Fezzzzzzzzz

Fiza: ☺

Dhruv: Wassssuuuuuup

Fiza: Have you been drinking?

This was so not the tone she wanted the conversation to take. And yet.

Dhruv: Some. There was a frat party.

Fiza: Hmm. Those super-secret ones where you behead chickens and have orgies?

Dhruv: Nothing that exciting. What's up with you?

Fiza: Nothing. Just thought I'd say hello.

This conversation was a bad idea. The timing couldn't be more off, in every way.

Fiza: Okay, then. Goodnight.

Dhruv: Huh? You pop up like this after ages and then just leave?

Fiza: I said it's nothing. Just thought I'd say hi.

Dhruv: You're getting weirder by the day, man.

Fiza: Haha. Yes. Lucky you. 'Night.

She had done it again. Taken a spontaneous moment and overthought the joy out of it.

The next day, Fiza was back at D.K.'s office, more in command of herself. This time he had someone with him: her father's lawyer, Suleiman Merchant. He went into the legal implications of her inheritance with painful emphasis on every little detail, sagely nodding his grey head as he went along. The bottom line was: she would be given access to a fund from which she could make withdrawals as she wished.

'Okay. So who will supervise everything?'

D.K. smiled. 'Supervise what?'

'The account. And the money, once it's been withdrawn.'

'It's yours. We're just facilitating the process,' the lawyer assured her.

'But I know nothing about setting up bookshops!'

'I'm a mechanical engineer. Suleiman here is a corporate lawyer. I think you're best qualified,' D.K. explained.

'But I'm ... twenty-two.'

D.K. turned to Suleiman, who read the look and left the room on the pretext of a meeting. He then walked over to Fiza's seat and patted her on the head. This gesture from a near-stranger would have made her uncomfortable under other circumstances. But here was someone delivering a posthumous message from his friend, her father, and trying to allay her doubts.

'Beta, I know this is all a bit strange for you. But I feel so proud right now that Iqbal's daughter – Iqbal and Noor's daughter – has turned out to be ... so smart and confident. Sometimes life is kind. And you have to be kind to yourself.'

Fiza focussed her gaze on the little, pebbly water fountain sitting on a sideboard by the door, studiously avoiding eye contact with D.K. Was that coloured cellophane paper, or little electric lights at the bottom? She tilted her head slightly to find a telltale plug connected to the back of the contraption. So the fountain ran on electricity, she thought to herself, trying hard to avoid reacting to the kind words from the still-unfamiliar man.

'You don't have a deadline. This is yours,' D.K. continued, noticing Fiza's attention wandering. 'You can use it as and when you like. And if you need any help or guidance, we are always there. Iqbal was a good friend. A very good friend. And in his absence, I'll do anything you need.'

'Thank you, D.K.,' she finally muttered, wondering whether an absence could leave behind yet another absence. 'Where do I need to sign?'

The lawyer was called back into the room. Fiza presented her ID and bank documents. And in a few minutes, it was all done. She was the inheritor of a small fortune and a cherished dream.

Once the paperwork was dealt with, D.K.'s driver drove Fiza back home. Stepping out of the car into the rainy September afternoon, she wasn't keen on another intense exchange with Noor, but it was pouring outside. Still, she thought it best to stay away until Noor had to leave for the studio. She headed for the Gaiety-Galaxy-Gemini cinema complex close by, and walked into a show of the much-talked-about hit, *Dil Chahta Hai*. The movie had just begun, and Fiza treated herself to a packet of samosas and a choco cone ice cream.

After a couple of pleasurable hours at the familiar theatre, Fiza walked back home in a gentle drizzle. It was already dark when she reached Little Flower.

She walked up the two floors absently, in desperate need of a hot cup of chai, but even before she could get into her apartment, she heard the TV blaring.

'Did you hear?' Noor asked breathlessly as soon as Fiza walked in.

'What?' Fiza asked with rising dread.

'New York.'

The pictures on television were surreal. Two planes had crashed into the iconic Twin Towers of the World Trade Centre. There was smoke, panic and rubble everywhere. Screeching ambulances. Crying survivors. Catatonic reporters.

'New York ...' Registering the personal significance of the distant images, Fiza ran into her room. She turned on the computer while looking for a number for Dhruv's university. The strange conversation from the previous night was playing in her head like a bad dream. Clicking furiously, she realized she should ring Dhruv's parents to get some news, and to see how they were doing.

'Hello, Aunty, this is Fiza.'

'Hello, Fiza,' replied a lifeless voice at the other end. 'We haven't heard from him yet.' At this, the voice cracked. Fiza was unable to think of anything that would bring relief. In fact, she couldn't think of anything to say at all.

'Fiza?'

'Yes, Aunty. Is Uncle with you?'

'No, he's in Calcutta on work. My sister has come over.'

'Okay. Please take care of yourself. And I'm sure Dhruv will call you soon. We were chatting just last night...'

'What did he say? Did he say anything about his plans for today? Was he going out?' Mrs Banerjee asked desperately.

'No, Aunty, it was a very short conversation.'

'Okay, if there's anything you remember, please call. Maybe we can track him...'

Fiza immediately regretted telling Mrs Banerjee about their chat. She had provided fresh material for speculation, without being able to offer any solace.

'Yes, Aunty. Everything will be fine. Don't worry.'

'Yes, yes. Call me if you hear anything ... if you remember something...'

'Of course. Bye, Aunty.'

The pictures on TV were shocking. Nothing made any sense. Fiza tried her best to observe every face captured by the shuddering cameras. What was happening? Why wasn't Dhruv reachable? What day of the week was it? In a flash, the world had lost all meaning. But it wasn't the world that she was worried about at the moment. All she cared about was Dhruv. Why hadn't she spoken to him longer? Why didn't she tell him she missed him? Why was she not with him right now?

'Fizu, look. They're actually speaking to people on the scene,' Noor said over the screaming TV.

Fiza turned away. If she looked at the TV screen, he would appear. As if she was the one creating this horrible reality with every fresh thought and gesture. Noor relayed the stories to her anyway.

'Ma, please don't! It's horrible.'

'You have to face reality.' This bewildered Fiza. How could one get instantly accustomed to a horror such as this? Noor was beyond reckoning.

Just then the phone rang and Fiza rushed to lift the receiver.

'Hello?'

'Hello, is that Fiza?'

'Yes, Aunty.'

'Fiza, he's okay. He went off to Staten Island for the afternoon. He's fine. He rang from a booth after hearing the news. He's okay,' the voice said, choking with emotion.

'Oh, thank god. Thank you, Aunty. This is just the best news ...' she mumbled as the TV kept flashing brutal images accompanied by a frenzied commentary.

Noor shut her eyes in relief and put the TV on mute.

'I haven't been able to breathe these last few hours! Tell that Dhruv I've never prayed like this for anyone in my life. And I don't even remember how to pray. I just kept chanting something.'

'I'll send him an email,' Fiza replied, unable to prolong the moment of relief. For her, the crashing towers had brought back the blood-soaked memories of the Bombay riots chillingly back to life.

The next few days at the university were a blur. Fiza was lost in a reverie, going through the motions of her workday with minimum involvement. The terror attacks consumed her thoughts night and day. And within the greater horror, she relived the anxious moments before hearing from Dhruv's mom. She tried to assess what her feelings were at that time, but all she got was a mass of confused emotions. She couldn't quite classify them under love. Sure, Dhruv had broken it off with her. But she wasn't the least bit inclined to renew the relationship – even after the time apart, the distance between them, and the 9/11 scare – she was sure of that.

'I am an invisible man,' the professor droned on, a few weeks after that dark September day. Mulk Raj Anand's *Untouchable*, filled with the angst of centuries of caste oppression, was the text of the semester. Fiza tried to focus her thoughts on loftier matters than her thwarted romance, but a few words into the professor's monotone, she began to drift away again. This time, she was summoned by fantasies dominated by books. Shelves filled with volumes of Faber & Faber poetry, which she had never been able to afford. The elegant grey spines of Vintage Classics. The cheery orange of Penguin. She saw her future like an abstract painting – a swirl of colours and shapes.

The bell rang and the class emptied out like a train compartment at Churchgate station at 9 a.m. Students dispersed, some moving to the next lecture in another classroom, others heading to the insipid canteen for half-cooked aloo bhaji with dry rotis. From across the empty room, Kavya Dwivedi flashed Fiza a smile. She had been together at college with her and Dhruv, the trio hanging out together after lectures every other day. Fiza assumed Kavya had heard about the break-up from Dhruv – Kavya had sent her a thoughtful SMS mentioning it – and wondered whether she should share her big news about the inheritance. *But what if this is some elaborate hoax?* Fiza thought to herself absurdly. The paperwork was done and she had no reason to doubt any of it. But who was to say real life wouldn't catch up with a second plot twist to cancel out the first? This was not the time for unbridled optimism. There was never a time for unbridled optimism. She waved hurriedly to Kavya, pointing helplessly to her watch and yelling, 'I'll call you!' Then she abandoned the rest of her classes and boarded the bus home. Back in her room, she switched on her computer to find a mail from Dhruv.

Fez,

Mom spoke to you, I heard. I was a bit surprised you didn't try to reach me yourself. I must have received dozens of calls and mails from random people. Anyway. I'm only writing because you sprung up on chat the other day. I think it's best you didn't try to reach me. It only unsettles me. Does no good.

D

This was getting to be a bore, thought Fiza. When does a relationship actually end? This mail was as good a point as any. There was nothing terrible about what Dhruv was saying. She had briefly thought she would lose him forever in the Twin Towers collapse, but when the danger had passed, so had her longing. That must count for something. Goodbye, Dhruv, she typed. The mouse hovered around the send option for a moment before she clicked on it. It felt like closure.

Instead of heading to university the next day, Fiza decided to pay her old college professor a visit. Frances D'Monte was the kind of person you never forgot. In her thirty-odd years as head of the English department at St. Xavier's College, she had inspired and petrified her students in equal measure. Frances had a sharp eye and an unforgiving tongue, one that burned through the pages of poetry anthologies and bruised the egos of generations of students. If you were one of her chosen ones in a classroom – like the crème de la crème of Miss Jean Brodie – the three years you spent studying Eng Lit would be life-changing. Fiza was one of the chosen few – the one to whom Frances gifted postcards from the Bombay Natural History Society, whom she treated to the occasional chicken omelette at Tea Centre in Churchgate, and even rang on the phone to ask if a particular lecture had gone well for the class. What made Frances special was her unwavering devotion to her students. She was acerbic at the slightest provocation, but if you were one of those struggling with course work, she would be gentle and accommodating. It was mostly the brash ones out to conquer the literary world that brought out the venom.

Fiza made sure she reached college during the long recess. It was when Frances would loom large over the staff room, smoking her Camel cigarettes, surveying the corridors of the college like an empress from her throne. A reclining wooden chair with cane matting had carried her not-insignificant weight – and stature – for decades.

'The prodigal daughter returns,' said the familiar nasal voice when Fiza got close.

Fiza smiled meekly – that's all she could muster in the presence of Frances. As fond as they both were of each other, there were invisible boundaries that Fiza dared not cross.

'How are you, ma'am?'

'As well as you can expect with Father Dan in charge,' Frances said with her trademark eye roll.

Father Daniel D'Costa was a Jesuit priest straight out of a Monty Python sketch. An exemplar of piety, he had recently banned the women of the college from wearing sleeveless clothes, and from walking too close to the boys. Fiza wondered if he had posted sentries at the chapel yet. Frances and Dan were as different from each other as one could imagine. While the professor encouraged students to reason and rebel, the priest called for obedience and deference. The result was an eternal war, with weapons that ranged from petty jibes to ugly politics.

'What's he gone and done now?' asked Fiza playfully.

'Oh, nothing that can't be fixed. Or broken.'

Fiza sensed there was a plot being hatched. The English department's annual festival, Ithaka, was where the entire year's bickering usually came to a head.

'Ithaka?'

Frances smiled. 'We're putting up Jean Anouilh's *Becket*. With the prostitute and the pope being played by the same actor.'

'That's ... that's just terrific, ma'am,' Fiza laughed.

'We do what we can. How's it going at Kalina? Bored to death yet?'

'Getting there. It's all so...'

'Pointless. Don't get me started with the UGC and the staff appointments. They've invited me to conduct a few guest lectures. Not sure I'll go this year. But then it's so close to my house...'

'Oh, please come, ma'am. It's like a morgue out there.'

Frances flicked some ash into the potted cactus at her feet and smiled wryly. 'It's good to see you. Paperwork at the office?'

'No, just to say hello.' There were still fifteen minutes to go before the bell would sound. But Frances always arrived outside her lecture room five minutes in advance. So Fiza had to be quick.

'Ma'am, there's some news I wanted to share with you.'

'Don't tell me you too have decided to get married and take up Chinese cooking and give birth to cabbages that I'll have to educate.'

'No such thing, ma'am,' Fiza laughed.

'That's a relief. The only time I hear from ex-students these days is when they're getting married to some investment banker or advertising guru. Or if they want me to get their child into college.'

'Then this won't disappoint you, I think. I've received some good news lately.'

'Hallelujah! Go on.'

'My father, whom I didn't know at all, recently passed away. And he's left me money to set up a bookshop here in Bombay.'

'I'm sorry about your father...'

'Thanks, ma'am, but like I said, I didn't know him.'

'I lost my father when I was three. I'm not sure I'm over him yet,' Frances replied.

Fiza paused at the thought. One of these days, she would have to confront this father business that everyone went on about. But she was always so busy dealing with the mother business.

'Anyway, this is wonderful news,' Frances said with the touch of warmth that lay just beneath the sardonic persona. It was what Fiza liked most about her.

'Thanks, ma'am.'

'So where are you looking to set it up?'

'Oh, I haven't given it a thought yet.'

'So you're not interested, then?' Frances said, an eyebrow slightly raised over her glasses.

'No, no! It's not that. It's all so sudden that I don't know what to make of it.'

'Dear heart, is the money in an account that you can access?'

'Yes. We sorted that out yesterday. My father's friend, who's handling this stuff, called in a lawyer. The money's legally mine,' Fiza said.

'So then it's real. Now you need to decide whether you want to set up a bookshop using the money that you have, or go visit Vegas, or donate it to a cat shelter. It's really quite simple. I'd love to sit and chat with you, but I've got a comatose second-year class to enthral with Gatsby.'

'Oh, yes, of course. I'm so sorry. Thank you for the chat.'

'Good to see you. It's lovely news. You'll be great at it,' Frances said, patting Fiza on the shoulder.

And just like that, the bookshop that had appeared out of thin air was turning into something real.

CHAPTER FOUR

*P*aper *Moon*. That's what she would call it. When Noor would sing the jazz tune to her when she was a little child, it made Fiza feel like everything was right with the world. They even had a record of the Ella Fitzgerald version.

> *Say it's only a paper moon*
> *Sailing over a cardboard sea*
> *But it wouldn't be make-believe*
> *If you believed in me*

As she grew up, Fiza began to find the song sentimental and annoying. It was too sweet and dreamy for her. But when she studied *A Streetcar Named Desire* in college, she came across a passage where the troubled Blanche DuBois sings the song in the bathtub. She sourced a copy of the Elia Kazan movie and sank deep into the dark and conflicted Southern world Tennessee Williams created. The 'silly' song took on a whole new meaning.

Now she was an adult on the cusp of fulfilling a dream that was not really hers, but which was beginning to work its magic despite all resistance. The song made sense all of a sudden. Noor's smoky vocals, the wistful lyrics, the perky melody, the piercing image of Blanche – something about it was right. Yes, she would call her bookshop *Paper Moon*.

That first phone call from D.K. and the events that followed had changed something in Fiza's home. In what had so far been a universe of two, a third, invisible presence had made itself felt. An alien landing in their territory, bearing strange gifts. What was odd for Fiza was how her world had suddenly expanded infinitely. And as a result, she felt light years away from Noor.

Noor was partly responsible for this change. Even now, weeks after the Day of the Phone Call, she hadn't fully processed the information. Years ago, she had found a place in her head to put Iqbal in, decided what to feel about it all. And in certainty, there was comfort. Now it was all back to the drawing board. Not only did his death mess up the equation, this unexpected generosity – if she could call it that – left her with no way to respond. To begin with, there was no one to respond to. Even in death, after all those years of distance, he had managed to unsettle her.

As October wound down to an oppressively hot end, the two women in the little apartment were renegotiating their relationship in countless small ways. Fiza could sense that the policy of containment now had to be replaced. In a single moment, her life had taken a dramatic turn. And she knew herself to be the least dramatic person of all. Noor had said nothing to express displeasure at the prospect of the bookshop. But Fiza realized that for the first time in her life, she needed more from her mother. She wanted active support, shared enthusiasm, a strong push. Noor, meanwhile, was behaving like Iqbal was wooing her daughter away from her, but she was too proud to articulate her insecurity. As always, it was Fiza's lot to interpret events occurring in her mother's world and head.

One evening, when the dry heat was waving a dusty goodbye, Fiza was watching nothing in particular on the television. She had spent hours surfing the net, haphazardly researching bookshops and publishers, and decided to call it a day. Noor walked in a little later, absently muttering something about Bharti's husband, Mahesh.

'What happened now?' Fiza asked, thankful for the opening into a neutral subject.

'Oh, same old. Not interested in anything but golf or the stock market. Worst use of money and spare time.'

Fiza smiled at the cliché. Golf had long been a point of contention in that marriage. To upset the stereotypical marital equation, Bharti was unusually fond of his parents. *Mahesh Uncle is a nice guy*, Fiza had always thought. Too much niceness, but too little joy.

'Bharti Aunty should go off on a holiday, maybe.'

'Hmm. I was telling her the same thing. She constantly stresses about Aunty and Uncle, even though they have enough help. And, touchwood, they're doing fine. Major guilt complex that woman runs on. Never able to do something just for herself.'

This was good. They hadn't spoken this much at a stretch in days. Fiza offered her mother the packet of masala chips that lay half-eaten in her lap.

'No, no. We went and had some paani puri at Elco. I needed to go to Khamisa. But they didn't have my size. So I've given an order.'

Khamisa was the old-fashioned lingerie store on Hill Road where bespectacled men sold austere cotton brassieres to exacting middle-aged women. The stitching around the cups, the adjustable straps, the conical contours – it was all an ode to the charmless 1980s. The old faithfuls often brought their young wards there for that most embarrassing of purchases – the beginner's bra. After that first awkward experience, the little women would invariably turn to less puritanical underclothes stocked in happier establishments.

Noor, for all her complexity, had simple tastes. Chaat and ganne ka ras. Paan and gajra. Rajnigandha and Bata. She was both easy and impossible to please. It was all about the moment.

'So ... how's it going with ... the bookshop plans?'

This was a big, big step forward.

'I'm still trying to make sense of it. Reading up on the business. It's going to take some time...'

'Hmm. And will D.K. help?'

'He has offered help – even his office, for the initial months. Which is quite sweet,' Fiza replied quickly.

Noor stiffened a bit. There was only so much she could offer at the moment. And now she had run out. 'So ... university?'

'Anyway the lectures are unbearable. And the play is done. A few months more, then the finals. I don't see any problem.'

'But your record—'

'I'm sure I'll do fine in the exams. Not like they make any difference, these scores.'

Before the conversation could spiral into darkness, Fiza flicked on a light. 'Do you want some naariyal paani? I'm going down to get some.'

'Hmm, okay. No malai.'

Fiza ran down the two short flights of stairs. On the pavement was the trusty Ismail, radio stuck to his ear. 'Ismail, two please. Ek mein patli malai.'

'I will give you, madam.'

'Very good, Ismail! You have learnt very fast.'

'I am trying, madam. Soon I am reading. Long books.' He said this with full conviction, which made Fiza check her laughter.

There was so much that she had learnt from the unlikely teacher herself. He had told her how it was best to drink straight from the coconut – straws were no fun. He had even taught her how to scrape off the malai on her own. Lean and dishevelled, an eye lost in a childhood accident, Ismail had moved to the pavement outside Little Flower some five years ago. The corner around the streetlamp was his kingdom. Neighbourhood watchmen, vendors and cleaners all collected around his moped with the attached cane basket for meals and chats. He somehow made his ragtag subjects feel like nothing was as bad as it seemed. At night, he pitched his mosquito net and stripped down to the bare minimum, sleeping soundly on the margins of an insomniac city. For some odd reason, Fiza always felt safe in her home with Ismail downstairs. The housing society had never had use for a watchman.

Back in the apartment, the TV had been switched off and Dave Brubeck was in the house. Jazz meant good things. Fiza poured the coconut water into a glass and offered it to Noor.

How many such glasses had been exchanged between mother and daughter over the years. Juice and milkshake, neembu paani and lassi. A drink for every occasion. A drink to make anything better.

'You know, Ismail's gotten really good with his English. He's so happy about it. It's great,' Fiza said, trying to make the most of the conversational breakthrough.

'Really? But what's the use?' Noor replied dourly.

'English is the first step. There are so many other jobs he can consider. Maybe even scale up his coconut business.'

'He sells coconuts. There's no scaling up. This English business is just timepass.'

Sensing another scrap coming on, Fiza deftly changed the subject. 'I visited Frances today.'

'Oh, that's nice. How's she doing?'

'She's okay. I told her about the bookshop.'

'Oh.'

'And she was really happy. Thought it was a great idea. Told me I shouldn't waste too much time thinking about it. Just start with the work,' Fiza said, finding the segue she was looking for.

'Okay, that's good for you.'

It was getting difficult to continue doing this. Fiza's natural compassion for her mother was somehow non-existent in this area. Why couldn't the woman for once work out her sordid emotions and make it easy for her child?

'So you're not happy with this whole thing?' Fiza finally asked, unable to keep the elephant out of the room.

'What thing?' Noor replied, stalling.

'You would prefer that I said no to the money and we went back to our old life?'

'Was it so bad, this "old life"?' Noor replied, giving up the pretence.

'But this has happened. There's no point ignoring it.'

'I'm not asking you to ignore it.'

'So what *are* you asking me to do, Ma?'

'Why must you fulfil that man's dream? Why can't you just do something else with the money? Or keep it in savings?'

'Because it's my dream, too.'

'*Your* dream? I've never heard about it until now!'

'I don't mean it literally.'

'Okay, so please explain to your *literal* mother what you mean.'

'Forget it.'

'This arrogance – this also comes from him.'

At this, Fiza got up from her chair and walked into her room, shutting the door behind her. Noor could not believe what had just happened. A conversation such as this would have ordinarily ended with Fiza calming things down and making them better.

Sitting in bed with her eyes closed and mind racing, Fiza had a quick and disturbing thought: *Am I shutting the door on my mother so I can let my father into my life?*

Excel sheets. She had tried to run far away from them, but they had finally chased her down. Fiza sat at an old, slow PC that D.K. had graciously allowed her to use at his office. She was finding it difficult to carry on with her research at home. Here, at least, things were peaceful. D.K. was visible on the other side of a glass cabin, smiling encouragingly between meetings and briefings. D.K. Batliwala ran a real estate business, but for his species, he showed some remarkably human traits. The safari suit, gold-plated pens and leather briefcase made him look the part. But he had always spoken to Fiza with great politeness, even affection. No slickness or subterfuge. She realized he was fulfilling a friendly obligation, but it was clear that he did it without the slightest strain of resentment or annoyance. *They must have been really good friends*, she thought, *Iqbal and he.*

The day was moving along unexceptionally. When Fiza looked up at the clock, it was already 3.30 p.m. – the time she would usually be heading home from university. Already, it seemed like those dull, empty days were from another era. She hadn't noticed just how jaded she had become. The heady days with Dhruv and the buzz of college had wound down to joyless months at the Kalina campus. It was impossible to go back to that now. The thought made her smile with relief.

Sipping the oversweet elaichi chai from the machine, Fiza saw a flurry of activity in D.K.'s cabin. Thinking it rude to stare, she lazily rolled her mouse over the sheet she was working on. Not knowing where to begin, she had drawn up a list of publishers with their addresses. A simple Google search about bulk rates for bookshops led her to a host of book distributors. Their offices and warehouses were invariably located in the snaking streets of old Bombay. Godowns where books were stored and sorted before they could be delivered to retail stores. The publishing websites also introduced her to catalogues with long lists of books, only a fraction of which interested her. Which brought her to the question – what sort of books would Paper Moon sell?

Lost in thought, she didn't notice D.K. waving at her, calling her into his cabin. Suleiman Merchant was seated on one of the swivel chairs facing D.K. Fiza walked into a quiet room with a question looming over it. *Now what?* She panicked inwardly. *It's too soon for the dream to end.* Thankfully, D.K. got to the point straightaway.

'Is the research going well?' he asked with a smile.

'Yes, I mean ... I'm getting to know about ... Yes.'

'Okay, that's a good start. If you think you're ready to go for it, then an excellent opportunity has come up.'

Rolling her chair forward, Fiza waited for him to explain.

'There's this property in Bandra that has been under dispute for around a decade. But the family has finally come to a settlement. It's an old mansion; they don't want to sell off any part of it, which would anyway be too expensive for us. They want to lease it out, and have already received quite a few offers. Mostly restaurants, ATMs – that kind of thing.'

Fiza nodded.

'They want the property to start maintaining itself. Since I know the family quite well, we can offer to take it on rent.'

Fiza realized she hadn't said anything and forced out an 'okay'.

'It's been lying vacant for a while, so it will take some work – repairs and all. But it's fully worth it, because of the size and location.'

'Where is it? And how big?'

'You know that Khoja Florist corner?'

'Yes. I studied at Carmel Convent close by.'

'Oh, Carmel girl! Nice. My sisters used to go there. So, yes. Next to Khoja, opposite St. Andrew's, there's this...'

'Old, empty villa. With arched windows. Yes, my school friends and I used to make up stories about what must go on in there.'

'That's the property. On Hill Road, just before Bandstand. Ranwar village, technically. It's looking like a bhoot bangla these days, but you won't get a property like that, beta.'

Fiza was trying not to seem ungrateful, but the place did look decrepit and abandoned.

D.K. smiled. 'Maximum one-and-a-half months and everything will be *chakachak*. You don't worry about that. Structure is solid. And we can get the owners to chip in with repairs also. Standard rules before putting a place up for rent.'

At this point, Fiza wasn't sure what she should worry about. Inheriting money was one thing, making high-stakes financial decisions was quite another. If she said yes to this offer, it would mean she was committed to the bookshop. That she'd agreed to become an entrepreneur. But those were things other people did. Fiza was suddenly dizzy as the full impact of the situation kicked in.

D.K. sensed he had rattled Fiza, but his business sense prevented him from loosening his grip on the moment.

'I know this is a big decision. But in some areas, you will have to bank on people with more experience. I don't know much about the book business. But property is in my blood. I can tell a good deal from miles way. And this is not just a good deal – this is like a blessing. They're only considering this because the older son – one of the heirs – is a big reader and artist-type. There are no speed breakers right now. We should seal the deal before everyone returns to their zidd.'

'Can I see it sometime soon?' Fiza asked weakly.

'Of course. Abdul will take us.' D.K. called for his driver, and in a couple of minutes they were driving out of Prabhadevi, past Shivaji Park, straight down Cadell Road and turning left at the Lucky Biryani corner onto Hill Road.

When they arrived, Fiza was struck by how charming the place was. The cobwebbed villa that was a part of her childhood landscape suddenly took on a new life. A key was arranged from a neighbouring building and Fiza was soon inspecting the bungalow. She had always found the flowers at Khoja to be too expensive. And now she was surveying property right next to it, with a realistic chance of taking it up on rent.

'Look, you can see Armaan Khan's house from here,' D.K. pointed with a grin, trying to rouse Fiza's interest, though she was keener on the St. Andrew's cemetery that was visible from the same window. The first burial she had ever attended – of her Chemistry teacher, Mrs Pinto – had been at that church. The entire class had been taken and she remembered feeling solemn, even moved by the ceremony.

The walls were peeling and the pink-and-green mosaic floor was well worn. Everything smelt musty. The windows rattled. But something about the space compelled her to stay. When the ten-minute inspection had turned into an hour-long exploration, D.K. knew he had convinced the young lady with his friend's furrowed brow and patrician nose. The rest of her appearance – tall frame, curly hair, deep-set eyes – was all Noor, he thought.

'So what do you think?' he finally asked. 'I know it will take effort, but trust me, this is a once-in-a-lifetime opportunity. You'll get something shinier and more modern, but this kind of charm, at such a location and at this rent—'

'Let's make an offer, D.K.,' Fiza cut in, growing in confidence and cheer by the minute.

CHAPTER FIVE

At 11.37 on a sunny Thursday morning, Fiza Khalid signed her name on a green rental agreement, with a hundred-rupee note printed on its front. The mansion was a charming remnant of Bombay's past, a stone's throw away from the seaside promenade where the space-starved gathered to exhale over peanuts and bhel. Frisky burqas fluttered against hopeful beards. Blaring Discmans – the CD version of the Walkman – propelled walkers forward. Noisy teens goofed around, while affable men in topis and turbans relived memories on benches donated by departed Rotarians.

When the registration formalities were completed at the Bandra Court, Abdul Bhai dropped Fiza back home in D.K.'s Accent. Stepping out of the car, she was greeted by Ismail, the man with no fixed address in the city.

'Hello, madam,' he said cheerfully, as he scooped out the patli malai for a customer.

'Hello, Ismail.'

'Very hot today, no?'

'Yes. But there is some wind at least,' Fiza replied, carefully calibrating the sentence so he would understand.

'Yes. We have to be happy.'

The watchman from the polyclinic next door was feeding Rani, the resident stray, a roti laced with chicken curry. A group of painters was busy with the salon soon to open on the ground floor of Little Flower. A couple of gas delivery guys sat on the footpath, taking a chai break. The street was doing its street thing.

'Yes. We have to be happy,' Fiza whispered, repeating the casual wisdom of the pavement prophet.

'The clock is ticking now.' That's what D.K. had said as soon as they had left the registration office. The pressure was already on. But for a business to launch, a plan needed to be in place. Fiza had neither experience nor interest in designing interiors or crunching numbers. *When would this become about the books?* she wondered.

Every day that passed made Fiza feel like she was up against it. After the big blow-up, things had calmed down at Little Flower, with mother and daughter meeting each other halfway. Showing Noor around the property, Fiza tried her best to be imaginative and optimistic, to dream it up into existence.

'This is lovely, Fizu! All these years of fighting, and they finally rent it out, haan? Ammi used to be friends with the mother. They used to play baddie at Bandra Gym. Can't believe my parents let the membership lapse.'

'Yes, we were very lucky to get the place,' Fiza replied enthusiastically.

'I'm impressed with D.K.'

Noor complimenting a friend of Iqbal's was a big concession.

'Yes, none of this would have been possible without him,' Fiza reiterated.

'We had all taken a trip to Ratnagiri once. He used to have a farm there. Great mangoes. It was his aunt's. Nice lady. Very elegant. Chiffons and pearls kind of thing. But he turned out to be a safari-suit walla.'

As Noor's thoughts meandered, the two found themselves at the first-floor window that looked out onto the sea.

'Fizu, I'm sorry I wasn't very...'

Fiza tried to forestall any sentimental declarations. They had a way of turning dark very quickly. 'No, it's okay. This was all very sudden.'

But Noor went on. This was not spontaneous rambling. She had thought about what she should say.

'No. I should have been more – accepting. This place is lovely. I couldn't even have dreamt of gifting you ... You know, I tried to put some money together, but after the singing stopped, it became very difficult.'

Fiza was moved by this rare admission of frailty.

'You deserve every bit of this, Fizu,' she went on. 'Whatever happened between us, he is ... was ... your father. Now it's too late ...' she said, looking around the place.

All this while, Fiza had resigned herself to an unequal relationship with her mother, and a non-existent one with her father. All of a sudden, the facts of her life had begun to rearrange themselves before her. Her father was present. Her mother was showing signs of acceptance, where once there had only been bitterness. Fiza was beginning to feel like she could be in the driver's seat of her own life after all.

'We really lucked out with this place,' she repeated with a smile.

'Oh, is that Armaan Khan's house?' Noor said, pointing to a nondescript building in the near distance.

'Yes, sadly.'

'Haha. What's he done to you, Fizu?'

'Nothing. Wouldn't allow him anywhere close.'

'His loss.'

'Eww. I'll have some chai while you're filling your lungs with tar.'

And so the two walked down the spiral staircase, opened the wood-panelled door and stepped out into the salty Bombay air.

Staring at the floor plans of the property at D.K.'s office, Fiza had an epiphany. She was not, in fact, an architect. The realization liberated her. She would hire one who would make sense of these plans that were driving her to despair. But she would step in when it came to picking the cushion covers. Cushions, she had decided, would be ample. The mosaic floor was perfect, once the cracks had been fixed. The arched windows already had wooden frames. Ooh, rugs. And lamps. And chai. And music. But she was getting ahead of herself. The technical drawings and load-bearing beams and walls prone to leakage had to be dealt with first. *When, oh when, would this become about the books?*

She walked up to the machine that dispensed the elaichi confection, making a mental note to never have such bilge served at her bookshop. Mr Merchant was pouring some out for himself.

'Things are progressing well?' he asked in his halting manner.

'It's going well, I think. I *hope*. Trying to get people together. Hoping I won't miss anything out.'

'And the interior decoration?'

'Yes, that's a challenge right now. I need a good architect.' She thought perhaps she should ask D.K. His firm would surely know some people. And then it struck her. Marcel! It *had* to be him.

Marcel was a designer friend of Dhruv's parents, with whom she had always got along. For years, they had hung out at the lavish parties that the Banerjees were famous for. Marcel was a spirited raconteur who could bring even the dullest gathering to life. He and his partner Vikram were the people she gravitated towards at those endless soirées involving fancy whisky and microscopic canapés. Dhruv would be circulating, refilling people's drinks and basking in all the attention – it was easy for him to mingle. She was usually the loner in a corner.

Marcel, known universally as Marc, was of mixed French and Parsi descent, and raised in Calcutta, the only product of that ethnic combination, he proudly insisted. No one had the heart, or method, to test the theory, and it became part of his folklore. Fiza realized she'd never really needed to seek him out before, so when she got his number from Mrs Banerjee, she decided to go with the formal 'Marcel'.

'Ooh, Fiza. How lufffley to hear from you! But who is this Marcel? Do you know him? How have you been? Broke our poor bloke's heart, I heard, naughty girl,' he replied exuberantly. That he brought up Dhruv straightaway made matters easier for Fiza. He was the kind of person who made these generous allowances in conversation.

'Hello to you too, Marc! And how's Vikram?'

'Good attempt to change the topic. He's well. Away on another snorkelling trip. Lucky bastard.'

'Oh, wow. That *is* lucky. And why didn't *you* go?

'It's all so – *wet!*'

'Yes, that is an inconvenience underwater,' she laughed.

'So what brings you to the other side of my temperamental cell phone? I dropped it in a punch bowl and it's never been the same after.'

'Well – I had a question, more of an offer. But I was hoping we could meet and talk about it.'

'Sure, sweetheart. That way I can pull out all the juicy goss about Baby Banerjee. Muhahaha.'

'You'd be disappointed. No gossip. But can I interest you in some chai?'

'Better still. Come over and I'll make you this orange cocktail with some vodka I've been saving for a while. Waiting for the right company.'

'Done. When's good?'

'Come this evening, love? Around seven?'

'Sure. Thanks so much, Marc.'

'I missed you, baby. Ta.'

Break-ups were miserable things, no matter who left whom. Thank goodness for people who understood.

Fiza had visited Marcel and Vikram's apartment only once before, when the couple had thrown an anniversary party for the Banerjees. For a designer's home, it was refreshingly devoid of design flourishes. Faded rugs languished on the Kota stone floor. You didn't have to worry about what you stepped on. Everything was lived-in and welcoming. When Fiza walked in, she saw Banana the Dachshund curled up on a wicker chair. Up on the living room wall was a giant painting – a Rothko-esque work that gave the room an air of lightness and warmth. The quality she wanted her bookshop to have.

As she stood staring at the painting, she was jolted by Enrique Iglesias's *'Don't turn off the lights'* blaring out of the open kitchen. 'Sorry, but I'm really tripping on this one. And Vikram can't stand him. So allow me this indulgence while he's away.'

'Indulge all you like. I quite like this one, too,' Fiza said, walking towards Marcel.

He hugged her extravagantly and got to work on the promised cocktail. 'So tell me everything, loveliness. I've missed you terribly at those shiny evenings at the Banerjees. I adore them, but you know how it can get with those suits and pearls. Need some young blood, non?'

'Yes, you and Vikram were my saviours on so many occasions. But, for once I actually have something quite exciting to report.'

'Oh, thank god. I've been dying of boredom. Tell, tell.'

'So ...' began Fiza, clearing her throat, 'my father, whom I didn't know at all, recently passed away and willed me a bookshop.'

'Which bookshop? And I'm sorry about your dad,' replied Marcel.

'Well, I should have been clearer. He left me money to set up a bookshop. And just the other day, I rented a property.'

'Okaayy, *this* I was *not* expecting,' he said while dunking a slice of malta in the long-stemmed glass as a final touch. Bolting across the room, he handed Fiza her drink and raised a toast.

'To Fiza, giggling partner at boring parties, femme fatale who's left our poor Banerjee boy high and dry, and literary proprietress. Who'd've thunk?'

Fiza's first meeting with D.K. had been dominated by Iqbal's death. And even now, months later, she hadn't really celebrated the bookshop news. But here, in this happy living room, clinking glasses with a man wearing bunny slippers, here it was: a vast, unalloyed happiness that could only erupt in silly laughter. Literary proprietress, not quite. But bookshop girl – that she could imagine.

Enrique morphed into Ricky Martin, glasses were refilled and Banana expressed a cursory interest in the absurd humans around him. Settling into the couch, Fiza explained the purpose of her visit.

'So Marcel – Marc,' Fiza heard her second cocktail saying, 'we've got the place, but haven't a clue what to do with it.'

'Who's the *we*, baby?'

'Oh. A couple of friends of my father's. One's into real estate. Another is a lawyer.'

'All this sounds very big league. But getting to the point ... where is this fairy-tale bookshop that's appeared from thin air? Please, please don't say Madh Island. I love you, but I will not step on that ferry ever again. I've never felt more French than when the stench went up my nose. Revolution and all be damned – please don't go all pleb on me.'

Marc's exaggerated elitism was enacted for laughs. And Fiza found him genuinely funny.

'No, Marc. It's not on Madh Island. It's near Bandstand, actually. So you're safe.'

'Oh, thank heavens. Go on. What's the catch? Your father's will says you can have the money only if you marry the local bootlegger's arms-dealing third son, to whom he owed a kidney, hearing which you dropped the Banerjee chhele like a chingri that's been rid of all juice?'

'Wow. That's quite a picture. And I thought *I* was sharing exciting news.'

'Okay. I'll zip it. Go on.'

'I want you to design the place.'

Marc drained his second drink in one long gulp. Then in a tone of mock relief, he whispered, 'I thought you'd never ask.'

'There has to be a striped awning. Red and white. Under that, we'll have the used books. On a handcart. I know someone on Reay Road.'

Marc began his inspection from the outside, with Fiza taking notes as he spoke. Design was not her thing and she needed to make sure she understood everything Marc was suggesting. One thing she was sure of: she had to surround herself with people who knew their job. To defer to the experts. This wouldn't work if she played the queen bee.

'There's got to be seating between bookracks. No fuss. Just a little wooden seat topped with a cushion. The mosaic's good. But we'll need to fill up the cracks here and there. And magazines? What shall we have for magazines?'

'I guess...'

'We'll have lovely little brackets in the wall. Letters of the alphabet. And oh. We have to get those revolving bookracks from Chor Bazar. Lamps, rugs, cushions, mats – you can take those.'

'You mean *I* can select them?'

'It's *your* bookshop, Fizz. *Something's* got to be you.'

Fiza smiled. She was still too nervous to enjoy this, but fear was already giving way to excitement.

They climbed up the spiral staircase that ran along the side of the room and Fiza announced joyously, 'And here's the children's section.'

'No, doesn't work,' Marc said, caressing the wrought-iron railing.

'What? But it's – the *children's* section.'

'Nah. Nada. Not.'

Fiza felt a tremor of annoyance for the first time since she had decided to let Marc into the bookshop plan. Composing herself, she asked, 'Okay. Why not?'

'The spiral staircase. It's too beautiful not to keep. And too unwieldy for children to use. Unless you want over-protective parents walking toddlers up and down all day long. Or worse – petrified nannies trying to mask the bump on the head of a precocious five-year-old who thought it a good idea to imitate the March Hare.'

'Hmm. You're right. It's not safe for little kids.'

'*Now* we're jamming. Safety first, love,' he said coolly.

This was not how Fiza had imagined it. But it was Marc's professional judgment over her whim. She could already see Marc agonizing over design details, and it hadn't even been five minutes since they had walked in. He was the real thing. And he *had* said she could pick the fabrics and the lamps.

Once on the upper floor, Marc plonked himself on the ground and began working furiously. She noticed a 2B pencil, the kind the art teacher would order the students to bring at school. With it, he made illegible squiggles and rough sketches in a red Moleskine diary with little checked pages. He occasionally ran up and down with his measuring tape, muttering numbers to himself. About an hour later, Fiza noticed it was time for lunch.

'Shall we have a quick bite, then?' she suggested.

Marc looked up disoriented, as if back from space travel. 'Huh?'

'It's lunchtime, Marc.'

'I could do with a beer.'

'Really? Okay. But where?'

'Yacht. Right across the church,' he said without missing a beat.

'Yacht bar? But it's – *grotty.*'

'Ooh. Now we're all delicate princess of the tower, are we?'

'No, no. Of course not. I'd be glad to. Just thought it was a bit—'

'Too real for me? Baby, I've been drinking there since you were on formula. The beef chilli fry is to die for.'

'Okay, then. Yacht it is. You surprise me, Marc,' Fiza said affectionately.

'Just don't let Vikram know I'm drinking at lunch again.'

Every morning of the next week, Marc and Fiza worked on design plans at the bookshop. At about two, they would take a break at Yacht, going over the drawings on the grubby tables of the bar. The little curtains on the window grills that separated them from the Hill Road traffic fluttered in the December breeze. Beef chilly fry, mutton biryani and Kingfisher was their staple order. The waiter made sure their stay was short. Seven days on this unsustainable diet and they switched to Café Good Luck, just ahead of Mehboob Studio, and a menu of keema pao, bun maska and chai. And if they were being health conscious, it was bhurji pao and Sulaimani tea with its daub of lemon.

When they returned to work, they'd take stock of the materials received and those on their way. The bookracks were being built. The sleeper wood both had wished for was too expensive to realistically consider, so they settled for a wood-finished laminate. Fiza realized she had to work out the business plan before she could take on big financial decisions. It was December already, and the days to the launch were disappearing like the potato chops at Hearsch Bakery at lunchtime. They were aiming for a mid-January opening. While Marcel supervised activities at the store, Fiza spent hours hunched over the laptop she had borrowed from D.K.

One Thursday afternoon, neither Marc nor Fiza noticed when lunch hour came and went. At about four, Noor walked in on the busy scene.

'Hey, Fizu.'

'Ma – when did you come in? Sorry I was…'

'Yes, your old friend Excel.'

'Just one sec. I needed to complete this column with depreciation of hardware…'

'Don't mind me. I've just got some frankies from Quality Picnic. And Thums Up.'

In a moment, both Marc and Fiza were tearing away at their mutton frankies from the Linking Road institution next to Metro Shoes, down to the juice at the bottom of the plastic casing. 'Now that's a real treat, Noor. You're an angel,' Marc said, licking his fingers.

Noor and Marc had met at the Banerjees' a few years ago. He had requested her – goaded her – to sing. But Noor wasn't in the mood. She hadn't been in the mood for years now. Fiza wondered whether it had left Noor, the impulse that had defined her for so many years. Could something that deep disappear just like that?

'I'm going to leave before this dust kills me,' Noor said between coughs, fishing out a pack of cigarettes from her bag. Marc and Fiza had stopped noticing the incessant drilling and sawing and whirring and hammering. But to anyone else who entered the area, it was a war zone.

'Yes, not good for your asthma,' Fiza said, frowning at the cigarettes. 'I'll see you at home. Thanks so much for the frankies. They saved our lives.'

'I'll extract my pound of flesh, don't worry. Reserve a nice comfy seat for me by that window. I'll be the weird old lady at the bookshop people will point to from the street. Which reminds me – have you settled on a name?'

'Oh, yes. I keep forgetting to ask you. And we're together all day, every day! Have you?' Marc asked.

'Paper Moon,' Fiza replied, looking up to see her mother's reaction.

'*But it wouldn't be make-believe, if you believed in me ...*' Noor sang in a soft, deep voice, filling Fiza with a faraway feeling.

'Yes, that's where I got it from. You used to sing it all the time when I was little.'

'You remember that? God, Fiza. You were what, three or four? I was doing those recordings for the Tennessee Williams play.'

'*A Streetcar Named Desire*. You played Blanche, Noor?' Marc asked, wide-eyed and high-pitched.

'I didn't know you were in a Tennessee Williams play! Or any play, Ma,' Fiza gushed.

'I just did some recordings. They played the song at several points in the play. And the actress couldn't get it right. The director was a friend, so it just happened. It was nothing.'

'And from nothing comes this bookshop. Paper Moon. It fits. I love it,' Marc said, giving Fiza a bear hug.

'Thanks, Marc. Ma, what do you think about it?'

'You sure you want to name your bookshop after some jazz tune I used to hum when you were a baby?'

'Couldn't be more sure,' Fiza replied.

'I feel like I've named it. It's great. Paper Moon. And I'm serious about that chair by the window. Now I'd better leave you to your hammers and drills. Ta,' Noor said, putting the pack of cigarettes back in her bag as a return gift for Fiza.

CHAPTER SIX

Christmas was around the corner and Hill Road was in overdrive. Cheap Jack was brimming over with streamers and tinsel, balloons and confetti, thermocol snowmen and glittering angels. On the pavement outside St. Peter's Church, Christmas trees found temporary shelter. In little kitchens on Bazaar Road and Waroda Road, marzipans were being nudged out of rubber moulds. Rum-soaked fruits were making their way into cake mixtures. Sorpotel meals were being planned with families visiting from the Gulf and Canada. And across from Fiza's bookshop, Damian furniture store had put up its annual Christmas display, featuring a life-size Santa, reindeer and sleigh.

Fiza was ensconced in her little office in a corner of the upper storey of the bookshop. She had in front of her a sheaf of colourful book catalogues and a large mug of rapidly cooling coffee. Representatives of all the big publishing houses had started doing the rounds already. The bookracks had been fitted. Much of the other furniture had arrived. Electrical works were in progress. The Internet was up and running. The days of working out of D.K.'s office were behind her. Paper Moon was rising into view.

'Madam,' said the overzealous contractor one morning.

'Ji, Prabhudasji?' Fiza replied absently.

'Koi aaya hai aapse milne.'

'Achha. Main aa rahi hoon.' These interruptions were common. There was always a delivery to receive or query to address.

'Aap bolo toh main baat karta hoon. Koi kaam dhoondhne aaya hai, shaayad. Aapke type ka nahi hai.'

In the weeks that he had spent working with Fiza, Prabhudasji had turned fiercely protective of her time. He regularly filtered out salesmen he thought were pesky, or other visitors he deemed unnecessary. Fiza was grateful for his attentiveness, but knew he could take it too far at times.

'Nahin, main milti hoon. Shukriya.'

Climbing down the staircase, Fiza expected to see a book distributor's representative. Or maybe even a curious neighbour. She was taken aback to see someone who was part of her daily routine.

'Ismail!'

'Madam, yesterday I am delivering coconuts here and there and see you going into this office. But yesterday I was having no time. Today again I am delivering and thinking I should check. Your office, madam?'

'Yes. I mean no, not really an office. Come in, come in.'

Walking in, he noticed the bookracks on the wall. 'Bookshop, madam?'

'Yes, Ismail. My bookshop.'

'Congratulations, madam. When is opening?'

'Soon. I will invite you.'

'What I'll do in bookshop, madam? Serve coconut?' he joked.

This struck Fiza as a great idea. 'Yes! Coconuts. You will serve coconuts. I'll pay you at the end of the opening. Naariyal paani is a great idea.'

'Okay, done, madam. Tell in advance. I'll go now. Delivery at Armaan Khan's house.'

'Good to see you, Ismail.'

'Thank you, madam. Good afternoon.'

Now that the naariyal paani was sorted, she would have to figure out the rest of the plan for the launch. These little digressions were her favourite part of the whole enterprise so far. Returning to her desk, she logged into her email account. Every time she opened her mail, she instinctively expected to hear from Dhruv. But it seemed like 9/11 had made the parting final. She scanned the mails from book distributors with their endless catalogues, featuring prices and ISBN numbers. But that was not how she saw her bookshop. General interest books, sure. But it had to have a particular slant. Popular wisdom said her shelves should stock every bestselling author and genre. Diaries of yogis and housewives' kitchen secrets, businessmen's mantras and celeb biographies. She couldn't escape them. This was not, after all, Frances D'Monte's lit class. But it wasn't going to be the McDonald's of the printed word either.

No, she had to actually visit these distributors and select real books off physical racks. Feel them. Smell them. This bookshop was going to be curated. But she was going to have to be careful it didn't scare people away with its high-mindedness. Like a wedding buffet, it would have the mandatory butter chicken and kaali dal, but for those who wanted more, there was going to be roghan josh and bagaare baigan, too. And maybe even some shaahi tukda.

New Majestic Shopping Centre. The location of Fiza's first-ever book-buying spree. The fantastical name matched the surreal quality the visit held for Fiza perfectly.

India Book Distributors – who had in their line-up Penguin, HarperCollins, Vintage, Random House and other reputed publishers – operated out of a few warehouses in the city. Fiza was now in the basement of the office in Girgaum, Charni Road, in the old commercial hub of Bombay, where business was still run in the quaint old way. She was directed to the lower chambers of the building and welcomed in by an ancient employee who didn't waste much time with pleasantries. His boss was away, but he had been asked to assist the new bookshop owner.

The smell hit her first. In the airless basement, the whiff of paper and print was intense. Creaking fans were switched on in the large room, which had one function – holding thousands of books within metal shelves. No fussy displays. No signage. Just the racks holding books. And an industrial-sized trolley for her to toss them in. Charlie could not have been more pleased in the Chocolate Factory, nor Eve in Eden. Fiza did not want the moment to actually begin. She just wanted to stand there, forever frozen in a prelapsarian tableau of innocence.

But a second later, she found books entering the trolley of their own will, as if commanded by a Hogwarts spell. Virginia Woolf, Iris Murdoch, Muriel Spark – the holy trio were some of the first to jump in. Milan Kundera followed Amitav Ghosh,

Dostoevsky chased Mario Vargas Llosa in some kind of mad hatter's literary tea party. Nick Hornby and Sue Townsend added some laughs. Darwin and Nietzsche kept the rest in check. Rumi's loftiness, Calvino's bizarreness, Arundhati's Royness – things were getting along nicely when Fiza realized this had to end.

The square Ajanta clock on the wall looked at her judgementally. This was not about her stocking up a store with her favourite books; it was about stocking a bookshop with books that would sell. And the two were far from the same thing. Thus chastised, Fiza made her way grudgingly to the section that displayed airport thrillers and self-help classics. To allay her uneasiness, she picked multiple copies of the first four Harry Potter books – page-turners that the pundits wouldn't scoff at.

It had been three hours and twenty minutes since she had walked in. While raiding the bookshelves, she had had two cups of cutting chai and some Marie biscuits. When the staff broke for lunch, they invited her to join them. But she was best left alone, feasting on the books. She had no idea whether her selection was appropriate in variety, number or cost. She was treating this trip as simply covering the bases. Books that her bookshop must have.

Fiza realized that the man who had greeted her when she had arrived was the bridge between the management and the customer. She had already worked out the details of discounts, credit period and return policy. According to her research, a new bookshop would be offered about a 30 per cent discount on the selling price – not a bad margin for a business, D.K. assured her. The credit period could range between thirty and ninety days, which, again, didn't seem daunting at the outset. And most distributors had a 10 per cent return policy, with the number going considerably higher for coffee-table books, which 'moved' slower. D.K. explained that the discount was more or less fixed, with a 5 per cent leeway. But it was in the area of credit and returns where she would have to keep pushing for more. The results of that negotiation could decide whether the bookshop made money or not.

When she couldn't ignore the glowering clock any longer, Fiza called out to Kambleji, the floor manager. He saw that the trolleys had multiplied. The zeal of the first-timer, she interpreted his smile as saying. She wondered if she had blundered. The billing would make it all clear. But that would have to wait; she was to leave them to it. A pro-forma invoice would be readied. A suitably scary Latin-tinged phrase that merely meant a list of selected items and their prices. So she had one last chance to make amends – this wasn't a *real* bill. Not a rupee had changed hands yet. But this was also the time that distributors, always hungry for outlets, tried to establish a strong relationship with booksellers. Fiza would soon realize that the city was dotted with distributors in similarly airless offices and warehouses. And the numbers she was holding as sacrosanct were more flexible than she imagined. It was where she would have to exercise her business skills – once she had acquired them.

Back at the store, she noticed the electrical work had been completed. The lamps threw a warm and happy glow on the shelves and floor. Just then, her Nokia 3210 beeped. The SMS was from Bharti Aunty. 'Congrats, Fizuuuuu. I'll bring cake for the opening. God bless!' Naariyal paani and cake. And now some books, too. It was all coming together.

'I used to work at Bestsellers Bookshop, madam. But I want an opportunity in a new place where I can do more things. There the systems are all there. But no mazaa.'

Sudhir Dadarkar was well turned out in a crisp striped shirt and grey trousers. His CV was impressive: six years at Bestsellers, well-versed in PoS software, doubled as a floor manager, accounting background, lived in nearby Khar Danda. Very promising.

'How did you hear about this place, Sudhir?' Fiza asked, trying to contain her excitement.

'Ismail Anna. The naariyal paani wala,' he said, as if it were the most obvious reply.

'Huh? Oh, you know him?'

'Yes. He comes to my area to deliver. On his moped. My neighbour's mother is very sick. She needs naariyal paani every day. He supplies to those stalls at Carter Road also, madam.'

Ismail was everywhere, like some kind of one-eyed guardian angel on a rickety steed.

'Hmm. Okay. So, Sudhir, your work experience fits the requirement. But I won't be able to pay you as much as Bestsellers. We're just starting the shop and our budgets are different from those of established businesses.'

'No problem, madam. We will try working together. Three months? Then you see the work and we can decide on the permanent salary,' Sudhir said with the confidence of a professional who knows his worth.

'That's a good approach, Sudhir,' Fiza smiled. 'But are you sure? I don't want to make any promises and then disappoint you.'

'Don't worry, madam. We have to take some risk to move ahead. I left my job for better work. Better work will come if I will also prove myself.'

'Okay, Sudhir,' Fiza said, convinced of his conviction. 'So when can you start?'

'I'm ready, madam. I'll just need some guidance on first day.'

And just like that, Paper Moon's first employee got to work.

New Year's Eve, 2001. A whole year since the infamous marriage proposal. The beginning of the end for Dhruv and Fiza. This year, Fiza decided to stay in. Keep working at the store till late in the evening, then return home to bed like on any other day. Marc and Vikram had invited her over to a party at theirs, but she wasn't quite in the mood to field questions about the break-up, however well-intentioned the enquirer. And it wasn't yet time to speak about the bookshop, she thought. In just a few weeks, the place would speak for itself. She was in a kind of twilight zone, with her old life almost completely dimming from view but the new one still shapeless.

At about seven, Fiza decided to walk home instead of adding to the crazy Hill Road traffic. She felt her body ache, but thought the exercise would do her some good. At her old school, a wedding reception was in progress. Ever since the spirited nun from the Delhi branch had been transferred to Bombay, they had begun to let the school grounds out for private events. Funds were being collected to start a junior college section. She stopped at A1 Bakery, owned by a schoolmate's father, who had always reminded her of Tevye from *The Fiddler on the Roof*. She peered, as usual, into the dingy Vienna Store, where the faithful still bought bread and eggs, then walked past Holy Family hospital, where the nativity scene was trying to infuse some cheer outside the emergency department. Past Sona Stores, where last-minute party-planners were buying balloons and masks by the dozen. Past Elco Arcade, where teenage girls were haggling with mothers over the lengths of sequinned dresses. Past Bhabha Municipal Hospital, where an ambulance was rushing into Casualties. Past Stomach Restaurant, which, like all times of the day, had families on a budget tucking into their sweet corn chicken soup and American chop suey. Then through the lane that led to the Bandra Hindu Association park, where the obligatory junkies were gathering for their year-end fix. And finally, home. By the time Fiza walked in, she felt like she had run a marathon.

Noor was away for a few days. As usual, Bharti and Mahesh had gathered a few friends and left for their Karjat farm the previous afternoon. They were due to return on the second. Maria, the trusty cook hired as a young girl by Noor's mother back in the day, was on leave till the second. But there were some goodies in the freezer that Fiza now decided to explore: chicken biryani and shami kababs, her all-time favourites. Thawing and microwaving took the joy out of any meal, but Fiza thought she would develop an appetite once the food was hot on her plate. Maria's biryani was always perfectly spiced with the fabulous Shan Special Bombay Biryani Masala, imported, ironically, from Karachi. And her kabab recipe came from Fiza's nani, unmatched hostess of splendid

Eid lunches. As she took her plate out of the microwave, Fiza anticipated a nice relaxed evening, and some rest before the big launch. The books had begun to come into the store. And the next day, despite the January 1 holiday tradition, a computer software demo had been arranged. Sudhir would be at work, and so would she.

One bite into a kabab and something didn't feel right. Fiza found herself retching – not her usual response to Mughlai delights. In a moment, she was running into the toilet, throwing up the contents of her skipped lunch. She hadn't realized it, but she had been skipping meals often the last few days. Plus, she had begun to feel exhausted even after a couple of hours of work. But there was always so much to do, there wasn't any time to indulge these niggles. Now, at about 8.30 p.m. on New Year's Eve, Fiza couldn't ignore the symptoms any longer. She had already been sick three times since that first bite. This was strange. And it was too late in the evening to see any doctor, with celebrations on in full swing all over the city.

Putting away the untouched food, she popped an antacid and put on her slippers. Should she call someone? A few names came to mind and left almost instantly: Marc, D.K., Sudhir? Everyone from a life that hadn't even existed a few weeks ago. It didn't seem right to bother them on a night like this. So she picked up her cloth bag, threw in her phone and decided to head to Holy Family Hospital, where she knew she wouldn't be disturbing anybody's party plans. But even getting to the hospital in the traffic seemed daunting. To make matters worse, Fiza doubled over with nausea as soon as she reached the pavement outside her home.

'Madam, are you all right?' a familiar voice called out.

Fiza took a few seconds to compose herself before she could figure out where the words came from. Ismail was standing close to her, looking anxious.

'I'm ... okay, Ismail.'

'I'll bring water ... naariyal paani? It helps sick people.'

Fiza nodded a vehement no, too uncomfortable to speak. She sat down by the streetlamp, on the low wall surrounding Ismail's tree. In a minute, she realized she could not avoid asking for help.

'Ismail, will you please take me to Holy Family Hospital?'

Ismail flagged down an auto and ushered Fiza in urgently. The next thing she knew, she was being wheeled into the emergency department of the hospital, which she had walked past only about an hour before. The efficient doctor on duty asked Ismail for the details of the case. Fiza interrupted, saying, 'He was very kind to bring me here. But he needs to get back now. Thank you so much, Ismail. Aapke help ke liye. Sorry aapka time waste hua. Happy New Year.'

'Madam, aisa kaise? Aap tension mat lo. I am here only.'

Fiza's protestations were dismissed so fiercely that she resigned herself to the fact that this was actually happening: New Year's Eve in a hospital bed, with Ismail the Coconut Seller by her side.

Jaundice. The preliminary examination and queries revealed that she had been stricken with the Hepatitis E strain, which pointed at food contamination. Something she had eaten or drunk must have carried within it strains of faecal matter. It was a Bombay virus currently doing the rounds. The kind of illness that you only realized you had once it had knocked you down.

'So you're missing a big party with friends and all?' asked the resident doctor, trying to lighten the atmosphere. He was a slight, smiling man wearing a 'party' shirt, a belt with an ornate buckle, and elaborately faded jeans. *New Year's Eve look*, Fiza thought to herself. There must be some version of a celebration even for emergency room staff.

'No, I had no plans. So what's the ... prognosis, doctor?' In a medical set-up, Fiza's mental dictionary always offered the most formal-sounding phrases.

'Oh, big words and all, haan?' the doctor laughed while addressing the nurse who looked away tiredly. 'Blood report will come, then we will see what the levels are. Then we will start treatment. But there is no treatment.'

Curioser and curioser.

'No treatment?'

'No. For jaundice, you have to get toxins out of liver. Then only body will accept food. Till then saline. Otherwise all is coming out, no?'

All had, in fact, been coming out the last couple of hours.

'You can go home if you want. Home care is also good.'

Fiza thought about the empty house. With Noor and Maria gone, and her being unable to retain even water, it all looked grim. And there it was again.

'Sister, sister. I need a kidney tray.'

And that decided it. She would stay the night and then figure out the way ahead in the morning. The saline drip would keep her nourished. She would ask for an anti-emetic in the IV. She had this under control.

Meanwhile, Ismail had brought the registration form to her bed. After she managed to fill it somehow, she realized she had to pay the fee. She handed him her debit card, requesting him to do what was needed and to bring her the receipt. He said he had handled it, and she was in no position to argue. When the formalities had been completed, Fiza turned to her soldier with a warm smile. 'Ismail, thank you very, very much. Lekin abhi aap please waapis jaao. Warna mujhe neend nahin aayegi. Please. Aapne waise hi bohat help ki hai meri.'

'Arre, madam. Yeh toh duty hai neighbour ka. Theek hai, I am going. But I will come in morning. With fresh coconut water. I already ask doctor. He said you are allowed.'

'Okay, thank you. I will try to have it. Goodnight. And Happy New Year.'

'Don't worry, madam. Small problem. Morning all will become all right. Happy New Year.'

As Ismail left, the quiet of the room was broken by the shrill sound of someone alternately shrieking and weeping. In an instant, a young boy wearing a denim jacket, his hair spiked with gel, came into view. Around either arm was a friend, encouraging him to take small steps. And to keep breathing.

'I was wondering how a toxic case had not come till now. New Year's Special it is. Some booze or drug abuse. This one looks like cocaine,' the doctor said to a bored-looking nurse. 'Get ready to pump his stomach. All these spoilt Bandra children.'

Fiza looked around the room for a clock. It was 11.54 p.m. The contents of the boy's stomach were being pumped out in a bed not far from hers. Try as the doctor would, the shrieking boy would not be restrained.

Then, a loud burst of fireworks. *Spoilt Bandra children and their spoilt Bandra parents*, Fiza smiled to herself. The pumping was still on, and the toxic case groaned intermittently. On another bed, an old woman's broken foot was being bandaged. Two ward boys spontaneously broke into a hug, and a smile drifted over the room. It was 2002.

'Happy New Year,' Fiza heard from a bed a short distance to her left. The curtain had been drawn all this while, but now it seemed as if the patient had parted it.

'Happy New Year,' Fiza replied, trying not to look too curious. He was wearing a white kurta and faded jeans. Just a jhola would have completed the Xavier's look. But this apparition looked like he was in his mid-30s. Perhaps a writer. Or an NGO worker. Before Fiza could go further in her conjecture, he spoke again.

'Epilepsy. You?'

'Huh? Er. Jaun – Hepatitis,' she replied feebly. This was turning into a conversation. The boy whose stomach was being pumped was now writhing in pain, comforted by his friends between long howls. Once or twice, the supporting cast had already been told off by nurses for answering their phones too loudly and cheerily.

'Hmm. Had that, too. Can't drink for about six months after. Food restrictions. But overall, it's a good controlled weight-loss programme.'

This was now a proper conversation. Fiza literally had nowhere to hide. Characteristically, she had nothing to say to this stranger, but she made an attempt despite herself.

'Have you been here long? I mean, when did you ...' she stuttered.

'About fifteen minutes before you came in with your very resourceful coconut seller friend.'

Fiza felt exposed and nervous. This didn't feel right, in so many ways.

'Sorry, I think I'll try and sleep,' she said tersely.

'No, no. I'm sorry. I've been in these situations so often, I'm sometimes insensitive to first-timers.'

The frankness of the patient's manner made Fiza soften unexpectedly. It was a bad night for anyone who was there. And he was reaching out. She could make an exception to her talking-to-overfamiliar-strangers rule.

'Is someone you know around?' she asked.

'Around here? At the hospital? Nah. Not needed. I suspect I'll be discharged soon. This time I hit my head on the kerb, so there was a mild concussion. An auto guy brought me here. Little bump. I'll survive.'

'Have you always had it? The epilepsy?'

'Hmm. Ever since I can remember. Head full of bumps,' he said boastfully. So, did you have better plans for the evening before – this?' he said, gesturing to the brightly lit room with his free arm. The other arm was attached to an IV.

'Actually, no plans at all. I was in the middle of dinner when I got … sick,' Fiza said, trying to change the image in her head quickly.

'Yes. The nausea is what kills. Then the weakness. I had jaundice when I was what – sixteen? Fuck, that's almost twenty years ago. I read *War and Peace* the month I was laid up. Thought it would build character. Don't remember a word.'

'A month?' Fiza panicked. She didn't have a month. The launch was planned for the middle of January. 'But that can't be true of all cases.'

'Hmm. There have been freaks who've been known to finish the book in three weeks.'

'No, I mean ...' Fiza replied earnestly.

'Yes, sorry, I know. You're in hospital. Not to scare you or anything, but most people don't get to this point.'

'I only came here because I was ...' She stopped herself from completing the sentence. She realized she didn't need to.

'Yes, when you're alone, it's best not to take chances. If only my bloody illness would be so polite as to give me an indication. But it's always a surprise.'

'That must be hard.'

'It could be worse,' he said with a shrug.

The nurse on duty came around to check the epileptic's IV. Seeing that it was almost through, she went back to the doctor's station and shared the notes she had taken. The doctor nodded, seemingly happy with the condition of the patient. The nurse returned with a smile.

'Sir, you can go home now.'

The patient looked towards Fiza for a fleeting second. She thought he winked at her slightly, but the idea was too preposterous to believe. Then he did something even more surprising.

'Sister, I'm beginning to feel this intense pain in my head. Here on the right side, just above the eyebrow. Problems with vision also,' he said, opening and shutting his eyes rapidly. 'I'd be more comfortable if you checked all was okay. Maybe I can stay overnight for observation?'

The nurse looked worried. 'Okay, I will tell the doctor.'

'If it gets unbearable, I'll ask for a painkiller. My threshold is quite high, normally. Thank you, sister,' he said in a schoolboy voice.

'But you just said you'd be discharged soon,' Fiza said, genuinely perplexed.

'Either you're modest to a fault or you're feigning ignorance, Miss Hepatitis. Hey, that almost rhymes!'

Just then, a big wave of nausea came over Fiza. The epileptic called for the nurse, who was quick to provide the kidney tray. There wasn't much left to puke out. The nurse told her there was anti-emetic medicine in the drip; she just needed to be patient. When the discomfort had passed, Fiza turned towards her neighbour.

'Thanks for calling the nurse,' she mumbled.

'Least I can do, considering my attempt at wooing you made you sick to your stomach.'

'Now *you're* being modest,' said Fiza, surprising herself. 'Were you serious? About that month in bed?' she said, switching modes.

'A few weeks at least. Why? Travel plans?'

'I have a bookshop to launch in a couple of weeks.'

'Where?'

'Down the road. Next to Khoja Florist. Do you know it?'

'Miss Hepatitis, you fascinate me. I could not have asked for a better New Year's Eve companion. Thank you. But riveting as my company is, I think it best that you rest now. Goodnight.'

The howling boy was now asleep. One of his friends had left; one stayed. The doctor was on the phone, wishing his family a Happy New Year. Fiza shut her eyes and almost immediately drifted into a deep and dreamless sleep.

CHAPTER SEVEN

10 February 2002. Paper Moon was born. And the celebrations had begun.

Marc had brought his old gramophone player. Noor had carried records. Jazz wafted in the air, blending with Bharti Aunty's baking. Chocolate cake and blueberry cookies, straight out of an Enid Blyton book. In the little compound outside, close to the handcart on which the second-hand books were stacked, Ismail served thirsty guests naariyal paani. Fiza had invited Frances to declare the bookshop open. She had arrived in a stunning black silk sari with a red border, and her trademark necklace of skulls.

At about noon, D.K. and Suleiman Merchant walked in with a bouquet of flowers from Khoja Florist next door. The overpowering scent of pink tiger lilies soon mixed with the smell of fresh print and perfume, a fragrance Fiza wished she could bottle for future use.

'Well done, young lady. You've done such a wonderful job. Iqbal would be so proud,' D.K. said, allowing himself this little burst of sentiment. He had been careful to keep the relationship with Fiza professional despite all the loaded history. But here, at the bookshop his friend had dreamt of setting up, he was overcome by memories. This was exactly Iqbal's kind of place.

'You made it possible, D.K.,' Fiza replied, holding his hand tight for a few seconds. It was a silent but eloquent gesture, not lost on D.K. Noor, who was standing nearby, chatting with a neighbour from Little Flower, caught the moment and smiled. Then she walked over to where her daughter stood with the man she had known from another lifetime.

'Hi, D.K. I like the French beard.'

'Hello, Noor Abbas. You should tell Sumaira that. She hates it,' he replied, as if continuing an old conversation.

'Uh-oh. Why isn't she here?'

'Bad knees. She's going in for surgery soon.'

'Oh. Give her my regards. And thank you for all the help with … with…'

'What are you saying, Noor! Iqbal always—' he began, but was interrupted by a clinking glass.

The Banerjees had just walked in, and Marc was in his element.

'Toast, toast, toast. Time to make a toast, ladies and lads. And since the presiding angel of the bookshop is recovering from a bout of Hepatitis that she insensitively contracted at just about the worst time in history, we'll be raising glasses of naariyal paani instead, her poison these days.'

Fiza tried not to blush. Being the centre of attention was not her thing. But with Marc, such flourishes had to be endured as cheerfully as possible.

'Here's to Fiza. Fizu. Fizzy. Fizz, who's smelt every book you see in this place. Yes, smelt. Even the musty ones on that handcart outside. Sometimes I think she doesn't even read. Just sniffs them and puts them away, like some kind of book hound. Anyway. Whether it's the twenty-seventh book on that shelf there, or that cushion on the seat there, or the painting on the wall there – it's all been hand-picked, sniffed and arranged by her. She's a slave driver. Lily-livered. And a bit of a literary snob. But we love her. And we love Paper Moon. Noor, your little princess...'

Fiza shut her eyes tight, unable to withstand any more praise. She cut off the extravagant tribute, saying, 'Here's to Marc. And D.K. And Suleiman sa'ab. And Sudhir. And my mom, Noor. Here's to Paper Moon.'

The Banerjees, meeting Fiza for the first time since that fateful New Year's Eve in Alibaug, had carried a bottle of fancy champagne. A few others had brought wine. This was now being poured into paper cups, and the crowd around Ismail's coconut stall was finally dwindling.

'Fiza, this is beyond our wildest expectations. We're so proud of you, darling,' said Mr Banerjee, overcome by genuine emotion and his second glass of champagne.

'This is just ... Dhruv has to see this,' Mrs Banerjee added. Could they have done something to keep those two together?

'Yes, Aunty. I hope he'll visit soon. How's he doing?' Fiza asked, overcompensating for the awkwardness with a forced lightness.

'We told him we're coming over for your launch. He was really surprised. Didn't know anything about it,' Mrs Banerjee replied.

'Yes, I've been caught up with all this work. And I figured everyone would know once it was launched. I'm so glad you could make it. Marc has been such a rock of support. Especially after I took ill...'

'You've lost more weight. Don't work so hard,' Mrs Banerjee said, picking up on Fiza's discomfort and changing the subject. Then she walked towards Marc, who greeted her exuberantly. His partner Vikram, a handsome combination of broody and athletic, with a beard speckled with grey, was busy with the philosophy section, filling a cane shopping basket with books.

As Fiza approached Vikram, she noticed Frances smoking by herself near the cart outside. She decided to walk over to her instead.

'So what do you think, ma'am? Will it do?'

'You know, every now and then my students surprise me. Maybe it's all worth it, day in day out on the local train, the philistine principal, same old syllabus. Maybe it all makes sense,' Frances replied.

'You know, when I came in that day and spoke with you in the staff room, that's when it came together in my head. I didn't even know whether I'd be doing this for sure. Now it just seems...'

Just then, Frances and Fiza found themselves face to face with an apparition in white. It was becoming difficult for Fiza to conclude even a single conversation, what with familiar faces popping up all around the store. But here was an unknown one. A clean-shaven man in a Lucknowi kurta, carrying a single red rose. Like someone at an Urdu mushaaira in the 1950s. Fiza had seen this man somewhere, but couldn't place him immediately.

'It's the stubble. It's gone,' he said.

'Huh? What stubble?'

'I'll leave you to your gentleman caller, then. I'd be failing in my duties if I didn't even pretend to browse through the books,' Frances said, walking back into the store, leaving behind a trail of tobacco and a woody scent.

'Kitaab khaana mubaarak,' said the visitor, handing her the long-stemmed red rose. It was her favourite flower.

'Shukriya,' she replied, puzzled and slightly amused. Whom did he remind her of?

'Mind if I take a look? Got any Archie comics? I have a weakness for them.'

'Er, no. Not yet anyway, sorry. But we have Garfield, and Calvin and Hobbes. And Asterix, and Tintin.'

'Highbrow, huh?'

The epileptic! He looked completely different.

'So the penny drops, Miss Hepatitis.'

'I'm Fiza Khalid. And you are?'

'Pleased to make your acquaintance.'

'Is this supposed to be a mystery, your identity?'

'Perhaps. Not sure yet.'

'Okay. So the children's section is downstairs. Along with magazines and comics. You'll find general interest books upstairs. I hope you find what you're looking for.'

'Hasn't worked yet for Bono...'

Fiza was disarmed by this overfamiliar stranger. He had taken her by surprise that night at the hospital. And now he was here at her bookshop, making corny U2 references. How did he even know about the store? Had she told him about the place? Her memory of that night was foggy.

The mellow afternoon was flowing into an evening of possibilities. At about four, Kavya walked in carrying a potted plant as a gift. Fiza felt a twinge of guilt; Kavya did all the work in the friendship. Then a couple of other college friends, Arvind and Daniel, walked in and went over to mutter nervous hellos to Frances. Fiza rescued them on the pretext of giving them a tour of the place. Once the others had drifted away, Fiza and Kavya found themselves giggling in a corner, remembering one of Frances's withering putdowns. She had called Arvind a 'blob of protoplasm' when he had looked vacant in reply to a question in class. After the tour was done, they stopped by the window on the upper storey.

'How's it going at university?' Fiza asked, not wanting the bookshop to dominate the conversation.

'Dull as ever, Fizz. I barely go myself. I've enrolled in a film appreciation course at XIC. Busy with that now.'

'That sounds great. I've been meaning to join a film club, but it just never happens.'

The stranger in white was back. 'Sorry, I'm told that you can see Armaan Khan's home from here,' he said, pointing out of the window in a vague direction.

'Not really. But you can see the Andrew's cemetery.'

'Yes, yes. A good substitute,' he replied tongue-in-cheek.

'Sorry, Kavya. This is a gentleman I met in hospital. And I think he's in need of a book. If you'll please excuse me, I'll see how the billing counter is doing,' she said, avoiding the increasingly insistent stranger.

While Sudhir attended to a customer, Fiza flipped through the bill book. Sudhir and she were still not fully comfortable with the retail software, so they had decided to start off the old-fashioned way. Now she was leafing through a thick sheaf of carbon copies – a strange new pleasure. When the customer had left the counter, Sudhir turned to Fiza, beaming. 'Twenty-five thousand upwards, ma'am. It's a bumper start.'

Fiza looked all around her. The place was overflowing with books, music and laughter. Her mother was there, her colleagues, her professor, her friends: everything good about her life, distilled into one place. She felt Dhruv's absence, but his family made up for it, in part. She was still an avowed existentialist, but one who was compelled to believe in uplifting twists of fate.

When all the guests had left, Fiza, Sudhir and Ismail stayed on to clear up. Fiza was still weak from the jaundice, but insisted on making sure everything was in order for the next day. They had ended the day with a sale of ₹38,372. This was a promising start. But she had been warned by D.K. that opening-day sales were never an indication of what was to come. The first month would be an education. She would see what was selling, what was in demand, what was lacking. Sudhir was the voice of experience. And there was the matter of hiring more staff, which they would begin to address from the next morning onwards.

But this was not a night meant for worry. Everyone who had walked in, from family to passers-by, had walked out pleased. The way the store looked and felt, the books on display, the attention from the staff – everything made people want to stay. The lower storey even had a kitchenette that would soon turn into a café. For now, it was geared to serve tea, coffee, biscuits and basic sandwiches. Fiza flipped through the visitors' book and smiled at the jottings. Among the copious lines of praise and the odd suggestion, one entry caught her eye. It was written in the Arabic script, which Fiza identified as Urdu. A professor had been hired by her grandfather, the academic, when she was quite young. But that didn't go very far. It was still difficult to find an Urdu language teacher who didn't tilt towards religious instruction.

This was puzzling. The only visitors she could think of who would be conversant with the script were Noor, D.K. and Suleiman Merchant. But they were all familiar with her ignorance. She tried to make sense of the words, but apart from a stray letter here and there, she found it indecipherable. Stranger still was that it looked calligraphic. Like the work of an artist. She would make Noor read and make sense of it. While these thoughts were running through her head, she remembered the stranger in white, and his 'kitaab khaana mubaarak'. First the chance encounter at the hospital. Then this slightly worrying appearance at the bookshop. Now a message in a script she did not understand. Ordinarily, Fiza would have had no patience for such riddles. But she found this particular collection of events intriguing. She shut the book and decided it was time to call it a night.

The shutters opened at nine, and by 9.30, Paper Moon was ready to sell books. The morning's first visitors were a young couple from St. Andrew's College nearby, sussing the place out. Soon, they settled into a corner, leafing through a Dan Brown.

'They will never buy, madam. They will only come and sit,' Sudhir whispered conspiratorially.

'But Sudhir, it's a bookshop. People should want to come and spend time here. You can't always expect people to buy books.'

'Correct, madam. But many faltu people will just do timepass.'

Fiza realized what he was saying from a business perspective. But the last few years, the city was starting to get increasingly polarized. The Irani cafés and dosa joints, where people from all backgrounds mingled over affordable treats, were giving way to swank eateries and clubs, designed to keep people out rather than in. She didn't want Paper Moon to turn into yet another gentrified public space, like a pretty doll in a glass case. And everyone who worked there would be trained to welcome guests, whether they came in for shelter from the rain or to browse without intending to buy.

Arranging books on the cart outside, Fiza made a mental note to talk to Sudhir about the way she saw the bookshop and its guests, without it turning into a socialist sermon. Her thoughts were interrupted by the ubiquitous Ismail, grinning as he made the turn at the Khoja corner.

'Big success, madam, yesterday. All guests happy. Some asking for Hindi books also. I said I think only English,' he beamed.

Right from its inception, Fiza had envisioned the bookshop to be English-oriented. But she also wished for it to speak different languages. The trips to the regional book distributors had to be made.

'Okay, madam. Going for delivery. Not so lucky to be in bookshop whole day. Thank you for stall yesterday. Reading, writing – I love. Okay, goodbye. See you later.'

A thought struck Fiza as Ismail scootered off. She was looking for staff. He was interested in books. And who could stop her from being offbeat? He could shift his coconut stall to the area outside the bookshop during the day. That way he could take charge of cleaning and maintenance. He could return to his base on the pavement in the night. In his spare time, he could work on his reading. This could work.

'Sudhir, I have an idea about the store's maintenance,' she said as a lady with a walking stick walked purposefully towards the revolving rack with the new releases.

'Yes, madam? I'll ask the watchmen in nearby buildings?'

'No, I was thinking of Ismail.'

'He knows someone who can work here?' Sudhir asked, confused.

'I was thinking of offering him a job. Store maintenance. He can sell coconuts outside, and work on his reading and writing whenever there is time.'

'Madam, all this is very good for Ismail Anna. But we have to think about the store.'

'Sudhir, this store is about the people who work here. And who visit. We can give it whatever form we choose,' Fiza said firmly.

This would take some time and effort. For now, she was pleased with her brainwave. All Paper Moon needed now was someone to come on board and assist Sudhir in managing the sales and software.

'I think we should place an ad in the paper for additional floor staff. What do you think?' Fiza said, careful not to let Sudhir feel he was being left out of important decisions.

'Yes, that is the best way. Local paper,' he agreed.

'Okay, so that's what we'll do. I'll get on it today.'

The first afternoon that the store was in operation was uneventful. People walked in and out, casting curious glances. Some complimented the design of the store. Others complained about the absence of their favourite authors.

Fiza and Sudhir filled the request book diligently, promising customers they would follow up. Fiza still didn't know how this worked. Which distributor was likely to provide which title at the best rate. But she took heart in the fact that since that first binge at New Majestic Shopping Centre, she had developed a more restrained approach to book-stocking. And now that Paper Moon was in business, she could respond to the requests that came in, rather than pre-empt them.

Bunches of flowers were still strewn about the place. D.K.'s lilies. A bouquet of carnations from her neighbours at Little Flower. A bunch of white daisies from Vikram, who had left with Sartre, Nietzsche and Kierkegaard. And a single red rose from Mystery Man, which she had dropped into a wine bottle acting as a water-filled vase on her desk. Fiza was unused to casual male attention after all that time with Dhruv. And she hadn't really had the time to think about the romantic question since the break-up. How did one think about such things? Being the object of a stranger's interest seemed vaguely troubling to her, and she tried to drive the thought away from her head.

'He's quite a hottie, Fizz. And he's clearly interested. Bookshop romance. Ah, such a warm and cuddly feeling,' Marc had said at the launch. Fiza had laughed away the suggestion, saying it meant nothing. It was just the backdrop that sparked the interest.

'But you said you first met at a hospital. That's clearly not a romantic setting, even by your gothic standards,' Marc had reminded her.

That was, in fact, true. The first time they had met, Fiza was a mess. And she hardly exchanged a few words with the man. She was still shaken by the fact that he had turned up at the bookshop. At the moment, he was halfway between a stranger and a romantic interest. This was new.

The question didn't bother her for too long. After that sudden appearance at the launch, the stranger had vanished. About a fortnight later, Fiza asked Noor to decipher the Urdu message over dinner. It was a quote from the poet Faiz, Noor informed her:

> *Woh log bahut khush-qismat thay*
> *Jo ishq ko kaam samajhte thay*
> *Ya kaam se aashiqui karte thay*

No name had been attached to the quote.

'So there's some artist type who's chasing you now? Better beware,' Noor ribbed Fiza about the cryptic guest.

'Uff, Ma. It's just a little verse.'

'With obvious romantic connotations. "Lucky were they who thought of love as their life's work or saw work as their beloved",' Noor translated off-handedly. 'Who is this?' she prodded.

'I don't know,' Fiza lied.

'Hmm. Have some lauki. She's made it well.' Noor's non sequiturs were legendary.

Fiza loved her veggies. But there was something about the gourds that she couldn't quite hack.

'How's the staff hunt going?'

'We've interviewed a few people. Just hasn't worked out for some reason. It's either the timings or fear of software, or something or the other. I was thinking of placing an ad at National, Andrew's, MMK. Maybe students coming in part-time could work out?' Fiza replied.

'Hmm. College kids is a good idea. And who's cleaning up the place? Still the bai from the next building?'

'At the moment. But I think we need someone there through the day. I had an idea about that. Ismail,' Fiza said nonchalantly.

'Who?' asked Noor.

'Our Ismail.'

'The coconut seller?'

'Yes, Ma. Is it *that* surprising?'

'Next you'll say Maria will handle the billing counter.'

'Sure, if she wants to train.'

Noor picked up her plate and left for the kitchen.

'You can't just pick someone off the street and give them charge of your business, Fizu.'

'Who's giving him the key to the Crown Jewels? It's just a cleaning job. Plus, he was the one who took me to hospital when I was throwing up in the street. If I could trust him to do that—'

'That's different.'

'And why is it different? Because I didn't have a choice at that point?'

'It's really difficult to get through to you when you get on this high horse. Just trust my instinct on this. He's not the kind of guy you want in a bookshop,' Noor insisted.

'He's friendly, polite, and really interested in books. I would think that's the perfect kind of person to have.'

'Do what you want. You always do,' Fiza heard Noor say faintly over the sound of water splashing on her plate.

Fiza thought it best to clear up the table once the kitchen was empty. She walked into her room annoyed, and was surprised to find a package on her bed wrapped in Noor's trademark Sunday newspaper. She opened it gingerly. Such gifts were reserved for birthdays or special occasions; this was unanticipated.

Fiza wasn't prepared for what she saw. A black-and-white picture in a wooden frame. In it, a bespectacled, serious-looking young man in a checked shirt, cigarette dangling from lips, held a book in one hand and a baby in the other. The baby was frowning intently at the book. It was wearing a cotton dress, with one strap fallen off the shoulder. This was the earliest picture she had seen of herself. The only one with her father. With this picture, his return to her life was complete. She wanted to step out and ask Noor about it. Where had she hidden this all these years? What made her share it now? But she already had the answers to her questions. And the tears were flowing too freely to make coherent conversation possible.

The next morning, Fiza walked up to Ismail, busy adding up numbers in his dusty notebook. 'Ismail, can I talk to you for a minute?' she asked.

'Yes, madam. Any problem? Coconut not sweet?'

'No, no. That's all fine, I had an offer for you.'

Ismail was uncomprehending of Fiza's plan. He could not believe what he was being offered: a regular job in a fancy store with a fixed salary. And the truly magnificent thing: a legitimate space from which he could conduct his coconut-selling business. After fumbling for the right words and feelings, he finally said, 'Madam, I promise I will work hard and learn everything properly. You are giving me so much trust. You will be happy with what you decide.'

'I'm sure, Ismail. I think it will work out very well. But I need you to start quite soon.'

'Madam, I will have to inform customers about change of location. Can you give two–three days, please?'

'Yes, sure. You can take a week,' Fiza said, smiling.

'Take this, madam. A sweet thank you,' he said, lopping off the head of a coconut and gallantly offering it to his new employer.

When Fiza returned to the bookshop, the stranger had struck again. A bunch of Birds of Paradise greeted her at the billing counter.

'Ma'am, the Khoja delivery boy brought these.'

'But I hadn't ordered any.'

'There was a note. Here,' Sudhir said, unable to conceal a grin.

'I'm out of the country, but that shouldn't stop me from visiting. The flowers will be replenished every week. Do consider letting them stay. I'll try and pick the low-maintenance ones. I doubt you'd have the patience for any other kind. I.'

'I.' Even for Mystery Man, that was too self-indulgent a sign off. Unless it was an initial. All she had to do was walk over to the florist next door and the riddle would be answered. But where was the fun in that?

'Oh, ma'am. There's one rose also.'

'Thanks, Sudhir. I'll take that up to the office.'

Fiza poured some water into the empty wine bottle on her desk and dropped in the rose. She then took out the framed photograph that had so moved her the previous evening and placed it in a corner. The past and the future were engulfing her with an intensity that was beginning to unnerve her.

A few minutes later, Sudhir murmured in his professional voice over the intercom: 'Madam, someone has come for interview.'

'Please send them upstairs. Thanks,' Fiza replied, transporting herself to the present.

A teenaged girl with thick glasses, a frilly top and fitted jeans walked in.

'Hello, my name is Scarlett, but all call me Rosy,' she said softly while offering Fiza a sheet of paper. 'My bio data. I saw your ad on the college notice board.'

Rosy. Fiza smiled to herself, glancing at the wine bottle on her desk. The CV revealed that Rosy was an avid reader, had volunteered at the local library every vacation, and was looking to take up library science once she graduated.

'Why library science?' Fiza asked, placing the CV under the wine bottle.

'My mummy is a librarian, ma'am.'

'Ah. Is that why your name ...' Fiza asked, trying to break the ice.

'Yes, ma'am. My granny loved *Gone with the Wind*. That's why Scarlett. But Rosy is better for me.'

'And how are you with computers? Our system is fully automated. Inventory. Billing. Customer database,' Fiza said, speaking her newly acquired bookshop lingo.

'I will learn,' she replied in a quiet but determined voice.

'And what about timings?'

'I have college nearby till 1 o'clock. I will come in after that and stay till nine. But I will need some time to do my college work, ma'am. Whenever it's a slow time.'

'Of course. I'm sure we can work it out. There are plenty of slow times right now. But we're hoping that will change,' Fiza said with a laugh.

And so it was decided. Rosy was to come in from the next afternoon. The store was up and running with full-strength staff. *Time to get that café ready*, Fiza resolved.

CHAPTER EIGHT

It was a scorching May afternoon and Fiza was sitting at her desk, directing the vent of her little window AC towards her. The last few months, filled with stories coming in from Gujarat, had been severely distressing. Yet, here she was in her glass bookcase, seemingly protected from the horrors of Godhra, and the terrors of the world at large.

The customary ninety-day credit period had elapsed, and her first purchases had to be paid for. Sudhir had filed the invoices in order of payment. A couple of accountants had already begun to make polite calls. She had asked for a statement of sales, distributor-wise, to see how much they had managed to sell and from which vendor. Fiza had bought books in bulk those first few outings; payments would far exceed sales at this point. In fact, D.K. and his staff accountants had predicted that the store would break even only around the three-year mark. But with rent, overheads and sundry expenses, Fiza was already grappling with scary thoughts, which were exacerbated by the sight of a bulky man in a hoodie and cycling shorts standing right at her office door.

'I'm Armaan Khan,' the hooded figure said in an unidentifiable foreign accent. When she looked up, Fiza found the claim to be true.

'Oh, hello. Are you looking for a book?' she said in her best sales voice.

'I want that section,' came the reply.

'Sorry?' Fiza said, stepping out of her office. A man twice the size of the star was filling a trolley with books. Art history, how-to guides, artist anthologies, graphic design books, coffee-table books – everything.

'Er, okay. If you'd like, we'll keep you posted about new arrivals in art.'

'Yeah. Send them o'er, sweetheart. You know where I live. Or my boy will pick 'em up. No sweat,' he replied with a wink.

'S-s-sure,' Fiza managed to say. And just like that, Paper Moon had sold books worth ₹2,34,000 within ten minutes. It was the most expensive section; Fiza rued the fact that she hadn't stocked it better. She couldn't wait to tell Dhruv what had just happened. In a flash, she remembered she didn't have him around to share funny stories with any more.

Walking down the staircase, Fiza spotted Ismail, Sudhir and Rosy in raptures. The few minutes of the celebrity's visit were being discussed in meticulous detail, from his sneakers to his piercings. Sudhir seemed to be the most affected.

'Madam, I'm his biggest fan. I've watched all his films fifteen to twenty times. But I felt too nervous to ask for autograph.'

Ismail chimed in. 'Arre, I will get autograph for you. I go to deliver naariyal. Sometimes he is doing exercise in middle of room only. No clothes. Means, no shirt. Very good body. Good discipline.'

Rosy, who usually kept to herself and her bookshelves, was gushing. 'He loves art, ma'am! His paintings are really great.

Christ and all he paints. Now he'll keep buying from here. We should keep all the latest art books. And old ones also.'

In an instant, Paper Moon had turned into the Armaan Khan Fan Club. Fiza couldn't for the life of her see how a man-child with negligible acting skills and a legendary sense of entitlement could addle perfectly reasonable brains in this way. Her own mother was a fan. And this was a woman who once refused a drink from Paul Simon at a jazz concert! She just couldn't see it.

Afternoons were usually slow, so Fiza felt it would be harsh to break up the impromptu party. And the shop had done great business. Just a little while ago, she was stressing about writing out cheques to creditors. Suddenly it had become the easiest task in the world. She hated the fact that Armaan Khan had everything to do with it.

The languid summer months gave way to a thunderous monsoon. By now, the bookshop had its regulars. The old Sindhi gentleman who spent long hours there to escape both boredom and his daughter-in-law. He'd distribute zeera golis among the staff, and the gesture actually sweetened their attitude towards him. Then there was the young couple that had browsed through the Dan Brown on Paper Moon's first day. They had a vast capacity for silence, broken by sudden giggles. A lady from a building down the street visited frequently. She was recently separated from her husband and found her evenings painfully vacant. 'He was a nice man, but our stars didn't match,' she had volunteered on one of her early visits. Fiza was still trying to get used to strangers and their confidences. Vandana, a lover of astrology and tarot-card readings, posed a particular challenge.

Fiza had grudgingly created a small section of self-help books, but she drew the line at tarot, until Vandana took her up on the resistance.

'Bestsellers keeps so many tarot sets. Why you don't have any? There is such a big demand,' she said in her matter-of-fact way.

'Actually, we're more focussed on our books. Merchandising is not really the plan.'

'But it's not about your plan, na? It's about what the customer wants. There are so many books about tarot. And this is a bookshop. So why to be so judgmental?' she persisted.

This could be a long conversation. But the customer had a point. The bookshop was not about Fiza's worldview. And yet, stocking books and objects to do with the supernatural or religious disturbed her; it was a value judgment about a way of interacting with the world. Then again, this *was* a store, not a private collection. It had to cater to the needs of those with views that differed from hers. In the end, economics defeated philosophy. The customer is always right, even when she isn't.

The next time Vandana walked in, Rosy directed her to the freshly-stocked section on tarot, Feng Shui and Vaastu. Fiza realized that if she had to make the bookshop work, she would have to learn how to let her personal views take a back seat in many departments. The idyll of the 'independent' bookshop was already beginning to reveal its complexities.

Meanwhile, the insistent Bombay rains affected walk-ins. Everyone was focussed on heading straight back home after work. Why risk flooded streets and cancelled trains? Sudhir and Rosy took to making phone calls, updating customers about new arrivals and book requests. Ismail had now been tasked with book deliveries, too. One stormy evening, Fiza was thinking about shutting the store early so the staff could head home, when a bedraggled lady in a dripping wet salwar-kameez shuffled in.

'Bharti Aunty! Gosh. I'll just get you a towel. You're soaking wet. Clearly, the umbrella was useless,' Fiza said while running up to her office.

'Uff, I had no idea it would get this bad so quick. I was on my way to Mount Mary and this blast of rain just ... came! I asked the auto guy to stop. Thought I would stay here at the shop till the storm passed,' Bharti muttered.

'You still go every Wednesday?' Fiza said, handing her the towel and putting the umbrella away.

'Wednesdays I go to St. Michael's for the Novena. Mount Mary is for special favours,' she explained while drying herself.

'Oh, okay. I'll just pour you some chai from the machine.'

'That machine chai is quite hopeless. Coffee is better. When are you opening your café, yaar?'

'Arre, we're just trying to figure something out. The permission is there. I have to find someone to run it for me.'

'Call me, na? I'll sell my cakes and cookies and all. And make much better coffee than this,' she joked while taking a quick sip.

'That's wonderful! Why didn't you suggest this before?'

'What? Me? Mad or what? I was just kidding. Mahesh can't be left alone in the house.'

'Seriously, Bharti Aunty. You've been talking about running a catering business for years now. Here's your chance. Everything is ready-made: kitchen, customers, interiors.' Fiza was thinking as she spoke, but it was effortless. Emboldened by the fluency with which the ideas presented themselves to her, she went on. 'You figure out a menu that works. We can have a small oven. A little fridge...'

Bharti took another long sip of the coffee and exhaled slowly. She was beginning to see this take shape.

'You think? I'll ask Noor...'

'Bharti Aunty, this is not about Mahesh Uncle or Ma. Do *you* want it? If you do, we'll make it work.' Fiza had always found it easy to speak to her mother's friend. With her, there was never any fear of consequences, no heavy baggage.

'Look, the rain has slowed down. Let me think about this, baccha. Now I'll run to church,' she said, shaking off the wet umbrella in the bucket at the entrance for no logical reason.

'You know, just think of this as a special favour that the Mother has granted!' Fiza said, and was immediately embarrassed at the cheap shot.

'Oh, so *now* you believe in miracles, haan?'

'I believe in you – like that "*Paper Moon*" song,' Fiza continued. Somehow she thought it terribly important to convince Bharti about the café plan. It seemed right.

'Hahah. I'll think about the offer. That song has been stuck in my head ever since your opening day. The gramophone was a great idea. I'll speak with Noor and Mahesh. I have all these other things in life to think about. But it's good to know I still have options!'

'I'll harass you, Bharti Aunty. You know I will.'

'It's one of the big joys of my life. Now let me run before another toofan strikes. Thank you for the coffee.'

The gently humming air conditioning was keeping the oppressive October heat at bay. Fiza was taking a break from work, reading a Faiz anthology by the picture window. Mystery Man's quote in the suggestions book had stoked her interest in the poet. '*Bol ke lab azaad hain tere…*' wrote the poet of revolt, of dissent, of questioning the status quo. Fiza looked up from the book, contemplating the post 9/11 world. How everything had changed, in a sense. Her generation had only heard twice-removed stories of the World Wars and of Partition. Then Babri Masjid happened, dividing Fiza's city forever. Now there was the gore and gloom of Gujarat. Every generation thought of itself as unique. Of negotiating historical events without precedent or the possibility of recurrence. Yet, how was this rapid descent into madness any different from the countless ones that had previously occurred? Was it just a difference in context? And where had Mystery Man disappeared to? The flowers were replaced week after week, as promised. And she could see also that his promise of unfussy seasonal varieties was being kept.

On a whim, Fiza decided to walk over to the florist and put an end to the suspense. Climbing down the stairs, she saw Bharti Aunty, now a couple of months into her role as café hostess, using a French press to serve a customer some Malabar coffee. The ground floor was filled with the aroma. Fiza decided to abandon the visit to the florist and request a cup instead.

After her initial reluctance, Bharti Aunty had taken to the café idea enthusiastically. She pored over all the details with Noor, and her husband provided more encouragement than she had expected. Now the little kitchen was serving not just coffee and sandwiches, but also cakes, desserts and other little treats. Regulars sank into their favourite chairs, bit into eclairs and brownies, and chatted over steaming lattes. Soon, the chef was inspired to experiment in the kitchen. She came up with dainty macaroons and delicate pavlovas. But on days when Fiza hosted book events, samosas and jalebis from Punjab Sweets at Pali Naka were passed around, and the chaiwala close to Mehboob Studio was summoned to serve his adrak and lemongrass confection. Just the previous day, the book club had been discussing the snacks more animatedly than the book of the month, *The Remains of the Day*.

It had been eight months since the launch and things were moving along smoothly. Fiza had nothing to complain about, and that was exactly the kind of thing that made her think twice. She had no experience of running a business of any sort, so all she was going with was a general sense of well-being. There were daily sales targets that they rarely met, but the one-off book binges made up for the slow days. They were not making money yet, but thanks to the café, they were on a steady course.

One pleasant November morning, Fiza arrived early at the store. After straightening a few shelves out, she began to leaf through the previous day's sales at the billing counter. Something occurred to her as she flipped through the filed bills. She had, or so she thought, successfully recommended a copy of *The Catcher in the Rye* to a customer herself. Yet, she couldn't find the book mentioned in any of the bills for the day. Rosy and Sudhir were meticulous about these matters. For the first time since the launch, Fiza was struck by a sense of doubt regarding her team.

Sudhir walked in at his usual time and was surprised to see Fiza at the counter.

'Good morning, ma'am. Today you will do the billing?' he asked with a smile.

'Yes, maybe I should. Just to keep in touch with sales,' Fiza said, somewhat awkwardly. She didn't want to make any false allegations, nor could she let the matter slip. A book had been sold, for which there was no record. This spelt trouble. Big trouble. Her head was filling quickly with horrible images.

'Sudhir, will you please look at the cartons lying upstairs? The ones that have come in from Rajesh Books? Check them against the invoice and classify them into sections, please. Thanks.'

She needed some time to go through the bills by herself. Rosy would come in by the afternoon. She would then confront both her and Sudhir about the matter. But first she would look for other discrepancies.

In about an hour's time, Fiza was sitting with her head in her hands, having made no headway in her investigation, but with fears and misgivings multiplying rapidly. Sudhir was still upstairs with the cartons. Bharti Aunty would be arriving soon. Ismail was standing outside at his stall. She decided to go have a word with him.

'Ismail, how's everything going? The work? The people in the bookshop?' she asked with a crinkled forehead.

'All is okay, madam. There is some problem?' he asked, sensing her anxiety.

'I don't know if there is a problem. I might need your help to find out.'

'Of course, madam. Tell me.'

'It's about the billing. There is a mismatch. I mean – I remember a book being sold recently, but I can't find it in the bills.'

'Oh, that's a big lafda. Very dangerous. What you think, madam?'

'I was hoping you could keep an eye on the billing counter. But quietly. I don't want this to become a big...'

'I understand. You want to see if customer money is going inside drawer or inside pocket,' he whispered.

'I don't have any proof. That's why we have to be careful.'

'Surely, madam. I will be quiet watchman. If there is any problem, I will find out for you. Trust is good. But too much trust does dhanda chaupat.'

'Thank you, Ismail.'

When Rosy walked in in the afternoon, Fiza wasn't her usual self. She stayed inside her office and stepped out only for a cursory glance every now and then. She didn't have the heart to address the issue just yet, even though she knew she couldn't delay it. Stressed and anxious through the day, she was happy to see Kavya at her door just before closing time.

'I'm so glad I caught you. I had a meeting in the area for a short film I'm working on, so I just took a chance.'

'I'm *so* happy to see you, Kavi, you have no idea. We're closing soon. What plans for later?'

'Nothing. If you're free for dinner, we can go somewhere nearby. Drinks toh you're still not allowed, na?'

'It's been over six months now. So I think I'm allowed a rum or two. Toto's?'

'Where else?' Kavya laughed.

Toto's Garage Pub at Pali Naka was Fiza's favourite dive. It was where she would spend evenings with Dhruv in a haze of smoke, to which neither of them would ever add. Dhruv carefully – and ineffectually – concealed his smoking from Fiza. The pub's car theme was bizarre, the food comforting and the music safe. The manager spotted Fiza walking in and said with delight, 'Oh! Welcome, welcome. I thought you forgot all about us after your bookshop and all.'

'That's not possible, Mr Acharya. This will always be home.'

Before she could sit down, the co-owner, Mr Bhatia of the dark glasses and bright shirts, took a seat at her table. 'Ab yaad aayi, bookshop girl?'

'Arre, I'm so sorry. God knows where the last six months disappeared.'

'Aur ladke ka kya haal hai? He's enjoying McDonald's and petrol pumps? Aur kya rakha hai America mein? Ask him to come back after his course, haan.'

Fiza smiled weakly in response. The day had already been difficult; she didn't want to make it any worse by spilling the news of her break-up to the pub gang. A few minutes later, when Mr Bhatia had left the table, Kavya was already halfway through a pint of draught. Fiza took her first sip of rum in months – Old Monk and Thums Up with a slice of lime and plenty of ice.

'So – you won't believe what I discovered today,' Fiza said, buoyed by her first few sips.

'Fizu, sorry, but the last time you said you discovered something, you had lost your father and inherited a bookshop. Now what?' Kavya said artlessly.

'No, no. This is not that kind of news,' Fiza laughed nervously. 'Someone is stealing from the bookshop.'

'What? You mean books?'

'Now that I hadn't even thought of! Thanks, Kavi,' Fiza smirked.

'Oh. But book pilferage is a big thing. You must have a CCTV, Fizu. You're too trusting.'

'I think you're right. But I have a human spy on the case right now. Ismail. He's going to see whether Sudhir and Rosy are actually presenting bills for all the books sold.'

'The naariyal guy? How do you know *he's* not the chor?' Kavya asked while signalling for another beer.

'Because I know. And he has no access to the billing.'

'Hmm. That's a tough one,' Kavya said, sipping her glass of draught. 'You know, Fizu, you look quite washed out. Have you even eaten something today?'

'Have I? I'm not sure. I think I forgot about lunch in all this mess,' she replied absently. 'I must be hungry. Sausages?'

'Sure. And I feel like having that chicken omelette-in-a-bun thing Dhruv loves … loved,' Kavya said, correcting herself sheepishly.

'He's still alive. You don't have to tiptoe about him around me. How's he doing?' Fiza said while catching the waiter's attention. 'Deepak,' she said. 'Sausages?' he asked, in a display of perfect communication.

'He's good. Meeting some hotshots while completing his course. His father is better connected than I thought.'

'Hmm. And any – you know – love interests?' Fiza asked, while trying to appear casual.

'Fizu, sometimes you talk like you're in a Jane Austen novel. Who says "love interests" any more?'

'Sometimes I feel we're still in that world. Just the appearance has changed. It's still girls vying for boys. Parents playing the social game. High-teas and Christmas dances.'

'He's coming down for Christmas,' Kavya said suddenly.

'Oh.'

Deepak placed the plate of sausages between the two glasses. Fiza sank her teeth into one, chewing on the thought

of seeing Dhruv again. Him standing in the bookshop she
set up from scratch; she couldn't help but find the thought
thrilling. Dhruv was always the go-getter, the enterprising
one. And out of nowhere, she had ended up with a dream
business. The sixteen-year-old in her was gloating.

'So will you meet him?' asked Kavya.

'Kavi, it's been a rough day. Can we speak about lighter
things, please? What's your short film about? The one you
mentioned earlier, at the bookshop?'

'Funeral rites in South Asia.'

The two broke into their signature synchronized laugh and
ordered another round of drinks.

Fourteenth November. Children's Day. Fiza had planned
a big party for her little readers. They came in dressed
as characters from books. Little witches and wizards,
caterpillars and princesses, strutting about the store. A Mad
Hatter – complete with top hat, pocket watch and jacket
– made an appearance. The embarrassed mother told her
how the elaborate costume was actually created for a school
play and she was happy she got another chance to use it.
Fiza had got the store crew to dress up, too. She had come
in as a pirate, with an eyepatch and cardboard sword; she'd
made Kavya borrow the props from a cousin in primary
school. Sudhir came in his Santa Claus outfit, misreading
the brief for a fancy dress. Rosy wore an animal suit, halfway
between a bear and a squirrel. And Ismail wore a Batman
mask. Bharti Aunty had avoided the costume threat by
volunteering to do a storytelling session. She had made the

kids special treats – jam tarts and chocolate bombs, mini idlis and chutney sandwiches.

After the storytelling session, the kids were served kokum sharbat from a punch bowl. When '*Bare Necessities*' blared out of the speaker, they broke into a mad dance. Fiza had never liked children before. These days, she realized, her favourite activities at the store revolved around them. Kids around books weren't all that bad, she decided. Taking a break from all the action, Fiza retreated to her office and opened the daily sales register online. Outside, Rosy was catering to a mother-and-child duo. Fiza went through the sales records for the last few days and glanced outside again. She noticed something strange. Walking away from the customer, she saw Rosy lifting the head portion of her costume and slipping something in. Fiza immediately went up to the customer and requested to see the bill that had just been presented to her. It was exactly what she was afraid of. All bills at the store were now computerized. This one was a fake – torn out of an unauthorized booklet. Was it just Rosy, or was Sudhir in on it, too?

The party was just wrapping up, with the last of the kids leaving with their parents and minders. Fiza realized she couldn't lose another moment, another rupee. She walked downstairs and interrupted Rosy, who was chatting with Sudhir.

'Rosy, may I see you for a minute, please?'

The two walked slowly outside the store. Ismail was still in his Batman mask, adding up coconut sales for the afternoon. Fiza requested that he step inside and give Bharti Aunty a hand at the café. Then she sat Rosy down on the low wall separating the store from the florist.

'Rosy, I want to do this as gently and quickly as possible. I saw what you did with the customer upstairs. Please don't try and deny it – I've been suspecting something was wrong for a few days now, and today I have proof. I want to know how long this has been going on and who all have been involved.'

After a pause that seemed to go on for hours, Rosy dropped the head portion of her costume to reveal a few currency notes. It was an absurd sight. A pirate sitting in front of a bear that was balancing money on its head. She handed the notes over to Fiza and said in a small voice: 'I'm sorry.'

'What happened, Rosy?' Fiza said with as much compassion as she could muster. Somehow, there was no relief, only pain at the discovery. There had to be more to the story. This wasn't the Rosy she had come to know.

'What do you need the money for? Is there some kind of crisis? Tell me, Rosy.'

The girl fixed her stare at a bunch of lilies at Khoja behind her. Her eyes were dry, as if by an act of will. Crying would have been a luxury under the circumstances.

'I wanted to collect 4000 rupees, ma'am. To buy new prescription glasses for Mummy. The number has gone up and she's not buying because all the money went into waterproofing before the rains. She's been having headaches every day. Can't even work properly. I thought I'll borrow – take money – from the shop and, and once we'd bought the glasses, put the money back … little by little, every month, in petty cash, when salary comes. Give back more money than what I took.'

Even though she had asked Rosy to tell the truth, Fiza wasn't expecting a moral dilemma. What Rosy was doing was 'wrong'. And yet her intent, and her plan to compensate, was endearing. *Do they tell you how to handle this in business school?* Fiza wondered.

Regaining her composure, she asked Rosy to hand her the fake bill book. Going through the leaves, Fiza quickly found that only a few had been used up, all bills together amounting to about ₹1500. So the damage was not as bad as she had imagined.

'Rosy, I want you to go back in, change into the clothes you came in wearing and excuse yourself for the day. I want to give this some serious thought, and I can't do that with you around.'

Rosy nodded feebly and walked into the store. A princess and a robot walked out, followed by two adoring mothers lugging bags full of books. Fiza felt a twinge of fear, wondering whether she should check their bills. Intuiting her doubt, Rosy turned back, walked over to Fiza and said, 'Ma'am, Sudhir did their billing. And he doesn't know anything about ... Only that bill you found today was wrong. You can check the bill book. The dates are all there. Only one bill every day will be...'

Fiza sighed and walked back in, desperately reaching for a chocolate bomb at the café counter.

CHAPTER NINE

'Hmm. This is quite unfortunate, darling. It was all going so well.'

'Tell me about it. The not knowing was really bothering me. Now that I know, it's a new kind of punishment.'

Fiza had called on Marc soon after Rosy left the store. She needed to speak to someone who didn't see the world in black and white. The incident needed a more nuanced approach.

'But you know what,' he said, popping a wasabi nut into his mouth. 'It's hardly the first time that a kid has broken the rules. How old is she, sixteen?'

'Older. Hardly a kid, Marc.'

'See, we can't go all IPC on this, Fizz. She's a good kid. And it seems like she's telling the truth about the ... lies,' he said, fidgeting with a bunny slipper.

'Yes. I guess. But the thing is: *should* we be okay with this? What kind of precedent does it set...'

'Who's the "we" here? The royal *we*? The great part about the shop is, you can do it your way. There is no "we".'

'I know what you're saying, but when Sudhir and the rest hear...'

'Wait, wait, waitaminute. *When* they hear?'

Fiza was suddenly struck by the feeling that she was the one seeing the picture in black and white.

'So what are you saying?' She noticed Marc's eyes were fixed somewhere close to her feet on his washed-out rug.

'The first thing I'm saying is, you need to get yourself a third pair of footwear. I know you think Kolhapuris and Batas cover all possible social occasions, but maybe open your mind to this radical new concept: shoes. Look at those poor heels!'

The digression dismantled Fiza's frown. 'Hmm. Now tell me what we should do about this ... *situation*.'

'*You* should do about this. *You*. Not *we*. Please get over the idea that you have to run this place out of a management guide MBAs jerk off to. Of best effing practices and shitty parables. She's a good kid, we both know that. You buy the story. It's more sad than bad. She's struggling with right and wrong, like all of us. Give her a chance.'

'Now you make me sound like a soulless zamindar type,' Fiza shot back in defence.

Marc jumped off the bar stool and sat beside her on the sofa. Then he returned his gaze to her feet saying, 'Actually, a pedicure wouldn't be amiss either.'

Fiza rolled her eyes in frustration. 'Why is it that I get properly hammered every time I walk into this place?'

'Maybe because St. Fiza feels she can be human here.'

'Uff. It was a rhetorical question. But maybe you're right. Maybe I'm just driving myself nuts trying to do things "the right way",' she said, using the air quotes she hated other people using.

'You're doing great, baby. And here comes Vikram. Let's not get him involved in this, please. He'll bore us with some quotes from Epictetus or Thomas Aquinas or something, and

arrive exactly at where we are now,' Marc said, greeting his
ragged lover with a fond smile to compensate for his words.

Vikram looked exhausted. He was shooting patchwork
for his latest nature documentary – *Wild Nights in the City* –
which was taking forever to complete. His mood visibly lifted
seeing Fiza on the chintz couch.

'Fiza! What a thing. I was thinking of you just today,' he
said, laying down his tripod and bazooka-like camera.

'Really? How come?' Fiza replied, walking over to hug him.

'No, no, no. Not before I disinfect myself. I smell like a
dumpster. Dhruv's here, by the way. Some assignment before
Christmas break. He dropped by at the shoot today. I didn't
really have much time then, but it was good to see the boy,' he
said before excusing himself and heading for the shower.

Fiza drained her drink and walked to the bar to refill her
glass. Marc sighed audibly, watching Vikram's receding back.

It was an unusually busy day at Paper Moon. All the seats of
the café were filled. The cash counter had been in active mode
pretty much since the shutters opened. The phone hadn't
stopped ringing. And Frances D'Monte had everything to do
with it.

Frances wrote a weekly column in the *Mumbai Banter*
newspaper about reading and writing. And on that particular
Wednesday, she had written about Paper Moon. Not just a
stray mention or a few lines of recommendation – an entire
column on Fiza and her store. A week earlier, Frances had
walked into the shop, filling Fiza with a familiar combination
of excitement and trepidation. She had asked if Fiza had some

time to spare and then gone on to ask questions about the
shop – how she had set it up, what plans she had for it, how
things had gone that far. Fiza found it surreal to be sitting in
a world of her making, speaking into a dictaphone, looking
into Frances's implacable eyes. In there, there was absolutely
no scope for flakiness or subterfuge. Now, when the piece had
appeared in the paper, she was charmed to see how she had
been quoted word for word.

'Ma'am, you actually wrote what I said,' she said excitedly
into the receiver after reading the piece.

'Yes, that's how it works, usually. It's called reported
speech,' Frances replied drily.

Fiza was surprised at the attention the store was receiving
thanks to the piece. Noor had cut out the article neatly, just
like she used to do with other columns and quotes she liked
in the papers. They would all go into an old coffee jar with a
rusty cap, which was never opened, except when there was a
new addition. It just lay there near the TV table, a talisman of
bottled-up wisdom. But she had other plans for Fiza's write-
up. She had it laminated and instructed her daughter to pin it
up at the store.

'But, Ma, when people are already at the store, why
advertise it?' Fiza complained.

'For once, just be quiet and do this, Fizu. Put it up where
people can see it. Not in some dark corner,' Noor insisted.

The conversation was redundant. Down at the store, Bharti
Aunty had already put up the article on the café soft board
using colourful push-pins. 'Paper Moon', said the headline
simply, exhilaratingly. It carried a biggish photograph – a
wide shot of the store, with Fiza sitting on her beloved Chor
Bazar bench, pretending to read Irvine Welsh's *Trainspotting*.

'Why couldn't you send a proper picture ya, Fizu? Can't even see your face properly. It's just books and pretty furniture.'

'Bharti Aunty, sometimes you and Ma sound exactly the same. It's never been my ambition to...'

'Fizu,' Bharti Aunty interrupted, looking awkwardly over Fiza's shoulder.

'What?' Fiza said, turning around.

It was Dhruv, but un-Dhruv-like. Beard and satchel. Black T-shirt and cork sandals. The globetrotter-comes-home look. He was carrying two books. One was a hardcover and the other, a paperback.

'Hey,' Fiza said, trying to appear calm despite a wildly fluttering heart. 'Oh shut up,' she was saying to herself under her breath, but it wasn't working.

'Hey,' Dhruv replied and handed her the books, as if it were just another casual meeting at the college library.

'Thanks. But you shouldn't have...'

He wrapped his arms around her in reply, pecking her gently on her cheek.

This was exactly what she had feared when Kavya, and later Vikram, had mentioned Dhruv's return. That his reappearance would bring back everything she was learning to leave behind, in a big, destructive whirlpool of emotion. There were leftover feelings that she had made her peace with. But seeing him at the store was making her think that none of the feelings had truly left.

She looked at the books in her hand while regaining her composure. The bigger one was a pop-up version of *Alice in Wonderland*. She had read about it in a magazine and gushed about it to Dhruv. Its exquisitely folded art – from the Cheshire Cat in the woods to the Red Queen's palace with all the card-shaped guards. The second was a Faber & Faber: *The Collected Poems of Louis MacNeice*. They had spotted it together at Strand, but it was too expensive at the time for them to even consider. She held the two books close to her, not daring to look at the inscriptions.

'Not too shabby,' Dhruv said, looking around the store. Then he turned to Fiza with a smile that had in it genuine pride. 'Not too shabby at all. How? What? When?'

The steady stream of visitors at the store did not stop, but it was as if Fiza and Dhruv had been frozen in a diorama. After the first few minutes, the conversation became easy. In a few more minutes, fun. The past year-and-a-half had been eventful for both. He was learning to find his place in a new city, a different world; she had built herself a new world altogether. And now they were narrating their stories freely, using a shorthand for jokes and references built over years.

At about seven in the evening, Fiza finally walked over to see how Sudhir was doing at the counter when she had the second surprise of the day. Mystery Man was walking into the store with that half-cocky, half-endearing grin that already seemed familiar to her. She instinctively looked behind her, where Dhruv was flipping through the pages of a Bob Dylan biography. The stranger's sudden reappearance had disturbed a very carefully assembled calm. She felt a ripple of discomfort – a mild panic – to see him resurface right at that moment, carrying with him the idea of possibilities, of the unknown.

'Begum,' said the stranger with that particular brand of confidence that stops just short of arrogance. 'Good to see the piece in today's *Banter*.'

'Thanks,' Fiza said hurriedly, feigning a lack of interest. 'If you'll excuse me, I have a customer to attend to upstairs.'

'Well, I'm a customer who needs attention, too,' the stranger continued in his usual insistent style.

Fiza called out to Rosy who was at the history section close by. 'Could you please attend to the gentleman here?' she said and walked upstairs.

'I'll be fine,' the stranger said to Rosy with a wink. Rosy and Sudhir exchanged a smile from across the room. 'Mr Gulaab' is what they called him on the sly, and secretly rooted for him, too.

The stranger walked across to the music section, where Dhruv was still rapt in the Dylan book. 'I love the bit where the interviewer asks what "*Like a Rolling Stone*" was about, and Dylan says, "It's about six minutes long". Or was that in another interview? Sorry, don't mind me,' he said, giving Dhruv a friendly nod.

'That sounds like him. I've never really got the lyrics. Something about Siamese cats and alibis ... quite trippy,' Dhruv replied. He was always up for an easy chat. And living in a new city had further sharpened his social skills.

'But that's the thing about Dylan. It's all about the words. Else, it's just a really pissed-off guy with a harmonica and an unbearable voice. One day, he'll win the Nobel in Literature and everyone will be buying those lyric tomes to make their coffee tables look smart.'

'I'm Dhruv,' came the reply, with an extended hand.

'Iqbal,' said the stranger. 'Nice to meet you. Great place, this. Come here often?'

'It's my first visit, actually. I was away when it opened. Heard a lot about it. It's run by my girl ... ex-girlfriend. So it's especially good,' Dhruv replied, establishing his affinity with the store.

Fiza had returned downstairs and busied herself with a customer looking for cookbooks. Every now and then, she shot a glance towards the two men, who had settled into a proper conversation. Bharti Aunty, who was behind the café counter, sensed the awkwardness of the situation. She walked over to Fiza and said, 'Fizu, naariyal paani?'

The two walked out and took their usual spots on the low wall. Sipping on a coconut, Bharti Aunty said, 'I know it's none of my business, but Dhruv has moved on.'

'Bharti Aunty, why're you saying this to me?' said Fiza, instantly annoyed. She was fiercely protective of her private life, of which her romantic relationship was the most heavily guarded centre. Right now, it seemed like all eyes were on her most intimate thoughts and feelings.

'I know, I'm sorry. I just thought, with the new guy … Anyway, you kids are smart these days. You know better what to do. Chalo, I think Table 2 needs coffee. So busy today has been, baap re.'

Fiza continued to sit on the wall, close to Ismail's perch, trying to make sense of the events of the day. Sudhir didn't have a minute to spare, while Rosy was busy taking orders and enquiries on the phone.

'Today is super-duper day, madam. *Sholay* level, after that news in paper. Your teacher is very powerful. Seeing her only I come to know. Some people have power in eyes, in voice,' Ismail rattled on. 'That sir is coming after many days no, madam?' he said, pointing his scythe towards the figure now heading towards the exit.

'Just met your ex. Sweet fellow. Feel you should give him another chance,' he said with a smirk.

Fiza had been accepting of the stranger's overfamiliar manner so far. But with this, she snapped. To add to her annoyance, she wondered why Dhruv would bring up their relationship with an absolute stranger. *Just like Dhruv to mark his territory*, she thought uncharitably.

'I don't mean to be rude, but we don't know each other at all. If you'd like to visit the store, please do. Sudhir and Rosy will help you. And the flowers – could you please stop that, too? They make me uncomfortable.'

Seeing Fiza outside the store with the stranger, Dhruv walked out, too. 'Thought you'd run off or something. Iqbal here was telling me all about his store connection,' he said, oblivious to the tension around him.

Fiza was stunned at the words. '*Iqbal*?' she uttered the loaded name with bewilderment. 'What store connection?'

'About how he grew up here – this mansion being his home. And how he was keen on renting it out to you. How he wanted it to be a bookshop rather than a bank or a pool parlour. Imagine, the house you've grown up in turning into a bookstore! There's a book right there,' he addressed these last words to Iqbal, who smiled politely.

'Yes, what a thing. Maybe someday,' he replied. 'Sorry, but I've got to go. I've left a request with Rosy. She'll call when the book comes in. Great meeting you, Dhruv. Good luck with the assignment,' said the stranger and walked away. Then, jumping the low wall, he stepped into Khoja Florist. Fiza could see him mumble something to the man at the counter and make a payment. He was doing as he was told.

'So what are you doing tonight, Fizz? Toto's?' Dhruv continued.

'Sorry, not tonight. I have plans,' Fiza lied, finally taking charge of her day. 'But it was great to see you. And thanks for the books. And the chat.'

'Why so formal? Wazzup?'

'Well, you wanted me to stay away. Now I've done that, you're asking for something else.'

'I'm not asking for anything. Maybe a beer. I love what you've done here, Fizz. I never imagined you could—'

'Get out into the world?'

'Yes, sort of. This is all so … dream-like.'

'It was never my dream. But I know what you mean. Things have worked out in strange ways,' Fiza said, keen to end the conversation and be by herself to indulge the bad mood that had descended on her.

'Yes. Iqbal seems like a great landlord, too. That's such a big thing in Bombay. Ironic, his name.'

'Yes. A little too ironic?' she said, quoting from one of Dhruv's favourite songs and drawing a fond smile from him.

'Right. So I'll scoot. Folks have this thing planned. Feel like coming?'

Fiza tensed instantly at the offer.

'Relax. I'm kidding. You take your time. We'll figure this out,' Dhruv said, stretching out his arms for a hug from which Fiza swiftly drew away.

'I've figured things out, Dhruv. Perhaps you need to take the time.'

'You're letting pride get in the way, Fizz.'

'Of what?'

'You know you want us to be back. Why fight it?'

'Do I? And what's changed your stance? Dhruv, this is just a backdrop. Store, picture window, coffee. I'm still who I was.'

'Nah. It's all changed. You're a dreamer now. You've imagined a life for yourself. Not some PTSD version of life, where everything's about containment, about keeping shit together. You know, chatting with you today, you were talking about the future. You know how *radical* that is? I could barely get you to commit to dinner! Just look at all this. It's magic.'

Fiza had gone completely quiet.

'I know this must all be too much. But think about what I've said. Swallow that pride,' Dhruv said playfully.

It's not pride. It's closure, Fiza thought. 'Good to see you again,' she said.

'Bye, Fizz,' Dhruv said and realized he still had the Dylan book in his hands. 'Oh. I'm a book thief. Let's get this billed.'

'It's from me, don't worry about it.'

'Are you kidding me? I've walked into your bookstore for the first time ever. *Your* bookstore,' he said with his hands on her shoulders. 'I don't think I've ever felt this happy buying a book. This is fucking insane. You're a rockstar, Fizz,' he said, walking back to the counter.

'I. Iqbal. *Iqbal*,' Fiza whispered to herself absently.

Fiza decided to pay D.K. a visit the next day to get to the bottom of the landlord business. D.K. had handled everything on that front: the negotiation, the agreement, the logistics. The thought of this connection with the stranger – Iqbal – changed everything. And yet she didn't know what there was to change. If Paper Moon was originally his home, then he was an integral part of the store and, by association, her life in it. The idea seemed oddly reassuring. Had Dhruv not appeared out of nowhere, would she have allowed herself to be happy about this revelation? Dhruv was eager for a reconciliation. Paper Moon was opening up her world in ways she wasn't sure she was prepared for.

'Yes, the Ali Khans. The owners, what about them? Is there some trouble? Don't worry about it. We're on a strong footing. Tell me what happened,' D.K. said, getting into protective mode straightaway.

'No, no, D.K. Not at all. There's been no problem. It's just that one of the family members, Iqbal, has been visiting.'

'Oh, okay. He settled in London long back. Must be here for some work. Very talented fellow. Very creative. I keep reading about him here and there. You know, he was the one who convinced the family to give us the space. They would have got more rent from some MNC, but he wanted it to be a bookshop. Your family knows his family,' D.K. said, relieved there was no trouble with the landlords.

'Yes. Ma said something about Nani and his – Iqbal's – grandmother playing badminton at the gymkhana. That's all. I just wanted to confirm he was who he was saying he was.'

'Yes, Mrs Abbas and Mrs Ali Khan were legends at the club. You won't believe the glamour. I think Yusuf sa'ab used to visit just to … Anyway, that zamaana was something else. But you're becoming a proper businesswoman. Background check and all. Good, good,' D.K. laughed.

'That sounds scary!' Fiza replied. 'Okay, I better head back to the store.'

'Give my salaams to Iqbal when he drops by. Nice guy. Tell the staff to be extra good to him. We should have him on our side. Better to be safe in property matters.'

Riding in the cab on the way to the store, Fiza decided to reach out to Iqbal. Even apologize for her rudeness the other day. Without the information she now had, his interest seemed unusual. Now it all made sense. The familiarity he had displayed wasn't troubling any more. And what really warmed her was the fact that he hadn't used his landlord status to woo her. He was going about it the hard way, the old-fashioned way. Before entering the store, she decided to pay Khoja Florist a visit. Play by *his* rules this time.

'Hello. I'd like to send Mr Iqbal Ali Khan some flowers. Would you have his address?'

'Yes, ma'am. This was his house,' smiled the old man at the counter, pointing to her store. Books, flowers and coincidence had laid the foundation for a classic romance. There was nothing for Fiza to do but to obey the laws of the genre.

The salon on the ground floor of Little Flower was now in operation. Fiza decided to cheat on her usual beauty parlour, where the owners and beauticians had known her since she was little. For as long as she remembered, the walls of Zahra Beauty Parlour off Hill Road had glamorous images of Rekha on its walls. And once, just once, she had encountered the icon at the parlour, having her luscious hair washed, her little dog Pishti on her lap, like old-style royalty. But this one downstairs was so much more convenient.

'Ma'am, so much tan! Not doing bleach or what?'

Fiza immediately regretted her decision. At Zahra, they wouldn't question or judge. In fact, her mocha skin and irrepressible ringlets garnered praise from the staff. Now she found herself to be the recipient of admonishment and advice when all she wanted was a simple hair trim.

'No, thank you. This is the actual colour of my skin. It's not a tan,' she replied in a pretend calm voice.

'No, no. This is tan only,' the beautician persisted. 'But it will go, madam. You just see. It's powerful bleach. Burns the skin.'

Fiza had quickly grown tired of this assault. She offered the slightest of smiles while nodding her head, picking up a magazine lying before her. 'I'M STILL A VIRGIN,' screamed the headline on the cover, accompanied by a picture of Armaan Khan mischievously chewing on his own vest. Fiza sighed and flipped through the pages to find a photo feature of actresses in swimwear being looked at amorously by men in suits; a section on the stars' favourite veggies (including the Big B's preferred bhindi preparation); and an in-depth Q&A with music composer Anu Malik in which he described his creative process. It was this or the beauty police, so she kept up the pretence of unwavering interest.

'*Aise kaise kiya?*' shrieked a voice from the neighbouring chair. It belonged to an aggrieved lady who was pointing to her eyebrows with a mixture of rage and sorrow. A petrified beautician was hovering over her with a pair of scissors in her hands and thread between her lips, which had now fallen to the floor.

The shrieking lady flew off her chair and landed right in front of the billing counter, where the owner of the salon was blowing her freshly painted nails dry. 'Look at this!' she screamed, pointing to her forehead. 'So thin! I just told her to remove the extra hair. What is this? Bloody idiot, your girl!'

The owner, who had been smiling benignly from her perch thus far, was failing spectacularly to calm the customer down.

'It's not looking bad, ma'am. We just have to thread this little ...' said the beautician meekly.

'You want to thread *more*? You'll shave off the whole thing. What I'll do then? Big disaster this is! How you can do this to your customers?'

Fiza was trying hard to pretend like she didn't know what was going on, but that charade ended when the screamer yelled in her direction.

'Look at this! Joker, I look like!'

At this point, Fiza had no option but to take a better look at the apoplectic lady. Her hair was covered in strips of foil; below her bare shoulders hung the floral parlour smock; her nails were painted a shocking purple. It was tough not to agree with her. And Fiza hadn't had the chance to examine her eyebrows yet.

Fiza responded by lowering her gaze, not wanting to give anything away. In a second, she told her hairdresser that the trim was done. Then, quickly throwing off her cape, she rushed to the counter, hoping her intervention would save the owner. By now, the mortified beautician was in tears. Fiza hurriedly paid for the half-finished trim, suddenly grateful she ran a bookstore, where the possibility of customers turning into wailing banshees was rather limited. Then, with uneven hair and spirits, she left for the store.

'Good morning, ma'am,' Sudhir said in his usual upbeat manner. 'Your friend has come, from yesterday.'

Fiza's pulse quickened. He had received the flowers. Amends had been made. Walking up the spiral staircase, she caught the back of a familiar head. It was Dhruv's.

'Hey!' she called out.

'Hey,' he replied, leaving the *Esquire* magazine he was flipping through on the cane chair. Then, walking up to Fiza with an embarrassed grin, he said, 'I'm sorry about yesterday. Got carried away, as usual.'

'Let's step inside,' Fiza replied, leading the way to her office. The last rose she had received from Iqbal was now wilting in the wine glass. She made a mental note to dry it up and turn it into pot pourri, so it wouldn't have to be thrown away.

'It's cool, Dhruv. This is how it's always been,' she said, settling into her swivel chair and turning her PC on.

'What's always been?'

'Ideas occur to you. You get over them. You have new ideas. You return to old ones. Things keep happening. But in the meantime, life goes on for the rest of us, too.'

'Look, Fizz. I've already apologized for barging in and making it … intense. But I won't be sorry for still hoping.'

This was incontestable. And yet this hope, this reappearance, had occurred at a most inconvenient time for Fiza. Just when she had gone into forward mode.

'Look, a lot has changed and I don't want to …' Fiza began, unable to avoid an explanation, however slim.

'Reconsider?'

'Please don't make this hard, Dhruv.'

'Is there someone else?'

Fiza found this question to be intolerable. The force with which Dhruv was approaching the situation showed a glaring lack of respect. He had offloaded his thoughts and hopes on her, without bothering to see if she was prepared.

'I'm sorry, Dhruv. I have a lot of work to catch up on. You're welcome to sit in the café,' she said, running the mouse over recent sales reports.

'Thanks. That's sweet. But I didn't really come here for the coffee. Oh, I almost forgot. Here,' he said, handing Fiza a leather CD carry case. Fiza opened it to find at least a dozen compilations from Dhruv's precious collection wedged into plastic pockets. CDs he'd spent nights burning and listening to on loop. CDs he'd insisted he'd never part with, no matter what technology brought next.

'I can't. First those books. Now this. I know what these mean to you.'

'Right. Go figure.' On his way out, Dhruv picked up the *Esquire* he was leafing through earlier and headed to the counter downstairs.

Fiza went through the CDs with copious markings – black-marker squiggles naming the songs, albums and arrangements. Dhruv had always been thorough. She knew he was going to put up a serious fight.

CHAPTER TEN

Fiza's head had turned into a battleground, invaded by amorous armies. All the energy and excitement that had filled her bookshop days so far was now being sucked into an exhausting spiral of thought, a black hole of confusion. How was she to get through to Iqbal and let go of Dhruv, all without seeming desperate or cruel? These were unfamiliar pre-occupations and Fiza wasn't enjoying them in the least. She needed to get away. And so she rang Kavya, who was looking for a break herself. On a crisp December day, the friends made their bleary-eyed way to the airport before sunrise. At 5.35 a.m., they were up in the clouds, determined to extract all the rest and relaxation three days in Goa could offer.

The air hostesses commenced their hurried service – it was a short flight, always before time at that unearthly hour. Kavya was thankful for her weak cup of coffee as Fiza flipped through the in-flight magazine, suddenly awake. The Konark Temple, the flower market on Dal Lake, the spice market of Cochin. Enticing pieces scripted to tempt captive travellers. Fiza quickly lost interest in the glossy offerings, casting a bored look at the back page generally reserved for snappy interviews. 'Huh?' she blurted out. A strange, unclassifiable sound. 'What?' Kavya said, leaning over. Iqbal Ali Khan, artist, stared back at her.

'I've seen this fellow somewhere,' Kavya yawned. 'Can't place him. Quite hot. You know him?' she asked before requesting for another coffee. 'Sorry, ma'am. We'll be landing soon,' the air hostess replied with a fixed smile. Fiza was relieved that Kavya hadn't recognized Iqbal from the Paper Moon launch.

'No,' she lied. 'Thought he was someone else.'

'Who?' Kavya persisted.

'No one you'd know. Not important.'

'Achha. So Dhruv ...' Kavya began.

'Yes. He came over to the store the other day,' Fiza broke in, eyes scanning the interview. He was an installation artist. He was travelling with a show conceptualized in London. He liked tacos. His son had hooked him on to them. Fiza read the line over and over. His. Son.

'Oh, you didn't tell me,' Kavya said with a frown.

'I was busy with work, Kavi. It's all been a bit hectic,' Fiza heard herself say. Her mind was galaxies away, and as heavy as a planet.

By the time the duo had touched down in Goa, Fiza had made a decision. This was a getaway, and the interview in the magazine had made it all the more necessary. When it came to Iqbal, it had been like this from the start. Drips and drabs of information. Suspense and drama. Sudden appearances and revelations. This was not Fiza's idea of fun. Already, the bookshop was a bolt from the blue. There was only so much excitement she could handle. This trip was going to be about her and Kavya, and the life she once knew.

About half an hour after they had arrived, the friends found themselves at the trusty Martha's Inn, the little boutique hotel close to the iconic Martin's Corner Restaurant in Betalbatim. South Goa was Fiza's idea of bliss, and this was her pocket of heaven. The girls checked into their rooms – Fiza was uncomfortable sharing, and Kavya was an old enough friend to understand that. Both decided to hit the bed instantly and meet at the little dining area by the pool when they woke. When Fiza sauntered out at about 9.30 a.m., Kavya was halfway through a bowl of fruit.

'Been here long?' Fiza asked cheerfully. 'I was knocked out.' She had a vague, sleepy memory of being bad company in the morning and was determined to make it up to her friend.

'I couldn't really sleep, so I walked down to the beach. Was nice and calm. Jogged a bit,' Kavya said, generously accepting Fiza's unsaid apology.

'Wow! I feel human only after that nap. I was knocked out for two hours, imagine! We have to stop taking these inhuman flights. What's good?' she said, pointing to the breakfast buffet.

'I asked for poached eggs. They gave me boiled ones instead. Had them with hash browns and baked beans.'

'Ah, let me inspect.' Fiza poured herself a cup of tea and took a look at the modest spread. The decision was instant. She'd ask for an omelette and have it with some aloo bhaji and sausages. Then end with some watermelon juice. Ah, Goa. It never failed.

'You didn't answer about the Dhruv thing. What was it like, meeting after so long, and in the bookshop and everything?' Kavya went on.

Fiza contemplated a deflection, but thought it would be unfair. 'It was okay, I guess. He was happy to see the place,' she said uninterestedly.

'And?'

'It got a bit heavy.'

'Wouldn't expect any less of you guys,' Kavya said while putting away her plate. 'Any talk of getting back?'

'Hmm. That's what made it heavy.'

Kavya knew better than to push further. Fiza's breakfast arrived and she dug into it with great interest.

'Fizu, you're a real character.'

'Means?' Fiza asked, digging her fork into a juicy sausage. Kavya saw a side of Fiza that no one else did. It didn't care for appearances or validation.

'By the way, Arvind's in Baga. Feel like making the trip north? I haven't seen him since the launch of your store.'

'No chance,' Fiza replied instantly. 'He'll want to do Tito's and Britto's and Curlies and what not. Too hectic. Pass me the ketchup, please.'

'That's true,' Kavya agreed. 'Okay, now if you're done with your banquet, let's head to the beach?'

'Yes. It's time to hit the gin,' Fiza said, wolfing down the last bit of her buttered poi.

It was 10.30 a.m. when the first glasses at the redoubtable Anri's Shack on Sunset Beach were clinked. The day was overcast and the sea was still, just the way Fiza liked it. After the first small drink, the two got into the ocean, feeling the familiar warmth of an Arabian Sea winter.

'Seriously Fizu – you *have* to get a new swimsuit. You've had this one from before college!'

'That's the thing about swimsuits. They last forever.'

'But fashions don't. God! Do you have to be a rebel about everything?'

'You know, Kavi, my mother said something on those lines, too, when I hired Ismail at the store. I didn't get what she was saying. I've never seen myself as a rebel. In fact, quite the opposite.'

A gentle wave suddenly turned rogue and hit both girls in the face. After the initial shock, they found themselves half-laughing, half-spluttering.

When they had caught their breath, Kavya replied, 'You're not one of those piercings-and-cocaine kind of rebels, obviously. But there's a very *anti* streak. Anti what, I don't really know.'

'Really? Anti? But I thought I was one of those sweet types.'

'For someone so bright, you can be quite clueless, Fizu. Watch out!'

But it was too late. The tide was literally turning and the girls were being lashed incessantly.

'Think we're safer with our G&Ts now,' Kavya suggested. They walked back to the shack, Fiza in her covered-up black bathing suit with a blue rim, and Kavya in her green bikini. With her close-cropped hair and dimpled smile, Kavya had always attracted attention in college. Now she was literally a head-turner, as Fiza noticed on the beach.

'Aunty, can we have some rawa-fried mussels, please,' Kavya said, before they could settle into their covered deck chairs, wrapping their yellow-striped beach towels around themselves. A black-and-white mongrel dusted himself off under a nearby table, and came and curled up by Fiza's side. The sky was grey–blue, mellow. The waves were growing impatient. As forms and colours splashed onto the canvas of the gin-soaked morning, Fiza bit into a mussel, her mind returning to the topic it most needed to escape from.

It was a Saturday night, which meant karaoke at Martin's Corner. Fiza had never attended a singalong that she had enjoyed, and contemplated leaving for another restaurant. But this time, she felt compelled to stay, since Kavya had been excited about trying the ox tongue on the menu all day. Despite all her intellectual departures from religion, Kavya had somehow not been able to shake off a few food taboos. It was visceral. But this was going to be her big liberation.

The two slid into their seats, as far from the little stage as possible, but even at their corner table, a speaker stalked them. On one of the tables facing theirs sat the mandatory interracial couple – an elderly white man with his thirty-something Asian partner. They had ordered their drinks – a Mojito for her and a single malt for him – and were scouring the menu, only to end predictably with the seafood platter.

'So – rum?' asked Kavya, almost rhetorically.

'Something else for a change?' replied Fiza, alarming her friend.

'Really? Cocktails, then. I'll have a Bloody Mary.'

'Tequila.'

'Umm, what?' Kavya replied, astonished.

'Ya. It's been a while since...'

'The worst drunken night in history. Do you not remember all the—'

'Yes, yes. The throwing up. The swearing I'd never drink again. The bump on my head. My calling Dhruv "male bourgeois scum". Trust me, I'll never forget. But I think I'm over it. I'll sip on it. Nothing will happen.'

'Famous last words,' Kavya chuckled, calling out to a waiter.

The couple facing them hadn't exchanged a word since they had arrived. Both were sipping their drinks, fixing their stare at different ends of the restaurant. Perhaps this was perfect communion. Or more believably, the final nail in the vacation coffin. The girls were elated at the sight of their starters. Kavya's ox tongue and Fiza's pork sausage chilly, with a basket of warm poi.

'Okay, so I'm going to do this,' Kavya said, rubbing her hands with childish glee.

'Yes, Kavya Dwivedi. But you have to realize, one bite and you're on the other side.'

'That's exactly why I'm doing it, I guess. But does it even count, doing it on the sly?' she asked, suddenly worried about her grand rebellion missing its mark.

'So what do you want to do – alert the local media? Enough of your tribe eat beef. Sadly, you're not a pioneer.'

'No one in my family, Fizu. Like no-one. For generations. You think my digestive system will be able to handle it?'

'Look,' said Fiza, serving herself a generous helping of the pork chilly. She loved that it came with potatoes at Martin's. Balanced the spicy-sour flavour perfectly. 'Sooner or later, we're all going to turn into ethical vegetarians. But before that dark day—'

'Let's live a little,' Kavya cut in nervously, serving herself a small portion of the tongue. It had been sliced in the manner of luncheon meat. No fuss. Just the meat, a few onion rings and a peppery masala. No veggies to assuage the guilt.

'Right. So here I go,' Kavya said, fork hovering around her mouth. Someone began to belt out *'Rhinestone Cowboy'* on the stage.

'You know, before you take that bite, you must know this is an acquired taste. Please don't judge all red meat by this.'

Before Fiza could finish her sentence, Kavya had swallowed her first bite of the forbidden meat. She looked inscrutable to Fiza. As if the transgressive act had wiped the humanity off her face. Then came a mild utterance, a murmured sigh.

'And?' Fiza asked impatiently. Kavya merely repeated the ritual of cutting the meat, piercing it with her fork and biting a chunk off the poi. This she did a few times, before saying her first words.

'I'm *so* going to hell,' she said, taking another lusty bite.

Before they knew it, the Goa idyll had ended. The friends were back on a plane home with exaggerated tans that gave the impression of a far longer trip. Fiza walked back into her flat on Sunday night to find that Noor wasn't in. She hadn't heard from Dhruv since that day at the bookshop. And the weekend had been peaceful and productive at the store, Bharti Aunty informed her. The trip had worked well. She had found a shelf in her head to place the bewildering short story that was Iqbal.

Noor was away for the night, watching a play at Prithvi Theatre, Fiza remembered. She emptied out her bag, putting away the clothes that needed washing. She had brought back some guava cheese for Noor, and a bottle of feni for Marc, who wanted to try out a new cocktail recipe. Then there were some cashews for the folks at Paper Moon. She put back the book she had carried – Milan Kundera's *The Joke*. She hadn't managed to read more than a few pages. This was unusual; holidays were where she finished books hungrily. In fact, she hadn't been reading at all these days. She was too distracted to engage with books.

Peeping into the fridge for leftovers, she was struck by a thought. Iqbal had never misrepresented himself. Yes, he had a son, but that did not automatically imply a wife or a partner. Fiza hadn't allowed him to get close, never asked about his life situation. The flowers had been sent, yes. Perhaps she needed to be a bit more forthcoming, show the interest she so clearly felt. Iqbal was supposed to be a closed chapter. But she had the worrying feeling that she was way more entangled in this than she cared to admit.

Before she could think better of the idea, she had texted D.K., asking him for Iqbal's number, saying it was about a book delivery. He replied almost instantly. Now that she was within reach of Iqbal, Fiza was hit by all sorts of sentiments. And each one of them fell under the category of blithering romance. For years, she had been in a quiet, everyday sort of love with Dhruv. Now, all of a sudden, there was this surge of conflicting emotions – one telling her to hold back, the next making it impossible to do that. The Fiza she knew would stay calm and allow the narrative to unfold at its own pace, accepting events as they came along. This alter ego was not interested in biding her time; she wanted something and was not coy about going after it. It was silly at one level, freeing at another. And most importantly, it wasn't like she had a choice in the matter. She was doing what she had to do.

'Hello. Did you receive the flowers? They were an apology, in case that wasn't clear ☺ Fiza.'

Her thumb hovered over the send key of her new Nokia 3210. Mustering all the courage she had, Fiza hit the button and desperately diverted her nervous energy to Snake, the digital serpent that climbed this way and that, inevitably finding its own tail and exploding. Fiza pressed the controls feverishly, focussing intently on the little black-and-white screen. Her heart was pacing and her fingers had gone cold. She used to wonder how Dhruv was often in paroxysms of delight and despair. Now here she was, like a lovesick teenager, hanging all her hopes on an SMS.

She didn't have to wait long. The phone beeped a few breathless minutes after her missive.

'Apology accepted. Beverage?'

Fiza found herself smiling foolishly. Her fingers were typing the words 'Sure. When? Where?'

'Now. Bandstand.'

It was like her fingertips were unconnected to her brain. 'Okay,' she typed, quicker than the speed of second thoughts.

'At the Armaan side in 20.'

Fiza jumped off the sofa and out of her apartment, waving to Ismail on the pavement as she rushed into an auto.

A nail paring of a moon hung in the sky, the kind that announces Eid to the faithful. Fiza began to stroll uncertainly on the promenade, hair blowing in the breeze, eyes darting across the street, feet fumbling. She had expected to see Iqbal there straightaway and was half-relieved, half-nervous about this time alone. What was she doing there? Had she lost complete control of her will? Before the questions could convince her to abandon the assignation, Fiza spotted Iqbal, buying something off a vendor. He walked up to her in his usual nonchalant manner, popping a few chanas into his mouth and saying 'Aadaab, mohtarma' with an exaggerated bow.

'Hello,' Fiza replied, unsure about how to proceed. Already, the rush of excitement was giving way to good sense. This was Bandstand, not the Empire State Building. No theatrics were required of anyone. From where they stood, they could even spot her bookshop. The light that she left on through the night cast a warm glow over the façade. It was familiar and reassuring, like the green light in Daisy's dock that comforts Gatsby. She suddenly remembered that Iqbal would have found a similar, even deeper, comfort in the sight. 'How've you been?' she asked as they strolled towards the Sea Rock end. The once popular hotel had shut its doors in 1993, one of three hotels to have been targeted by the serial bomb blasts. She had loved browsing through the coffee-table books in the lobby bookshop whenever she had the chance.

'Not too bad. Got this big bunch of flowers from an admirer,' Iqbal replied, chewing lazily.

'Admirer? You sure you're not reading too much into them? What did the note say?' Fiza replied with a half-smile, still avoiding eye contact.

'I feel I might be reading too little. Nice tan. Where you been?'

'Goa. With Kavya, a friend from college.'

'Lucky Kavya.'

Fiza sensed the conversation drifting into the banter zone – the easy route to stalling any meaningful exchange. But she had a lot on her mind that needed to be addressed.

'Why didn't you ever tell me about the house connection?' she asked while looking straight into his eyes, as if registering them for the first time. Dark brown. Thick eyelashes. There was even a prominent scar on the lid of the right eye which she had never noticed before.

'And cut out the suspense? Where's the fun in that?' Iqbal replied, crumpling the Gujarati newspaper the chana was wrapped in and tossing it into a penguin-shaped bin that screamed 'Use Me'.

'It's funny, I saw an interview of yours in the in-flight magazine.'

'Ah. What did it say? I never see those things once they come out. My chin always looks too big. And the words too small.'

'It was nice. The chin and the words. Especially the bit about your son and the tacos,' she said bravely.

'Ah. Yes. Ray's big on them,' he said, as if they spoke about his child every day.

'So, how old is ... Ray? School?'

'Eight. Between schools. I'd say he was being home-schooled, but his mother thinks my attempts don't qualify. Too much art and philosophy, she says. Not enough reading and writing ... that sort of thing,' he replied with ease.

Fiza flinched at the mention of the mother of his child, but quickly checked herself. She had agreed to this meeting and would make sure it didn't end abruptly. Moreover, she felt

Iqbal's overtures had earned her the right to get a few straight answers on important matters.

'I haven't seen either of them at the store. You should bring them over sometime,' she continued, seemingly unperturbed.

'Ray would love the place. His dadi's old home, now filled with new books. In fact, he's why I wanted the bookshop. The world has enough ATMs and fast-food joints. Bandra clearly does. Hardly enough bookshops. And they're disappearing fast. Maybe we'll all be walking around reading off cold little screens someday.'

'So ... why is he between schools?' Fiza carried on, not wanting to switch tracks.

'In full-on investigation mode, aren't we?' Iqbal said as they reached the Sea Rock end. Something they first assumed was a cricket- or cicada-like insect went tak-tak-tak. When they looked in the direction of the sound, they noticed a young man beating two little stones together furtively, advertising some kind of service. A few seconds later, they saw him approach an elderly man sitting on a bench, and begin giving him a foot massage. 'That looks like fun,' Iqbal said, pointing to the scene.

'Yes. But it can't just be about the massage. A bootlegger, perhaps?'

'Ooh. That's nice and noir, Miss Hepatitis.'

A sudden gust of wind took them by surprise. The sodium-vapour street lamps lit the scene below. Postprandial couples, and the occasional solo walker, ambled along the promenade. It was a scene straight out of an Edward Hopper painting. Fiza carried on her quest for a substantial conversation. 'So, about your son – Ray's – school...'

'He's in London, with his mother. Sila's from Pakistan, with a British passport; her mum's Brit. We've had all sorts of hassles with her living and working in India. We tried, I'll give us that. Somewhere down the line, we stopped. We're not together any longer.'

A wave slashed the boulders on the shore with force and Fiza began to feel the discomfort wash away.

'Nice name, Sila,' she said, looking for words that wouldn't give away too much emotion.

'Yes. She chose it herself. Her parents asked her to pick a proper name when she was about Ray's age. She wanted to be called Unicorn 7. They convinced her to go with Sila, assisted by a Toblerone bar.'

'And Ray. What's his…'

'Rehaan.'

'*Rehaan.* That's nice. So this new school, where is it?'

'Here in Bombay. Sila's been offered an artist's residency in Morocco. She's a sculptor. I find I'm happiest in Bombay. Or at least not as grumpy as I am elsewhere. Ray has roots here. It should all get sorted by Jan.'

The masseur was done with his client on the bench and approached Iqbal with his tak-tak-tak. 'Aaj nahi, ustaad. Kisi aur waqt,' Iqbal said warmly.

'That's nice. Which school? Somewhere close?' Fiza carried on with interest.

'That's the thing. It hasn't been easy figuring out someplace with inclusive classrooms. Ray's on the autism spectrum. Pretty much at the business end of it. And we're in the dark ages when it comes to children who haven't popped out of a Disney classic. Fun times.'

Fiza had a great urge to show some sign of affection. Maybe a nudge on the shoulder, a pat on the back or even a hug. But everything seemed patronizing and hollow. They had now strolled up and down the promenade a few times, but she was nowhere close to ready for the night to end.

'Do you feel like chai?' she asked while consulting the Casio on her wrist.

'Sure. But not that cycle one. It's ridiculous.'

'Okay. Wherever you like.'

'There's this tapri near Gateway that's pretty good. Not so far away on the bike at this hour.' He gestured to a Royal Enfield parked outside the Parsi Convalescent Home.

In a minute, Fiza Khalid and Iqbal Ali Khan zoomed away into the wakeful Bombay night, under the wry smile of a crescent moon.

CHAPTER ELEVEN

'Those IBD people had called again, ma'am. They wanted the balance payment. Non-stop they're calling,' Sudhir said just as Fiza walked into the store the morning after the charmed night. It was a pleasant December day, with that end-of-year feeling creeping into the city. A few overeager stores had already put up their Christmas decorations. Fiza had decided to hold out till at least the fifteenth, just a few days away. With the calendar year closing, suppliers usually went into overdrive, trying to neaten their books and end the year on a confidence-boosting note. For Fiza and her staff, it meant trying to keep up with pending payments, checking inventory and reaching out to holiday shoppers, from neighbourhood bookworms to corporate gifters.

'Oh, okay. Can you please bring the file up to the office? I'll write them a stopgap cheque. We'll pay off the rest when the Jamnabai payment comes in.'

Paper Moon was fast growing outside of the physical store. Exhibitions at schools, colleges and fairs had widened their customer base and even boosted sales. Fiza made sure that the books at these stalls covered a wide range. D.K. and she had worked out a pricing system that wouldn't hurt the store, nor fetch it big margins. The idea was to establish Paper Moon as the friendly neighbourhood bookstore that often visited the customer's neighbourhood. It was tough to manage the store and exhibitions with the limited staff and resources available, but with the help of Bharti Aunty, and sometimes even Noor, they somehow pulled it off.

Rosy took the file up to Fiza's office instead of Sudhir, and talked her through the pending bills. 'Here's the cheque,' Fiza said at last, tearing out a signed leaf. 'Thanks, Rosy.'

'Ma'am, here,' Rosy said, handing Fiza an envelope in return.

'What's this?' Fiza said, instantly worried it would be a resignation letter. With all the exhibition work and end-of-year stocktaking, this would be a big dampener. She opened the envelope while searching Rosy's face for an explanation. She found, instead, a 500-rupee note that she placed on the table, like a card in a poker game.

'What's this for?' Fiza asked, confused.

'I'm returning the money I stole from the store, ma'am,' Rosy replied simply.

Fiza was taken aback by the words. Not borrowed. Stole.

'This is not necessary, Rosy. Coming to me ... like this. Just put it in the petty cash, like you had said,' Fiza said, embarrassed on Rosy's behalf.

'I don't want to do anything hiding-hiding, ma'am. This way I know that you know. I feel I'm doing right,' Rosy explained.

'I told you to forget about the whole thing. You made a bad decision. We can move on now.'

'Yes, ma'am. But still. This is the right way. Every month I will pay part of balance amount. After few months, I will

be free. You will also know. Then there will be no confusion or
bad feelings. Okay, ma'am. Thank you, ma'am.'

Rosy had found a way to absolve herself, confronting her
guilt month after month, until, hopefully, it'd go away. Fiza had
no option but to heed her request. There was a grace in the
gesture that moved her. In her short time at the store, she was
finding herself among people and situations that taught her
more than all her years of formal education. It was a privilege,
Fiza thought, to be part of an intimate space, equally public
and private, bookish and living. She looked at the picture of
her father on the desk – both parent and patron, absent and
present.

Just as she was about to head downstairs to place the
money in the petty cash register, her phone beeped a couple
of times in quick succession. SMSes often came together, she
thought, as if travelling in pairs. The first was from Kavya,
saying she had received the funding for her next documentary
and that they should celebrate. The second was from Iqbal.
Fiza's face broke into a smile that she instinctively suppressed.
'Heading to London. Sila leaves for Morocco sooner than
we thought. Ray and I will see her off. Will text when I know
more. Xx'

The message was telegraphic and unapologetic. After Fiza
had read it a few times in an attempt to decode it, she realized
there was nothing to decipher. This was it. This was him.
She was one disconnected little fragment of his big world.
Fiza immediately regretted having given in to her impulse
the previous evening. With Dhruv, things had been up and
down, but there was no doubt that they were two people in an
exclusive, immersive relationship. As unsentimental as Fiza

thought herself to be, the relationship was built around all the familiar pillars of intimacy, communication and expectation. With Iqbal, it was like revving up and backing off at the same time. It made no sense.

Fiza climbed down the stairs to find Sudhir surrounded by cartons with books spilling out of them. He was bringing back the stock left over after an exhibition at the Jamnabai Narsee School in Juhu, where Bollywood celebrities – the Juhu–Vile Parle crowd – traditionally sent their kids.

'Right. So Rosy, Sudhir – and bring Ismail in too, please. Where are we on the inventory check?' enquired Fiza, fastening her untamed hair with a Nataraj pencil.

'Ma'am, we've finished history, health, art and children,' Rosy replied, counting the sections on her fingers.

'So that's way less than half, then.'

Just then, Ismail walked in in his usual urgent manner.

'Ismail – please check the books in these boxes against the pro forma invoice,' Fiza said, pushing a bunch of papers towards him.

'Certainly, madam. I shall.' Ismail had taken to improving his English using the primers at the store. The results, as now, were often exaggerated.

'Thank you. And everyone, we need to get this wrapped up by the weekend. We have the book release coming up. I don't want any cartons and lists lying around on that day. So let's head upstairs. Bharti Aunty will take care of the counter.'

Everyone did as they were told. They knew that look and voice; their boss meant business. Fiza followed the lot upstairs, happy that there was *some* stocktaking in her life that would yield conclusive results.

It was the week before Christmas, and Damian – the big furniture store close to the bookshop – was dressed for the part. This year, they had a snowman leaning on a Christmas tree, with Santa waving from behind. Everything was festive, snow flecked, colourful. It was a Saturday evening, and Fiza was walking back from chai at Good Luck with Noor, who had dropped in before heading to the FM studio. It was her producer's birthday and she wanted to gift him a book voucher. After the voucher and chai, she took a cab to town as a rare treat. For years, Fiza had insisted that her mother commute by cab, but Noor heard none of it. 'Fizu, there's a better way to burn a hole in my pocket,' she said while flicking ash off her Classic Mild cigarette. 'Can't afford both,' she laughed. Fiza had promised herself a hundred times that she wouldn't bring up the smoking, but found it impossible. Noor's room in the house was a smoking zone, with the rest of the place strictly off bounds. The physical boundary managed to keep the problematic discussion at bay. But every now and then, it erupted again.

Fiza was ambling back to the store, hardly a minute away, rereading the terse message from Iqbal. Crossing the road from the traffic island to the Mehboob Studio side, she found herself face to face with a fully kitted-out cyclist. Blocking her path with his bike, he said something that sounded like 'migraine'.

'Hey. Bookshop girl,' he continued. Fiza figured he had yelled out 'Meg Ryan'.

She had that suffocating feeling of no escape even though they were in the middle of a busy street.

'I need more,' said the cyclist.

'I'm sorry?' Fiza faltered.

'Art books. Done with the whole lot. Send them over. Or come over with them.'

'Ismail, the delivery guy, will be over with them. If you could just call the store...'

'Sweetie, send them all. Just now.' He whispered the last words and then waved his hand in an authoritative gesture.

Cringing at the moment, Fiza hadn't noticed what was happening around her. The star's bodyguards and the studio's watchmen were trying to contain a crowd that was fast getting out of hand. 'Beta, books leke aa ja,' the cyclist commanded one of his retinue. The next thing Fiza knew, she was being trailed by a 6 foot 5 man in a peacock blue pathani and camouflage cap, seeking Chagall, Toulouse-Lautrec and Souza.

The last two New Year's Eves had been pretty eventful. One had produced an unwanted marriage proposal; the next, a liver condition. This year, Fiza was determined to keep it quiet and undramatic. The staff had worked doubly hard through December, and Fiza decided to end the year with an in-house lunch, ordered from Lucky Biryani on popular demand. Extra potatoes had been requested and, as usual, weren't enough. Noor, Marc and D.K. had been invited, but none of them could make it, trying to squeeze in work or chores before the madness of the evening began. Bharti Aunty, despite being told not to bother with any cooking, had brought shami kababs and kheer. Every dish was wiped clean, and even the few customers who walked in at the usually quiet hour were offered little bowls of kheer, which were coyly accepted. A feeling of well-being coursed through

Fiza after the confusion of the last few weeks. Things hadn't worked out in the romance department, and the store had had its wobbles, but the scene before her brought her deep contentment.

When the party had wrapped up, Fiza had a surprise for everyone. They were to take the next morning off; she would handle the store herself. Which was just as well, since she had nowhere to go and no-one to see on either day. At about four in the afternoon, there was a sudden wave of excitement as the building next door began the sound-check for the party it was hosting in the evening. Apache Indian rang out of giant speakers at full blast, about a decade after his prime. A middle-aged schoolteacher who often visited the store did not approve.

'What is this hungama? New Year means gundagardi? Sheh!'

Fiza nodded meekly, secretly enjoying the music she hadn't heard since school. The thrilling days of the early '90s, when MTV and Channel V first introduced music videos to Bollywood-weaned teenagers. That steaming kettle in George Michael's '*Freedom! '90*' flicked a switch in her head that she wasn't then able to name. It was pure desire and sexuality.

'Yes,' she lied, because she liked the customer. 'What are your plans for tonight, Mrs Zariwala?' she said, trying to shift the focus from the Don Raja looking for a Don Rani.

'Building party is there. Tambola and whatall. They took donation, but rubbish khaana they give. So I'll eat my dinner and go downstairs. Achha, how much this is for?' she asked, extending a book of Tarla Dalal recipes.

'After the discount, it's ₹150.'

'Oh, why discount? You'll become a pauper like this.'

'It's from the second-hand cart outside. Got mixed up with the inside books,' Fiza laughed.

'Oh, like that. Looks new only. Chalo, my good luck. Happy New Year. I hope you'll stay here and not go thup. Who is there to buy books nowadays?' she complained, walking out of the store and halting an auto with a wave of her cane.

It would soon be two years since the launch of the store, and things had gone off smoothly, more or less. But every time someone raised a doubt, it multiplied itself inside Fiza's head, making her question her whole approach. *Should I be selling more? Marking up more?* She usually stopped herself going down the rabbit hole of fear by speaking to one of her cheering squad, but today was not the day to burden anyone with her private worries. The music had changed from Apache Indian to the more current *Dil Chahta Hai*. '*Koi Kahe*' – the New Year's anthem from the film – burst out euphorically and Fiza was tempted to give in to the mood of the moment. To hell with the doubts. She was young. The world was ahead of her. She would get on just fine. As the staff left the store one by one, she decided to make herself a cup of coffee and settle in with a book of poems in translation. She turned the revolving bookrack, contemplating Rumi and Dickinson, but finally pulling out *The Absent Traveller*. Ruminations of desiring women, translated from Prakrit and Pali. She headed for Sudhir's seat behind the counter, just to make sure she didn't miss any customer while lost in her reading.

A few minutes in, a group of tourists walked in, each carrying a few bags of shopping, from shoes to gadgets. 'Hullo, mate,' said a man in a fedora. 'Any chance we'll get a cuppa?'

'Hello. Yes, sure. The lady who runs the café's done for the day, but I can manage some French press, if you're okay with that?'

'Anything at all. Just need that shot of caffeine.' A freckled lady in a block-print kurta, and three kids of varying ages and lengths of blond hair, sank into whatever chairs were available.

'Say, you've got something to munch on?' the man asked hopefully. Fiza hadn't expected the last few hours of the year to throw a culinary challenge at her. But here she was, alone with a ravenous group of clearly big shoppers.

'Er, I can rustle up sandwiches. We've got salads and cold cuts...'

'One of each, please. And then some. We've been traipsing all over town and our car's got a flat. So we just need to regroup before we head into Caballa again.'

'You mean Colaba?' Fiza asked while quickly assembling mismatched ingredients.

'Yeah, yeah. That's the bunny. We're staying at the Taj. But we gotta fuel up before hitting the road again. There's a lot of road here in Mumbai to cover,' the lady said while browsing the new arrivals.

Fiza's absent traveller was quickly replaced by the hungry tourists. They made light-hearted conversation while she slapped ingredients onto slices, trying to make the plates look presentable. Meanwhile, the lady had picked up a few yoga and self-help books. The youngest child had run up the stairs, and the two older ones were asked to follow. In about ten minutes, Fiza had enough food to offer the bunch.

When the last of the sandwiches had been wolfed down and the coffee drained, the replenished squad hunted for more things to fill into their bags. Fitness bibles. Gardening hacks. Kitchen secrets. Efficiency boosters. The couple left no category of improvement untouched. The kids were more imaginative in their tastes, picking fantasy and adventure books by the dozen. By the time the driver had fixed the flat and the lusty shoppers had left, Paper Moon had rounded off year-end sales on an unexpected high. And to think it all hinged on Fiza's sloppy sandwiches! With Ismail absent, she began to put away the dishes, dreaming of the crisp white sheets she'd stretched over her bed that morning. As she stacked dishes, she heard the doors swing open, letting in the neighbour's party, now going through an ABBA phase. It was Dhruv, carrying a bottle of wine. Fiza hoped he was on his way to a party, dropping in to say a quick hello.

'You alone here?' he asked as she poured out the dregs from the French press.

'Yes. I thought everyone should have the evening off,' she replied, memories of their last meeting flashing annoyingly in her head.

'Everyone but you, you mean,' Dhruv said, memories of the last meeting far away from his head. His resolve had always triumphed over what he saw as temporary setbacks.

'I'll leave soon, too,' Fiza replied, tearing off a bit of the last slice of salami in the packet and tossing it into her mouth. 'Like some?' she said, offering Dhruv the remainder.

'Nah. Big plans?'

'No plans,' said Fiza, trying to keep the conversation to a minimum. Dhruv strode up to the café and placed the bottle of wine on the counter. 'It's the kind you like.'

Fiza glanced at the label. It was a brand they had had together on one of her birthdays. It was rare and expensive, and she instinctively recoiled from the grandness of the gesture.

'That's really nice of you, but I can't...'

'This resistance. It has to break, Fizu.'

So it's going to be yet another one of those New Year's Eves, Fiza thought to herself while lifting the bottle of wine and wiping the counter clean of crumbs.

It would soon be closing time and Fiza thought she could use the excuse to lock up and get away from the situation. Before she could say anything, Dhruv had seated himself on a café stool. 'Can I have a glass of your finest, please?' he said in a comic French accent, gesturing to the bottle before him.

'Sorry, we don't serve drinks. Also, it's closing time. So if you'll please allow us to lock up?'

'But, but, but, ma cherie ... It's New Year's Eve. It's ze time for ze wine and dancing and celebration,' he said, carrying on the charade.

'I'm sorry, monsieur. This isn't a club. It's a bookshop.'

'Oh, don't be so ... how do you say ... literal. It's not French at all. Let us have ze wine and forget about all these rules, oui? Just for one evening? You tell me what your heart desires. And I'll tell you what makes my heart sing.'

'My heart desires my home and my bed,' Fiza said, grinning.

'Oooohh. That is très disappointing. Okay, let's play a game, oui?'

'You mean *another* one?'

'Huh – ah, yes, yes. Very clever, ma cherie. You'll like this game. It's literal and make-believe, both. It's very *Papier Lune*.'

This made Fiza giggle. It was silly, but what could she do but play along? Take off the armour, call a truce for the night. She had had a bad time of it with Iqbal. And now here was the comfort of the familiar. If there was any pressure, she wasn't feeling it.

'All right,' she said, washing her hands in the sink.

'Okay, so you have to say "Oui, mon amour".'

'I am *not*—'

'Just joking, just joking. You can say "Oui, mon ami", yes?'

Fiza rolled her eyes and repeated the words. The party next door blared on. ABBA had morphed into Eminem. Fiza suddenly remembered to hang the *Closed* sign from the door handle. She decided to leave the shutters open, a sign not so much for customers as for Dhruv.

'Right. So you think you know this store very well, oui?' Dhruv said when she had returned.

'Er, yes. It's mine.'

They had barely interacted in over a year, but he could still push her buttons.

'Très bien, très bien. So you know *exactly* where every section is, oui?'

'Umm, yes.'

'Okay, so all I ask is you shut your eyes and I name a section. You 'ave to walk over to it and pick out a book. Simple?'

'How ridiculous. I'm not playing this silly game.'

'Uh, uh, uh. You doubt your knowledge of ze store?'

'No. I'm just not interested in this—'

'You feel you'll fail. It's okay, it's okay.'

'Dhruv, whatever this game, this role-playing is, it's not working.'

'I agree. You know what'll make it fun?' he pointed to the bottle gleaming on the café counter, reflecting the track lights on the ceiling.

Fiza was too tired to put up a fight. And the wine *was* tempting. She'd renew her anti-Dhruv vows on the first of January.

She walked over to the counter, picked up the bottle and gestured to Dhruv instinctively. He read the sign and took a Swiss Army Knife out of his pocket, drilling the corkscrew into the bottle.

'Just a gentle tug and pull, and ... voila. Mademoiselle, here is the most superior, most smooth, most delectable wine from the heart of Bordeaux.'

Fiza pulled out two Borosil glasses from below the counter and Dhruv poured into them, assuming the air of a sommelier. Then he sniffed the wine, swirled it around in the glass and took a quick sip with eyes closed. Fiza repressed a smile and took two long sips. It was rather good.

'Now that we have our sustenance, it's time to get to work. So, ze first section I give you, mademoiselle, is fitness. Just to get into ze ghroove. You have thirty seconds to reach and pick out un livre. Shut your eyes, please. Use your inner magnetic compass. And off you go.'

Fiza had a good sense of direction, though the wine was doing its thing. She felt a bit light-headed; that first glass had gone down quite quick. Exactly the kind of loosening up she needed for an evening like this. An evening she hadn't planned, and one that was rapidly getting out of control. In a few seconds, she had reached the fitness section and was pulling out a book. She went so far as to name the book she had picked, a popular hardback they usually placed in prime position.

'*5-minute Tums and Bums*,' she declared.

'Marvellous! Stupendous! Miraculous! Mademoiselle has shown that she has not just a great appetite for ze scarlet nectar, but also a nose full of iron. What a memory photographique. I am astounded. Dumbfounded. Unfounded.'

Fiza laughed openly now, pouring herself another glass. Dhruv was still halfway through his first.

'Now since mademoiselle has shown such great skill, we'll raise ze stakes, oui?'

'Sure. Go ahead. Take your pick,' Fiza said expansively.

'Yes, yes. I'm thinking of a challenge that befits mademoiselle. All right. The next section I pick is history. All those bloody battles and fancy wigs. Marie Antoinette and Robespierre.'

Fiza had always teased Dhruv about his French pretensions. A couple of levels at Alliance Française had made him confident enough to tick the French box in the 'languages spoken' section of his university application. Fiza ribbed him about his swagger, but secretly admired his self-belief. 'Easy peasy,' she replied now, and turned east.

'Ah – mademoiselle is hasty. But there's one more thing. You need to pick up a particular author. Let's say, who's that now, a Little History of the Clock?'

Fiza rolled her eyes. This was classic Dhruv, saying stupid things to be charming. She had it down pat. '*A Brief History of Time*. Science section.'

'Oh – yes, yes. So confusing, these geniuses. Saying history, meaning physics...'

Before he could even finish his sentence, Fiza had sped across to the section near the cash counter, eyes shut, stumbling here and there, too brisk too care. She felt for the book on the second shelf, laughing as she fumbled. Suddenly, she felt a book being placed in her hand. 'That's not fair!' she complained, opening her eyes. Standing in front of her was a figure looking at her with an awkward smile.

'Sorry, I didn't mean to interrupt. Thought perhaps I'd catch you before closing time – the shutters were still ...' Iqbal had lost his customary coolness. He had miscalculated and three people were paying the price. Fiza quickly seated herself behind the cash counter in an attempt to appear professional and decorous. The effect was comical. Dhruv, not knowing what to say, offered Iqbal a glass of wine. Iqbal, looking sheepish, said yes. The evening had turned into a farce. Fiza finally looked straight at Iqbal and said, 'Here for a book? Or just strolling around the old neighbourhood?' The same wine that had made her feel light-headed and silly a little earlier now made her sharp and bitter.

'I should have checked...'

'No, technically, you own the place. So feel free to walk in and out whenever you like,' Fiza continued acerbically.

Iqbal took another sip of his wine and looked apologetically at Dhruv. 'Happy New Year to you both. I didn't mean to barge in on—'

'Well, if we're talking about barging in, you're not the first one this evening.'

Dhruv looked up at Fiza, surprised. This was not the person he had spent the last couple of hours with. And to be called out in front of this stranger, who was clearly vying for her attention, was humiliating.

'Right. Have a good night, Fizz,' Dhruv said, walking to the door. 'And year. And life.'

Fiza expected Iqbal to follow Dhruv out and looked determinedly at the floor beneath her. Instead, in a kind of replay of Dhruv at the café counter, he took something out of the back pocket of his jeans and placed it at the cash counter. Outside, a car with screeching wheels and deafening music whizzed past the store, echoing the chaos in Fiza's head.

'What's this?' she asked coldly.

'A gift. It's a year since we first met.'

'An anniversary, then. How romantic. I'm sorry, I have nothing to offer in return. You see, I don't even know if you exist, leave alone ...' It was almost midnight and Fiza's phone rang. It was Noor. 'Happy New Year to you too, Ma. I can't really hear you with all the noise around. See you tomorrow for lunch? Yes, we'll decide in the morning.' This year, the Karjat plan at Bharti and Mahesh's hadn't worked out, so Noor joined some studio colleagues at a year-end dinner at Gaylord.

As if on cue, Iqbal's phone rang, too. 'Happy New Year, Ray. Did you have the black-and-white cookie? Ah, a muffin! That's super. I love you too, monkey. Now you listen to your ammi and finish off those greens real quick, okay? 'Night, squirrel. I'll see you soon.'

'You not going to check out what it is?' Iqbal continued, somehow boosted by the two phone calls.

'Iqbal, I'd really rather not,' Fiza said tiredly. 'What are you even doing here? Aren't you supposed to be in Morocco with your ex-wife?'

'Had to rush back for work. Which this jet lag won't allow me to finish.'

'Why are we doing this? Whatever this is. Was. Never was. Whatever. It's all so – fake. We are not part of each other's real worlds. I don't know why you're bothering—'

'Look, Fiza. It's strange, I don't think I've ever used your name before. Nor you mine.'

'Yes. Exactly what I was saying. Nothing about this is real.'

'Look, you have every reason to be upset...'

'Thank you for that acknowledgement, endorsement, permission. Whatever it is.' In one of her big blow-ups with Dhruv, he had called her a thesaurus. Here she was again, using words to shield herself from big feelings. She walked up to the café counter and poured out the remnants of the wine. She suddenly realized she hadn't eaten anything for hours, apart from that shred of salami. She felt tired, hungry and overcome by emotion. A frown formed over her forehead, and her will tightened along with it. 'Look, why don't you just leave, all right?' she said, walking back to the swivel chair at the counter, which she turned away from Iqbal.

'Sure. Let's lock up first. Let me take you back home – or wherever you need to be – and I'll be out of your excellent hair.'

'That's very gallant of you, but I'll be fine. This sudden burst of duty doesn't become you.'

'I mean it. I'll be out of your way. Just let me take you back home is all,' he insisted.

'Ha. The Disappearing Man threatening someone with a disappearance. That's new.'

Iqbal walked over to Fiza and pulled a stool close to her. Then he gently turned her chair, so she faced him.

'Listen, Iqbal. This might be fun for you, in some strange way. But you should know that I haven't had a great time of it with Iqbals in general.'

'Huh? You mean the name?'

'Yes. It's what you all do. You float in and float out, somehow leaving me among ... books.'

'Okay, I'm sorry for tonight, but I really have no clue what you're talking about.'

'I have a life, Iqbal, apart from this store. Something you know nothing about. You see this pretty picture ...' Fiza checked herself, not wanting to sound vain.

'Beautiful picture. A bit dishevelled at the moment, but that just adds to the charm,' Iqbal jumped in.

'See, this. This is exactly what I'm talking about. You come in. Smooth-talk me, *disarm* me – and that takes a lot – and then saunter off into your real life. And you expect me to play along. On loop. Shit. That was awful what I said about Dhruv. We were actually having a great time, you know. Till you walked in and unscrewed something in my head. That's what you do. Just when I'm finally pulling myself together, in walks an Iqbal, inseparable from this store...'

'I'm sorry, were you dating an Iqbal?'

'No. My mother was. I'm what came of it. I wouldn't have, if he could help it. But it didn't take much for him to move on. From the marriage, from the baby. From anything that was an inconvenience to him,' Fiza said impassively.

'Well, sorry to burst your Freudian bubble, but he and I are clearly different. I can't think of anything that could keep me away from Ray. But now's not the time.'

'He's a lucky kid,' Fiza shot back. Then, remembering what Iqbal had told her about his son's condition, she felt another pang of regret. 'I'm sorry, I shouldn't have...'

'No, you're right. He's lucky. We're lucky to have him, too. This is our story. Wouldn't trade it.'

Iqbal walked over to the water filter by the sink and filled two glasses. He handed one to Fiza, who took a sip and said unexpectedly, 'I'm really hungry.'

'I'm quite the chef. No, really. If there's anything lying back here ... Looks like it's been a busy day at the café,' he said, looking at the dishes stacked up.

'There was this Aussie family – don't ask.'

Iqbal put the electric stove on, gathered up some ingredients and tossed them together in a pan. Mushrooms, peppers, boiled chicken and herbs. A touch of olive oil. Shavings of parmesan. And a slice of warm bread on the side.

'It's not my best effort, I promise.'

'What about you?' Fiza said, digging into the plate with relish. The meal was instantly comforting.

'Nah. It's fun to watch. I mean it's nice to see you happy,' he said with a fond smile.

'I need to speak to Dhruv. That was not on, the way I behaved,' she said between mouthfuls.

'Seems like a great chap. And is clearly mad about you.'

'Yes. I care about him, too. Anyway, it's not for us to talk about.'

'Isn't it? I'm happy to. No, really. Not like some kind of asshole who wants to swoop in. If you need to talk about this, I'm here. Now.'

'Exactly. Yes. Now you see him, now you don't,' Fiza said while biting into a mushroom.

'It's what anyone can offer. The now,' Iqbal countered.

'Let's not get you out on a technicality. I'm not asking for forever. But finding out who you are and what you do from an in-flight magazine, that hurt.'

'Yes, I know. I have nothing to say for myself. What happened with your parents?'

'He left. Then he died. And now there's this bookshop he dreamt of. That's pretty much it,' Fiza said morosely.

'Dreamt of?'

'He left me this store – or the money for it – in his will.'

Fiza had finished the contents of her plate and was feeling much better for it. Iqbal was washing up, just like she had been when Dhruv had walked in not too long ago. She was feeling all the weight of the events of the day. Somehow, her father had entered this scene too, bringing with him the customary confusion. Fiza wondered how she had given over the charge of her mind to three men and a store. It suddenly felt unbearably stifling. Her father and the store were deep entanglements, justifying the emotions they brought with them. But the fleeting excitement of Iqbal's visits and the episodic comfort of Dhruv's friendship were too unsettling. She needed to take control of things. Not out of some deference to principle, but because this ad hoc situation was making her tense and unhappy.

'Iqbal, thanks for that. I really needed it,' she said, throwing a neglected lettuce leaf into the bin.

'Like I said – it's not my best. You have to try my French onion soup. I'm told it rivals Heston's.'

'I'm sure it's great. Listen, Iqbal—' Fiza said purposefully.

'Ooh. May I not, please? Let me take you home and we'll talk about this when—'

'No, this is the perfect time, actually. I'll admit I've been thinking about you. I've waited to see you walk through that door. To send me flowers. An SMS. You have to know how difficult it is for me to say these things. Anyone who knows me knows I'm usually rubbish at talking about feelings.'

'I'm flattered – no, thrilled – to hear this. Absolutely thrilled. It *was* the intention, you know.'

'Sure. You hit your mark. But I guess there's not much more that you want from this. You'll always be a part of this store, in a strange, exasperating way. But it ends at that. I don't know what I want. But I'm sure I don't want this. So if you could please respect that and step away from my life, I'd really appreciate it,' she said, and took a long sip from her glass of water.

'Wow. That sounds – final,' Iqbal replied. 'You really should try the French onion soup before you say these things.'

Fiza nodded, clearly not in the mood for appeasement.

Iqbal carried on. 'I don't agree with a word you've said, but what can I do? This respect thing is a tough one.' A group of drunken revellers shrieked 'Happy New Year' outside the store. Iqbal glanced at his watch, an old HMT he had inherited from his grandfather, with the big round dial and grey markings. It was past one. 'As you wish, Fiza. I think you're being overly reactive. You haven't even given us time to begin,' he said softly.

'I haven't? *I* haven't? You know, before this turns maudlin, let's just end it. Right here. I need to lock up. So if you'll leave me to it, please,' Fiza said, placing back the books she had moved during the game with Dhruv.

'Let me give you a hand.'

'No, Iqbal. I insist. Thanks for dinner. It was great. Now goodnight.'

'Goodnight. Just one thing – don't read too much into the name thing, please. It's going out of fashion, but if I had a

rupee for every Iqbal I knew, I'd buy a new name.' Iqbal looked
at his feet for a moment, then shook her hand and walked out
the door.

Fiza returned to the counter, neatening it up. Her eye
caught the gift from Iqbal that she had refused to look at
earlier. A leather bookmark from the British Museum, with a
tasselled edge. 'Second-hand books are wild books, homeless
books; they have come together in vast flocks of variegated
feather, and have a charm which the domesticated volumes
of the library lack,' it said on the side facing her. She turned
it around to see Virginia Woolf's famous melancholic profile.
She took a deep breath.

He had no way of knowing it, but it was her longtime
dream to visit Bloomsbury and explore the lingering history
of Woolf's world. She walked up the stairs, switched on her
desk lamp and placed the bookmark in her diary. She looked
at the picture of her father and her. It was saying too many
things, things she couldn't make sense of. She placed it face
down on her desk and walked down the stairs. Then she
switched off light after light, locked the door, climbed the step
ladder, pulled down the shutter and began to walk back home
through festive streets that had made a habit of mocking her.

CHAPTER TWELVE

'Madam, 2003 is bumper year for bijness. I'm telling you. All are saying. Bookshop will become double-tipple,' Ismail said to Fiza when she walked into the store the next morning. To make up for the previous day's absence, he had shown up earlier than usual to put things in order.

'Happy New Year, Ismail,' Fiza said, walking up to her office with a determined stride. It was a new year and there was nothing else to do but to begin again. She had made a mess of things the previous night, which became a symbol for the whole of the previous year. A mess of romance and a mess of her mind. But it was time to lift herself out of the indecision and frustration of the past few months and focus on the task at hand. Paper Moon was doing okay. But she knew she could do a lot more if she allowed it more space in her head. This was what the new year was going to be about. To stay focussed on the best thing that had ever happened to her.

'Happy New Year, Fizu!' Bharti Aunty said, as Fiza walked to the café. 'I hope there were no customers last night? I felt so guilty after leaving you alone, I can't tell you, beta. I realized, on festive days, people tend to just walk in here and there.'

Fiza smiled in reply. 'Nothing I couldn't manage, Bharti Aunty. You've taught me well.'

While Fiza poured herself some coffee, a lady in an ikat salwar-kameez, short grey hair framing her striking face, walked into the store. She carried with her a gentle whiff of tea tree perfume. 'I better get that. Rosy and Sudhir won't come in until much later,' Fiza said, leaving her coffee cup at the counter.

'May I help you, ma'am?' Fiza had cultivated a store manner she hoped sounded courteous but not intrusive. She hated it when she was disturbed while browsing in other bookshops; it was only when she asked for help that she liked to receive it. And yet, she couldn't stop herself from approaching this lady. She was a new customer and Fiza didn't want the missing staff to be missed.

'Hello. Are you Fiza Khalid?' the lady said tentatively.

'Yes, I am,' Fiza answered, bewildered. There was something about the lady – a quiet grace – that appealed to Fiza instantly. But she was sure she hadn't met her before.

'Thought as much. It's the same nose,' she replied with a fond smile.

'I'm sorry?' said Fiza. 'Have we met? Do you know my mother?'

As if on cue, in walked Noor in giant sunshades, complaining about the weather. 'It's January, for god's sake, and it's beating down like it's May! Someone give the weather the memo.'

'Ma! I was just talking to ...' Fiza chimed in, expecting her to solve the mystery of the elegant stranger who stood in front of her.

'You left before I woke up and I forgot to ask where we were going for lunch. Then I thought I'd just show up and we could decide,' Noor replied.

Fiza suddenly remembered her lunch date with her mother.

The tea tree lady let out a cough, which made Noor realize that her family scene was unfolding in front of a stranger. 'I'm so sorry. You have to show up at your child's workplace sometimes to be able to chat with them, even if you live together,' she said, speaking the universal language of parenthood.

The lady smiled politely, looking away from Noor. Fiza was now completely confused. *So she doesn't know Ma*, she made a mental note. Noor, meanwhile, persisted.

'That's such a beautiful pair of earrings. It's one of those antique Hyderabadi moti jadaau pieces. I was gifted a similar pair at my wedding and then ... Never mind. Should have kept the jewellery, in hindsight. Ha! They're stunning.'

'Thank you,' the lady said. 'They were a gift,' she said haltingly.

'Lucky you! An anniversary gift or something?'

'Yes, something like that. If you'll excuse me, I'll just pick up...'

'Oh, yes, sure. Sorry for keeping you. Just reminded me of a whole different zamaana. I'm Noor – Fiza's mother,' Noor introduced herself, seemingly drawn to the lady just as Fiza had been.

'I was just asking if the lady here knew you,' Fiza broke in. 'You were saying something about me having the same nose ... I'm confused.'

'I'm sorry, I must be leaving,' the lady said hurriedly.

'No, no. What you were saying before—' Noor said with sudden interest.

'It was nothing.'

'Fiza actually gets her nose and her intelligence from her father. She gets her curly hair and stubbornness from me, poor girl,' Noor said light-heartedly.

Fiza vaguely sensed a connection between the earrings and the comment about her nose. It had to do with her father. She was hoping her mother wouldn't get there.

'Yes, I agree about the nose,' the stranger whispered.

'Huh?'

'I'm Gayatri Iyer. Iqbal and I...'

Noor's face changed colour. It was as if years of buried history had jumped out at her from a Trojan Horse: the part of Iqbal's story that Noor had found too painful and humiliating to share with Fiza.

'Fiza, this is the person your father chose to spend his life with. The earrings look way better on you.' Noor addressed the last words to Gayatri coldly and walked out of the store. Bharti followed her, but Noor had already hopped into an auto and was out of sight.

'I'm sorry, what just happened there?' Fiza asked, shell-shocked.

A Hare Krishna devotee walked in, looking for Herman Hesse's *Siddhartha*. Bharti Aunty attended to him with a smile, concealing the pain she felt in sympathy with Noor. Fiza led Gayatri to the café and repeated quietly, 'I'm sorry, *what*?'

'It was never meant to be this way. Iqbal going ... like this. I always thought a day would come when we would all sit together and make sense of this ... distance. Bridges would be built. All that kind of thing.' She spoke in a soft, melancholic voice which complemented her beautifully lined face. The effect was of a painting suddenly coming to life. Fiza couldn't take her eyes off it. Here it was again, a glimpse into her father's life. He was real again.

'Did you two ... live together?'

'Yes. For decades. We met after he ... left Bombay.'

Gayatri said these words inexpressively, as if she had rehearsed them her entire life. As if stating them calmly like this emptied them of their horror.

'Okay. What? I never knew there was ... I always thought he was a loner. Someone who couldn't wrap his head around commitment.'

'We were never married,' Gayatri said feebly.

'That's not what I meant.'

'I know, Fiza.'

Fiza asked the lady if she could join her up at her office. Her face had turned hot and she could feel her throat going dry.

'I really didn't mean for it to ... In fact, I never wanted your mother to know I was here,' Gayatri continued. 'But she walked in, and there was that comment I had made about your nose and then she asked about the earrings – it all got out of hand very quickly.'

'Yes, that's the problem. My mother walking into the store today.' Of all the emotions Fiza was experiencing, the most dominant one was a deep empathy with her mother. Fiza had barely had any time to think about this, but she was already beset by an overwhelming despair. Noor had had to stand there, face to face with her biggest defeat. A defeat so big, she had never shared it with her daughter.

'I'm sorry. But I've only come here to make good,' Gayatri said, looking contrite.

'He's gone already. What's left to make good? How long will his death keep playing out?' Fiza retorted.

'It's not just about him.'

'Ms Iyer, I don't know what you had in mind, but it's not working.'

'I understand that. And I always told Iqbal...'

'I'd really rather not hear about your domestic bliss. Or intellectual companionship. Or political affinities.'

'It's not about Iqbal, Fiza. I'm not here to torment you, I promise. And it's not my place to offer any consolation. Or even apologize,' Gayatri went on, unwilling to give up now that she had come this far.

'Then could you please let me be?' Fiza was momentarily relieved to see the picture with her father still lying face down on her desk.

'I didn't want the conversation to go this way. I wanted to do this properly, but I can see there's no easy way. I wondered for years whether Noor would have told you. But lately, I've been convinced she hadn't.'

Fiza looked at Gayatri intently as she spoke.

'Fiza, you have a half-brother. He's an actor. Or trying to be one.'

Fiza could not stop a tear from escaping her eye. It slid down her face and she used the corner of her dupatta to wipe it off.

Gayatri instinctively extended her hand, briefly touching Fiza's. It seemed too intrusive, so she retracted. 'He was a good man. He just didn't know how to undo the damage he caused you and your mother. And god knows I tried. It almost tore us apart many, many times. But he was just too frightened of being rejected.'

'What's his name?' Fiza asked while clearing her throat.

'Huh?'

'Your son. My half-brother.'

'Vivek. After my father.'

'How old is he?'

'A year younger than you. He's twenty-four.'

'Ah.'

Her father, after leaving her mother and her, almost immediately conceived another child with another woman, and chose to live with them. The phrase had formulated itself and was hardening in her head with every passing second.

'I have a picture, if you'd like … It's about a year old.' Gayatri opened her wallet and took out a Polaroid of a tall young man in an olive-green T-shirt, faded blue jeans, uneven stubble on face. He was smiling wryly, arms folded across his chest, as if he were being forced to pose.

'He hates being photographed,' Gayatri said.

Fiza smiled weakly at the comment. Here was a mother like any other, eager for her son to be liked. The news had knocked the stuffing out of Fiza. Yet, seeing the face of this young man, seemingly from a more innocent world, restored her spirits in some way. She instinctively began to search his face for familiar features. Something of hers she could find in him.

'Can I see him?' Fiza said without thinking.

'Sure, but he's in London at the moment. Just out of drama school. Looking for acting jobs.'

'Ah. Okay,' Fiza said, her mind filling up with questions and images. This time, there were definite answers. He was a living, breathing person. What was she going to do about it?

After a pause, she added, her voice falling to a whisper: 'Does he know – about me?'

'Yes,' Gayatri reassured her. 'I told him after Iqbal passed away. I couldn't keep it any longer. He deserved to know.'

'Yes. We both did.'

'I'm sorry. It wasn't my story to tell.'

'I can't argue with that.' Fiza was back to being her measured self. She saw in front of her a lady who was trying to make amends for a man who had been too weak to do it himself. 'Thank you,' she said, gathering all the grace she had.

'Thanks for saying that. I know this will take a while to process, but you have to know this was not an unconsidered visit. I've thought about it for a large part of my life with Iqbal. I can understand Noor's hatred of me. Yours, too. But Vivek is blame-free in all of this.'

Fiza said nothing.

'He was very upset when he heard. He felt betrayed. It was what I expected. If I could go back, I would have done this a long time ago.'

'So ... does he want ...' Fiza began.

'I don't know, honestly. He's not the most open about his emotions. Iqbal and I are both like that. Iqbal was, I mean. It took him years to really speak to me about Noor.'

'What did he say about her?' Fiza asked.

'I don't think...'

'No. It's enough of not knowing. Now that we're speaking, let's really speak. What did my father say about my mother?'

'He had great regard—'

'Ms Iyer, please let's be frank. It would be very insulting to both of us if we were not. Not after all this.'

'He was in awe of her. She was some kind of superstar in his mind. He just didn't feel good enough,' Gayatri said, clearly unprepared for the question.

'He was jealous?' Fiza said incredulously.

'That's not the word he used...'

'Do you think he was? Of her talent?' Fiza prodded with rising emotion.

'He was too insecure about himself. She was a force of nature, in his words. If he stayed in it, he would get carried away into her world and lose whatever he thought *he* was. It was a clash of temperaments.'

'So he left over an idea about himself,' Fiza said coldly.

'Yes, Fiza, you could say that. But he was young, then; and it troubled him until the end. He didn't know how to correct it.'

'He could have called or sent an email or come over and taken it from there,' Fiza said unyieldingly.

'Yes, he should've. I tried. I think he tried, too.'

'Right. We'll have to leave it at that. What choice do we have? When is your – when is Vivek here?'

'No plans at the moment. He's busy with auditions and little gigs here and there. Plus, he works at a café.' The smile had returned to Gayatri's face with the mention of her son.

'Does he live with friends?' Fiza asked.

'His own place. Iqbal wanted him to have a flat in London. Viv's lived there since college. Loves it there.'

'Ma'am?' Rosy asked, knocking on the door gingerly. 'The IBD guy has come for payment.'

'Two minutes, Rosy,' Fiza said absently.

Gayatri took a quick look at her watch and got up. 'Gosh, I've been here far too long, taking up your time. This was all ...' Fiza took a long look at the earrings that had caused her mother such hurt. They truly were beautiful.

'I'm sorry, I haven't even offered you coffee.' After all the waves of intensity that the last hour had unleashed, the words sounded banal. But Fiza felt she had to say something placatory before Gayatri left.

'Nah, thanks. I think today can only be salvaged by a single malt,' Gayatri replied with a sad laugh. Then almost instinctively, her hand moved to the picture lying face down on the desk. 'Oh,' she said, setting it straight. Recovering herself a moment later, she added, 'You *do* have his nose.'

CHAPTER THIRTEEN

'Madam, you've ever been to my village near Kanyakumari?' Ismail's hometown was at the southernmost tip of India, reflecting well the man of striking qualities.

'No, I've been as far as Cochin. But never to Kanyakumari,' Fiza replied absently, pulling *Zen and the Art of Motorcycle Maintenance* out of the how-to section and placing it in philosophy.

'Oh, it's so close, why you never came to my gaon? That temple with the devi's mookuthi...'

'Mukuti?'

'Yes, that nose item you are wearing, no.'

'Ah, okay,' Fiza said, touching the little diamond on her nose, gifted by Dhruv. It was so unobtrusive, she had forgotten it was even there.

'Mook means nose in our language. You come to village, I will show you real beauty. Not like this sea. Blue-blue sea. Not like this fish. Proper fish.'

'Is your family still there?'

'They are there. My wife, Zulekha, and son, Mahmoud. Parents are off. TB, one after other. Used to smoke beedi.

Even when they are so sick. *I* never touch cigarette and all,' Ismail said, biting the tip of his tongue with his uneven teeth and nodding.

He had just finished unpacking three new 'cartoons' of books, and Fiza was marking the categories on the front page in pencil. Strolling over to the shelves to see if there were any duplicates of copies she was freshly marking, she often discovered books where they didn't belong. She remembered how she had once found Milan Kundera in the Indian fiction section at a big bookstore and swore she would never allow that to happen at Paper Moon. But mix-ups were common. Sudhir and Rosy had been trained to do the job, but Fiza found the exercise to be soothing. It had been three weeks since that unsettling New Year's Day, and her mind was still trying to find an anchor. There were brief periods of calm between alternate bursts of anger and despair. Noor had clammed up completely, refusing to speak about the matter, and Fiza knew better than to push her. She hadn't visited the store at all since the first of January, and their interactions at home were minimal.

But you knew about his family, Fiza kept thinking to herself whenever she saw her mother. *Then why this delayed response of hurt?* Noor, on the other hand, had not been able to endure coming face to face with Gayatri. Hiding Iqbal's biggest betrayal was as much about protecting herself as Fiza. This way, she didn't have to confront it. Just suffer it in her own head, her own way. But now the bookshop was like the scene of a crime in which she was both victim and perpetrator. Fiza, meanwhile, had absorbed her mother's share of hurt along with her own, and it was making her time at the bookshop unbearable.

The phone at the counter interrupted Fiza's reverie. Rosy answered. 'Hello, Paper Moon. Yes, yes. Yes, my ma'am is here. I'll just give her the phone.'

Fiza made an enquiring gesture. Rosy covered the speaker with her free hand and said, 'It's from Business Plus channel, madam. They want to interview you about the bookshop.' Rosy was beaming. Fiza put down the origami book in her hand and walked dispiritedly to the counter. It was great, if a little unnerving, to be interviewed by Frances for the newspaper. But the thought of business-related questions on camera was another thing altogether.

'Yes, this is Fiza. Yes, of course I know your channel. Yes, yes. That's a popular show. Next week, Tuesday? Yes, that should be okay. Recce tomorrow works, too. See you then. Thanks.'

Fiza had been asked to appear on the *Young Guns* show, which showcased entrepreneurs and innovators below thirty in diverse fields. Questions ranged from childhood dreams and career ambitions, to market analysis and break-even points. Fiza, in a stupor for the last few weeks, had now plunged into the abyss. This was the last thing she wanted right now, when her relationship with the bookshop – with her mother, with herself – was hanging by a thread. For the hundredth time, she blamed Gayatri for unloading this terrible burden on her. And for the hundredth time, she corrected herself. She had to know. But why couldn't this whole sordid saga have unfolded once and for all? Why couldn't Gayatri have told her when Iqbal died? Why this staggered release of difficult information? She would much rather have had the entire lethal dose in one go. But there was no accounting for emotion. Gayatri was beholden to Iqbal while he was alive, and to their son, now that Iqbal was gone. Even as she tried to sail towards a rational harbour, Fiza's mind was engulfed by a violent storm.

The TV crew arrived the next day to make arrangements. They scoured the store for photogenic corners and well-lit spots. It wasn't difficult, with a beautiful filtered light pouring in from the picture window on the upper floor.

'So, Armaan Khan lives here?' said the production assistant with a grin. 'You see him?' he asked, scratching his goatee.

'Yes, he's come in once. And orders books once in a while,' Fiza answered with an insincere smile that never reached her eyes.

'Oh, wow! Bodybuilding books?'

'No, art, mostly,' Fiza replied. She hadn't thought about him in a while. He had been involved in a drunken road incident after a high-profile break-up. And he still had people defending him as the poor-little-bad-boy with a broken heart. It was all too depressing.

'Okay, so ma'am, we'll come on Tuesday at 9 a.m. to set up.'

When they had gone, Fiza was left with a sinking feeling. She had half a mind to have the whole thing scrapped, but that would be unprofessional. It was just an interview, she told herself; nothing to get worked up about. At least they hadn't made any bothersome requests to do with clothes and make-up. This could work, she hoped.

On the day of the interview, Ismail had been asked to open the store early and to give it a thorough cleaning. Fiza arrived by nine, and was glad the TV crew wasn't in yet. She made herself a cup of coffee and took it up to her office. Switching on her computer, she glanced through the mails that had gathered over the past few days. She hadn't had the inclination to reply to any of them, which was very unlike her. She took the chance to catch up on the correspondence. It was also a way to keep nervousness at bay. The crew got in by 9.40 and began to set up the space near the bay window. They had requested two days of Fiza's time: one for the main interview, and one for candid shots around the store. But this was the day of the big shoot, with the anchor coming in shortly. Fiza drained her coffee and took a deep breath.

'Okay, ma'am, we're ready to go,' said the production in-charge after they had completed the setup.

Fiza seated herself on her favourite cushioned cane chair, with a look of vague distress. Sensing her discomfort, the goateed assistant offered sweetly, 'No tension, madam. Take your time. We'll roll aaraam se, when you are ready.'

The anchor, Sangeeta Murali, had walked up to the setup by now, and seated herself on an identical chair on the other side of Fiza. She was dressed in a business suit, in the manner of all the channel's anchors, and was pleasant and polite. Fiza, dressed in a floral salwar kameez and a green bindi, was a striking counterpoint, clothes-wise. After a few polite exchanges, the camera and questions began to roll.

'So, Fiza Khalid, was this a lifelong dream? Did you always see yourself running a bookshop in the heart of Mumbai?' the anchor began cheerfully.

Fiza was immediately circumspect. She had never, in fact, dreamt of such a life. It had all appeared out of nowhere. The thought made her seem like an impostor. But she had to supply an answer.

'No, I mean, it's every reader's dream, in a manner of speaking. But I didn't *literally* dream of this.' It was a tentative start. And who knew what was to come?

'Yes, I can imagine. But at which point did you say – okay, now I'm going to do this. How did the idea spring?'

This put Fiza further on the back foot. The idea sprang at her rather than from her. Iqbal, her father, was lurking in the shadows again. It was impossible to conduct this interview without speaking about him.

'It was my father's idea, actually. He always wanted to have a bookshop – that's what his friend D.K. told me.'

'Oh?' Sangeeta said, face crinkling in confusion. 'So, can you tell us a little bit about your father's dream – and how it became your reality?'

'He passed away a couple of years ago. And so I took it up as ...' Fiza stopped mid-sentence, as if dragged down by a terrible weight. 'I'm sorry, Sangeeta. Can we just move on to the store rather than speak about my father?'

Sangeeta signalled to the cameraman, who switched off his apparatus. 'It's just to establish some context, that's all. I don't mean to probe – you can explain this your own way. We can take a break and then try again, yes?'

'I don't think I can do it. I thought I could, but I'm sorry. I'll just not be able to ... to do *this*,' Fiza said, pointing to the camera.

'I'm sorry, we'll take it slow. Can we get you something? A coffee? Would you prefer another setup?' Sangeeta asked gently, wondering what she had triggered.

'No, you've all been great. This is completely my problem. I've been dealing with ... some stuff lately and I just don't think I'm in the right frame of mind to do this,' Fiza said apologetically.

'It happens. The camera takes some time to adjust to. We'll take it slow. It will be okay, I promise,' Sangeeta was speaking gently, but to Fiza, the whole scene had taken on a nightmarish quality. There were five faces and two cameras around her; she had nowhere to escape. All the guilt, regret and hurt of the last few weeks – and years – had emptied itself into this moment. She was helpless and all she could do was to continue sitting in her chair and not bolt out dramatically.

After a couple of minutes of apology, Fiza had convinced the anchor that the shoot was best left abandoned. The Paper Moon staff, who had gathered around the counter downstairs in high spirits, were surprised to see the crew descend the stairs with their equipment. A few minutes after the TV people had left, Fiza collected her things and told Sudhir that she was heading home, too.

February arrived like bad news. The weather was still holding up, and the daytime was beautifully lit, but Fiza had descended completely into darkness. Her visits to the bookshop had trickled down to twice a week, and even then she only stayed as long as strictly needed. She would sign cheques, cast a cursory glance at the shelves and discuss management-related issues with the staff, all without enthusiasm. At home, she had taken to staying in her room for long hours, reading whenever she could between troubled thoughts. Noor had begun to soften after the big shock of January, enquiring about why Fiza had stopped going to work. Fiza skirted the issue, saying the store was running itself quite well and she was just taking a bit of a break. But both knew this was much more serious. She had lost all interest in the store. Noor could tell that Fiza thought the bookshop had brought bad things into their peaceful lives. That they had been content before it exploded into their world, bringing all sorts of unwelcome things with it.

I've made a huge mistake, Fiza thought, *and one I can't undo*. She wished the bookshop would just disappear, taking with it the monsters it had unleashed.

One afternoon, determined to find a way out for Fiza, Noor returned to the store. A few customers were browsing in the aisles, and Sudhir was busy taking an order on the phone. *At least there's business*, she thought to herself. Settling herself into a chair by the café counter, she asked Bharti how things had been.

'You know how it is, Noor. The kids can take care of the place, but they don't have Fiza's touch. After that whole TV fiasco, everyone's morale is down. We're all trying to get the place back to normal, but it's not normal, na. Yesterday only one fellow came looking for some theatre books, and these kids had no idea what he was talking about. He was sweet only, so he left without complaining. But customers expect better service from us. All those write-ups and all ...' she explained worriedly.

'Hmm. I've been trying to get her out of this slump, but Bharti, she's reminding me of myself. I was like this after Iqbal left – you remember? I can't take it,' Noor said, fidgeting with the plastic lighter in her hand.

'But she's blaming the store. This place is her baby. Yes, money and all came from him, but this is her work, her story.'

'It's so complicated, Bharti. Now with this news about the boy—'

'But now what can she do? What can anyone do? The mess is there. It's best to just move on,' Bharti said in her usual pragmatic manner.

'I know she must be blaming me for keeping her in the dark. But I just couldn't … I can't explain why, but I couldn't. It felt like it was my fault that he left. My fault that she is without a father. My fault he chose another family.'

'Noor, this is all useless now. You *have* to talk to her, yaar. *Sometime* toh you people should talk about these big things. All this hoo-ha about bookshop, and underneath it all, pain and secrets.'

'I wanted her to do this. If I'd told her, she would never have taken up this offer.'

'End mein, it's best to tell the truth only, Noor. Look at *my* life. I didn't have to tell Mahesh about that time in Shimla. But I didn't really have a choice. Yes, we suffered; it changed our relationship, but what I had done had changed it anyway. Things happen in life. It's not neat and tidy,' Bharti said while leaning in.

'So what should I do now?' Noor asked, surprised to hear her friend refer to her big misjudgement in life, rarely brought up since that tumultuous time many years ago. 'It's not like confessing to adultery. Somehow this is … just deeper.'

'Tell Mahesh that,' Bharti snapped back.

'I'm sorry. I didn't mean to … I know how hard it all was.' Noor was stopped by a wave of her friend's hand.

'Tell her she has your support. Noor, half of this is her pain for you. She can't bear to see you hurt because of her. And now she's thinking this bookshop is making you sad. The whole scene with that stupid woman…'

'You know, I can't really blame Gayatri for any of this. Sometimes, all I want is to throw a … big fat book on his head or something. But the rogue got away,' Noor said through gritted teeth.

'*Rogue*? That's the kindest word you've used for him in all these years. Kya baat hai.'

Noor had that faraway look that signalled an important thought. A decision. 'I think she should go meet her brother. Her half-brother.'

'How can *you* decide for her? Plus, he's in London, na?'

'Yes. She should go. I'll get her tickets,' Noor said, her resolve strengthening with each passing moment.

'Go home and talk to her. Let her decide. Don't go deciding for her again, Noorie. Make her see that she has built her own life. This bookshop is not a bribe from her dead father. Families are mad and stupid. But we can't run away like this.'

Noor had already slung her famous blue handbag over her shoulder and was fishing out a cigarette from it. In it was a clutter of mints, keys, books, pills and an ever-changing assemblage of potions for the throat. 'Yes, families are mad. But enough of this drama. It's not about me and Iqbal, or about Iqbal and Gayatri. It's about Fizu and her brother. Later, Bharti,' she said, rolling the wheel of the plastic lighter before she had even left the store.

'May I pour you some more wine, ma'am?'

If someone had asked Fiza two weeks ago what she saw in her future, it wouldn't have been this. Ensconced in a luxurious British Airways business-class seat, flying to London. After much protest, she had finally relented and allowed Noor to gift her tickets for the journey. The London Book Fair was scheduled for early March, and if the meeting with her half-brother didn't go well, there was always the fair to look forward to.

Fiza pulled up the fawn blanket to cover her neck. She had Leonard Cohen on the headphones, a glass of Chardonnay in her hand, and a view of the clouds. The moment couldn't have been any better. She felt more relaxed than she had in ages. And now there was a menu to choose from, with one decadent offering after another.

Noor had arranged Fiza's stay at the home of Carole, a sculptor she had been friends with for decades. They had met at a formal dinner at a Delhi gallery where Noor, then at her musical prime, had performed at Carole's big art show, 'Faces within Faces'. Noor had never been a big fan of conceptual art, but there was something about those clay heads with glass features that spoke to her in a fiercely direct manner. Somehow, the friendship had survived the years and the distance, long letters and phone calls replaced by emails and texts of late. Carole even wrote Fiza a warm mail asking her to enjoy her home while she was away in Europe, firing a new collection. After her initial misgivings, Fiza gave in. The fancy tickets gave Noor so much joy that any resistance Fiza put up eventually withered away. Now on her own up in the sky, she felt a great sense of lightness and ease, free from guilt, free from expectation, free – for the moment – from the past and the future.

Carole had arranged for Fiza to be picked up at Heathrow by a cab she often used. Leaving the busy airport, Fiza was immediately struck by the silence around the city. The driver, Ali, was a first-generation Pakistani from Tooting, speaking in an accent straight out of *East is East*. 'You here for an outing, eh? Get all the sights in? Big Ben, Tower of London, St. Paul's?'

'I'm actually here to meet ... family. And to attend the London Book Fair,' Fiza replied cautiously.

Fiza arrived at the flat in Chelsea and found the key in the appointed flowerpot. The green door, complete with knocker and lamp, announced the quintessential central London flat. She turned the key with trepidation – here she was, on her first international trip, walking into a stranger's home. It all seemed a bit unreal. And what she saw around the flat confirmed that she had stepped into the set of a feel-good movie. She had the intense urge to share the moment with Marc; this was so his kind of scene.

It was one of those flats that you saw in uppity magazines, in which artists threw soirées, Salman Rushdie held forth, and crystal decanters were replenished every hour. Every inch of wall space was taken up by art, from classic landscapes to edgy multimedia. An exquisitely shaped bird sculpture enjoyed pride of place in the living room. But for all the art and knick-knacks, the place did not seem forbidding. It invited you to look, feel, even touch. All the same, she decided to keep a respectful distance from the beautiful objets d'art all around her.

Leading from the living room, a well-lit corridor opened out into doors on either side. Here a study, there a kitchen. The bedrooms, right at the end, were done up in beautiful fabrics, linen and silk with delicate embroidery and trimming. The bedroom she had been assigned had an electric fireplace, which she switched on immediately. She noticed a skylight on the roof and found a remote control by her bedside that operated it. Fiza sank into an easy chair by the fireplace, with a stunning woollen throw covering one of the arms, and exhaled deeply. Then, with the excitement of a child in a fairy tale, she skipped to the kitchen and opened the fridge. Sure enough, the shelves were neatly stacked with cheese and chocolates, custard and fruit. Carole had written to her saying Stella, the Filipino cleaning lady who came in twice a week, would look after her. But she wasn't expecting this kind of indulgence. She began mentally composing a thank you note straightaway but realized it was best left for her time of departure. With a little over a month to go, she was in no mood to rush anything.

Fiza decided to step out in the evening to form her first impressions of a city that she had built up in her head ever since she had learnt how to read. Carole had left her an Oyster card that would give her access to the buses and the Tube, the subterranean transit system that connected the city in magical ways. But this first day, she decided to walk around the neighbourhood and get the feel of the place. It was colder than she had expected, and after just a few steps, she had to go back in to layer up. Now Fiza was not just cosy in her woollens; it seemed like a warmth and happiness had enveloped her completely. So this was what it was like to be out in the world. She had been spectacularly lucky to be gifted this trip, and she would make sure she made it up to both her mother and her kind friend. But this was the time to drink in the moment, not overthink it. The neighbourhood was quiet but not without activity, with evening walkers being pulled along by all kinds of adorable dogs. 'There are dogs everywhere, even on the Tube, and in cafés and pubs,' she remembered Kavya telling her. As if on cue, a pub called Chelsea Potter appeared before her eyes, and it seemed apt to walk in.

Fiza seated herself on a bar stool and, in a moment, was being asked by a petite young girl with smoky eyes and black nail polish what she'd like to drink. Fiza looked at the blackboard listing specials and the wheat beer stood out. A couple of sips in, Fiza decided this was her drink. The bartender, Midge, laughed, insisting she shouldn't decide quite so soon. 'You're here now, love, doing the London thing. You've got to order some bangers and mash and get it out of the way.'

Fiza was still stuffed from all the treats on the flight, but felt Midge had a point. While she tucked into her sausages and potatoes which she clearly would never finish, she glanced around the place. Pretty much what she would expect of a typical British pub, and yet everything felt so different from how she imagined it. That special quality a place possesses – is it the air? – that words or pictures can never adequately prepare you for. In a corner, she saw some familiar faces: Jimi Hendrix and the Rolling Stones staring down from the walls. Midge explained how this was their pub in the '60s and '70s. 'That's why I pour beer here rather than in any of the other gazillion and one pubs in the city. I'm learning to play guitar. Like Hendrix.' She made this last statement while moving her fingers over the imaginary strings on a beer pitcher. Fiza wondered whether the young musician was being chatty because she felt like it, or because she was paid to. Whatever the reason, she was grateful for a friendly presence on her first day in the city. She was told she would find 'culture' wherever she went in London, but she hadn't expected to be accosted by it at the very first place she visited.

'You from Mumbai, luv? I'm just dying to come and see all those Bollywood hunks. Armon Can, yes?'

Fiza nodded and smiled, wondering when the curse would be lifted. Back in the flat, she washed up and got under the duvet, playing with the remote that controlled the skylight. Outside, it had grown dark pretty quickly. But, through the little glass window, she could see a patch of sky gathering stars. Inside, a lamp threw leafy patterns on the wall. Fiza knew it would be late at home, but she sent a message anyway: 'Thank you, Ma. This is heaven.' Then she fell asleep and dreamt of The Beatles performing at Hogwarts, while Kavya, Midge and she chugged giant mugs of butterbeer in the audience.

When Fiza woke up on Saturday morning, it took her a moment to register her co-ordinates. The night had been filled with a flurry of bizarre dreams and now it felt like she was jumping off a train onto still ground. She noticed that she had left the skylight open and a syrupy sun was lighting up the February sky. She woke up nice and toasty; perhaps she didn't need the fire in the night? Her mind was already adjusting to its new surroundings. And for no apparent reason, she found herself smiling as she walked out of bed and into the washroom in the new pair of striped blue pyjamas she had bought for the trip.

When she walked down the corridor to the kitchen, she realized she was not alone in the house. The leftover bangers and mash she had placed on the kitchen table were missing. A cheerful bunch of red roses had taken their place. Just as she was sniffing the flowers, a soft voice greeted her from the other side of the room. 'Good morning, madame. How was your evening?'

Fiza looked up to see a middle-aged Asian woman holding a box of washing powder. 'Hello, hello, Stella. My evening was

great, thank you. Sorry for ...' Fiza seemed to have picked up
the 'sorrys' hovering around the London air.

'No, no. No sorry, miss. Can I make breakfast? You'll have
waffles? Eggs, toast?'

'Eggs would be great. But I had packed some leftovers from
last night. That will do, too, thanks. Sorry. And my name's
Fiza.'

'No, no, Miss Fiza. You have fresh breakfast. You've had
long journey. Coffee is ready. I'll squeeze orange juice also.
We'll both have.' Fiza found it difficult to say no to anything
Stella suggested, and not just because they were perfectly
good ideas. For all her friendliness, there was a quiet authority
in her manner. Like she knew how things were done.

'The newspaper is outside on the table, miss. I'll bring
breakfast in few minutes.'

Fiza had never held an actual copy of the *Guardian* in
her hands, though she had long since made a daily habit of
reading it online. It seemed smaller than she had imagined it
to be, just like the city, so far. She knew this smallness was an
illusion, just like the infinite London of her imagination. Soon,
she was chewing on her toast and scrambled eggs, and taking
sips of strong coffee in between mouthfuls of news, just like
thousands of Londoners right at that minute. Fiza was acutely
conscious of the privilege of her situation, but made up her
mind to accept this stroke of luck just as gracefully as she had
learnt to take recent setbacks in her stride.

'Miss likes art?'

'Sorry? Art? Yes, I like art. Lovely work in this house.'

'My madame is artist. So she collects beautiful things. You
are also artist?'

'No, sadly not. I run a bookshop.' Fiza hadn't thought about the store ever since she had left Bombay. The thought of mentioning it here, hundreds of miles away, was strangely unsettling. Like she was playing truant.

'Oh, wow! Bookshop? What is name?'

'Paper Moon.'

'How lovely. So who is there now, when miss is here?'

'I have staff who run the place. Excellent people, like you,' Fiza smiled.

'Staff does not steal?'

'I hope not,' Fiza was surprised by the question. 'Why do you ask?'

'Madame had hired one part-time lady when I was in Manila for mother's funeral. She steals. Some nice painting,' she said scrunching up her nose disapprovingly.

'Oh. Did she get it back, the painting?'

'Yes, yes. Long story. Police and neighbours and all involved. See that painting of girl on horse? That one. When they took it back, thief cried and cried. She loved the painting.'

'That's terrible. I'm glad it's back, but it's terrible.'

'Yes, what to do? Terrible things keep on happening,' Stella replied and excused herself. Fiza was reminded of Ismail's take on adversity. Some kind of stoic wisdom that helps us take human failings in our stride. Like it's the norm, not the aberration.

After breakfast, Fiza cast a curious glance across the room, flitting from one precious thing to the other. She had saved the pièce de résistance, the abstract bird-like sculpture, for last. Now she moved towards it slowly, according the moment the attention it demanded. As she stood facing it, it spoke to her in a visceral way. The boldness of its form, the surprising use of colour, the playfulness – it was a work that appealed to her senses with great urgency. But what was it that the artist had intended by it? What was it telling her? Like with so much poetry she read, it whispered its sense to her, making questions about meaning irrelevant. Her thoughts went back to a quote from Iqbal in the in-flight magazine, answering the eternal question about the artist's intention by dismissing it altogether.

She wondered whether she was being overcautious with him. What if she tried a different approach? What if she didn't find this hide-and-seek with Iqbal bewildering, but merely amusing? He had caught her on the wrong foot a few times. But here she was, one step ahead, at least here, in this moment. She was in his city – he was too, presumably – and he didn't know it yet. What she did next was up to her. And the thought was empowering, even exciting. It hadn't even been a full twenty-four hours in London and she could already sense so many possibilities.

Her racing thoughts were interrupted by an SMS. It was Noor, replying to Fiza's message from the previous night, wishing her luck with her half-brother. Fiza took this as her cue to send him a text announcing her arrival in London. Something that made her intentions to meet clear without being too pushy. It was a tricky situation and she was counting on her brother being open to one meeting, if nothing else. There was no way for her to know his view on things. How he was in general. She didn't want to involve Gayatri in this; somehow it felt dishonest to speak about her brother behind his back. That she had a sibling was a strange new idea that was taking some getting used to. But ever since she had seen his picture that difficult day at Paper Moon, she could think of little else.

'This is Fiza, Iqbal's daughter', she began typing, but it seemed too grand.

'Hello. I'm Fiza, from Paper Moon. Your mother would have mentioned me, I imagine.' Too convoluted.

'Hello. This is Fiza Khalid. I'm here in London and was hoping we could meet. Do let me know if you'd be open to that. And if you are, when's a good time? Thanks.'

Then she took a deep breath and pressed the send button. Unable to bear the tension, she went into the study and pulled out the *London A-Z* guide she had spotted on a low shelf of the big white bookcase. In her mail, Carole had said it was surprisingly useful. Fiza began to leaf through the pages, but she had made up her mind already: she would spend her first proper day in London at the National Gallery.

CHAPTER FOURTEEN

Five minutes in, Fiza decided there was enough in the National Gallery to keep her interested for life. She would have to be disciplined about her time there. Schedule daily visits, if possible, exploring separate sections, without getting overwhelmed by the magnificence of the whole. Yet, on that first day, devouring the paintings of the masters like they were part of a rapidly vanishing feast, following the numbers painted on the walls, she made her way purposefully to a section that had captured the attention of a small gathering of visitors. The post-Impressionists had their own room and Fiza walked slowly in the direction of a cluster of paintings that created a hazy yellow effect on the wall. Right in front of the section, a young couple, presumably European, held each other tight. The woman was weeping quietly but continuously; the man held on to her, trying to conceal his own tears. Fiza first looked at van Gogh's *Sunflowers* through the eyes of this embracing couple, and was overcome by shared emotion. If she didn't allow herself to get sentimental here, there was no hope. Then, when she had summoned enough courage, she looked right at them. The familiar swirls and strokes. The yellows and whites. The history of the artist. The heat of the context.

The cooling effect of a century. It was a myth come to life. In its form, colour and story, it captured our messy, incoherent, too-short lives. Here was an answer, making every difficult question a thing of beauty. Fiza stood there for a whole fifteen minutes, reliving the countless sensations that the work and its artist's life evoked in her ever since she had leafed through the van Gogh issue of the Great Artist series. Then, unable to take in any more, she walked out of the building and towards the Underground, filled with a sense of wonder. *This is what a holy moment must feel like*, she thought.

As she was descending the steps to the Piccadilly stop, her phone beeped. She fished it out from her many-pocketed jacket, with no expectation. Her mind was someplace else, and any human contact seemed like an intrusion. Yet, when she saw the message, it made her heart beat faster. 'Sorry. Busy with auditions this week. Perhaps after, if you're around. V.'

There was no way for Fiza to know whether this was a genuine case of being busy or a very understandable resistance to her. Uncertainty seemed to be her lot when it came to relationships.

By the following Monday, Fiza had found her stride in the city and decided to pursue the elusive half-brother with a renewed vigour.

'Hello. It's me again. So does this week look any better? ☺' she typed hopefully.

No response for a few hours. Then, as she was contemplating the cheap sushi at a Sainsbury's, her phone replied: 'Figuring. Will let you know.'

A couple of days later, as she was getting a closer view of the Magna Carta at the British Library, her morning's message was addressed by the vibrating words on her silent phone: 'Not today. Sorry.'

'Hey. Does today look good?'

'No, I'm afraid.'

'Today?'

'Sorry.'

The conversation, such as it was, had trickled down to nothing. Under ordinary circumstances, Fiza would have given up long ago. But nothing was ordinary about this trip. Instead of backing off after a week of rejection, she decided to act with uncharacteristic confidence, calling Vivek on the phone. He replied on the fifth ring.

'Hello?'

'Hi, Vivek. It's Fiza.'

'Yes, sorry, I haven't been able to ...' said a deep, thoughtful voice on the phone.

'Don't worry about it. I'd have been weirded out about it too. My landing up like this and expecting a meeting.' Fiza thought it best to get to the point.

'No, work's been mad—'

'I know the phone isn't the best medium for anything, but I just wanted to tell you I had no idea about ... you. Not till your mother came into my bookstore a few weeks ago.'

'Right.'

'You *do* know that, don't you?'

'Honestly, I don't know what to think about the whole thing. Amma said some stuff ... Nooooo. Stop that, silly cat. Not my mom. There's an actual cat here that's—'

'Yes. I was worried only for an instant,' Fiza smiled at the interruption. 'Look, I don't know what to think, either. But I know I'd like for us to meet.'

'I'm not sure, to tell you the truth. Maybe just let things stay as they've always been?'

'But they're not like they've always been,' Fiza replied.

'I know. But it's too much. And it's not *my* mess, to be frank. It was his. I'm sorry, I didn't mean...'

Fiza realized this wasn't working. 'Sure. I somehow thought in all this mess, there might be something to salvage. But you're right. Maybe it's best to just carry on like nothing happened.'

'I'm sorry. It's all too ... *weird.*'

So her trepidation wasn't misplaced. All that press that irrational fears get, when it's the rational ones that upend us every time.

The next few days, Fiza's spirits were lifted by the overcast weather. There was unseasonal snow, and it was all anyone could talk about wherever she went. She hadn't really packed for snowy days, but the redoubtable Carole wrote in saying Stella would help her with all the warm clothes she needed during her stay. Fiza was touched by the kindness of her fairy godmother in absentia, and was finding it increasingly difficult to think of ways to express her gratitude. Maybe pick up an artefact for the flat; something beautiful from one of the museum gift shops. And so the chilly days trotted along, with Fiza doing her best to not be disheartened by the setback with

Vivek. She hadn't told her mother yet about the phone call, and was determined not to speak about it till she returned home.

One foggy afternoon, two weeks into her trip, Fiza walked into Monmouth Coffee at Borough Market, feeling every bit an insider in London. At the communal table sat a bunch of regulars. Fiza had already mastered the art of the polite hello that just about admits the presence of other humans while keeping one safe in one's bubble. She realized this rule did not hold at the pub or on the Tube, where the chances of being drawn into a conversation with strangers were far greater. In fact, just the other day, an elderly lady with a purple jacket on the Bakerloo line told her about her experiences working in drought relief in rural Maharashtra in the 1980s. Fiza was unfamiliar with the region, but the lady had sparkling eyes and a vivid memory.

'What's that wonderful sweet bread they have on festivals? Purra ... paaraapoo—'

'Puranpoli. Yes. I've never really liked it. But I'm craving it all of a sudden now,' Fiza had laughed.

London had begun to open up to her – or she to it. It was still odd for her to find the streets empty – which happened more often now with the inclement weather. And the silence of the traffic, the restaurants, the neighbourhoods. She remembered all the times visiting Europeans had described India as 'too much'. She wondered now if she was going the other way, finding it all to be 'too little'. She stepped out of her bus at Marble Arch one evening and walked towards Hyde Park. The place had planted itself in her imagination via Iris Murdoch's *The Word Child*. No, there was nothing little about London, she corrected herself. She made her way to the Peter Pan statue, watched families trotting along on horseback, and ended up at the Serpentine Gallery.

The exhibition didn't strike her as being terribly exciting; now that she had visited the National Gallery a few times, and Tate Britain and Tate Modern once each, she couldn't settle for mediocrity. Her thoughts went instinctively back to Carole's flat and its exquisite bric-a-brac. And, inevitably, to Iqbal.

Her failed meeting with Vivek had cast a shadow over the trip. She hadn't really expected an instant connection, but neither had she expected a complete drubbing. To reach out to Iqbal now would be to set herself up for disappointment all over again. The very risk made the idea appealing to her. This was growing into an annoying attraction that scoffed at reasonableness.

Fiza walked wanly around the exhibits – abstract art made up of grey blotches and blank spaces – without connecting with anything she saw. Then, suddenly lifting a mental barrier, she wrote Iqbal a text. Before she could think better of it, she had sent it off. Acting out of character had now become a character trait. She shook her head disapprovingly as the phone beeped. Then replied to the message saying 'Yes'. She would meet him at St. Pancras the next morning at 11.30.

When it was time to set out, Fiza was filled with doubt. This was not what she should be doing, she told herself. But it was too late to back off. She didn't want to seem afraid, but that's exactly how she felt. She put on a sweater, and carried a book in her bag in case she had to wait. Something told her to go prepared; Iqbal hadn't exactly inspired confidence with the way things had gone so far. This time, she had a back up. No expectations, and a book. She walked into the station and there he was, on the platform, unnervingly on time. Fiza suddenly wondered whether she should have bought a ticket for the platform; surely this wasn't allowed. The question was answered in the most astonishing way possible.

'So, you've got two options, both fairly viable ones, though I am, of course, biased towards one. The train – this train here – leaves in about fifteen minutes. It's going to Edinburgh. I'm assuming you've carried your ID. We might need it for the ticket – we Indians are good with things like that, no? I suggest I buy the tickets, we get on board and discuss the details later. It's a short trip; I've got to get back for Ray in two days. We stay at my friends' lovely home. Big enough for you to have your own space. We walk everywhere. I'd love to show you around. It's my city, really, though I've only lived there a year after college. So wha'd'you think?' Iqbal said as they approached the ticket counter. The ID wasn't needed.

Iqbal extended his hand, offering her a piece of paper that made no sense to her. Fiza looked at him in absolute shock, troubled by the sight of his bulging backpack.

'What? Are you insane?' she blurted out, looking at the ticket in her hand.

'So we've got just two minutes now. We can have a detailed discussion about my intellectual – and moral – failings. The journey's long enough for that – a bit over four hours. Though I suspect you might be done around Newcastle.'

'You *are* insane. I'll leave now. Enjoy your trip,' Fiza replied resolutely.

'I've even carried an extra jacket, pyjamas, toothbrushes, that kind of thing. In case that's what you were worried about.'

'No, actually. That's not what…'

'Look,' Iqbal said urgently, pointing to the overhead clock, 'this is actually the last minute. I'm going to hop on.'

'Please do.'

'Ah, well. It was worth a try. It would have been glorious. Bye, Fiza. If I get over my embarrassment, I'll look you up when I'm back.' Iqbal climbed into the compartment and walked down the aisle looking for his seat.

About to settle in, he was met by Fiza who had walked in from the other side of the compartment, shaking her head in disbelief. On her lips was the slightest of smiles.

Scotland was just as she had imagined it to be – cold, wet and magical. Once her initial apprehension had worn off, the train ride ran pleasantly along the track of books and art, food and music.

As they passed through the picturesque Durham, an ancient cathedral perfectly framed by the window, Fiza looked dreamily at the idyllic scene outside.

'So what brings you here? Much as I'd like to think it was me, I have a feeling there could be more compelling reasons,' Iqbal said, opening a packet of Kettle chips.

'The books. London Book Fair, actually.' Fiza thought it best not to delve into deep matters. He had already received a whirlwind version of her family history on that endless New Year's Eve.

'Ah. Of course, it's sometime now. In fact, I make it a point to visit if I'm here. Ask anyone,' Iqbal said with a lopsided grin.

Fiza smiled back. Far away from Paper Moon and her life in Bandra, Iqbal's cavalier claims seemed less dangerous. She was in a bubble here, protected from hope and disappointment. *What can I possibly lose?* was her guiding thought.

In the second big shock of the day, Fiza found herself at the Primark in Edinburgh. 'Does this look too stodgy?' Fiza said, putting on a greyish brown jacket under oppressive white lights.

'I've seen something close to this on the actor playing Macbeth at the Globe. What's it, corduroy?'

'I like it. Has a kind of rustic charm,' Fiza said defiantly.

'If you insist. Now can we leave this ghastly place? I can even *smell* the sweatshops in here. And allow me to ...' Iqbal said, taking the jacket in his hand.

'Not a chance!' Fiza said more emphatically than she had intended. 'Look, I'm here on this god-knows-what trip. But I'm paying my way through. Let's not even go there.'

Iqbal knew he shouldn't push his luck. They were lucky to find a queue with just a few people in it, and soon they were out in the dank February air, stepping into a landscape straight out of Harry Potter.

'So I thought we could ...' Iqbal began.

'The World's End. Old Town. Haggis, neeps and tattie scones,' Fiza said without missing a beat. She remembered the place from Kavya's holiday pictures.

'Wow. That's a very ... specific plan.'

'Yes. And I think we should walk. Are you okay lugging the bag?' Fiza asked rhetorically.

'Yes, ma'am. And you're warm enough in the jacket?'

'It'll do.'

And so the two set out on the famously undulating streets of Edinburgh, new friends in an old city. The Royal Mile – connecting the Holyrood Palace to the Edinburgh Castle – was the town's historic route, charming travellers with its cobblestones and cafés, churches and museums. A steady stream of cyclists and pedestrians went about their day cheerfully, stopping occasionally at the restaurants for meaty delights.

'It's all so ... J.K. Rowling,' Fiza said with a wave of her hand.

'Yes. Ray loves it, too,' Iqbal chuckled.

Fiza's hackles went up for the first time since she had seen Iqbal at the station. The son, in her thoughts, invariably led to the mother. And that was a dark space she preferred not to explore. 'I'd love to meet him,' Fiza said, making up for her thoughts.

'I think he'd love to meet you, too.'

'Is he here? I mean, there? In London?'

'He's with his mother in Spain at the moment. Back soon, though.'

'Yes, yes. You'd mentioned that before, back in Bombay,' Fiza said, recalling the conversation at the Bandstand promenade.

They had arrived at the pub and the conversation reached a natural ending. Fiza often said things in Iqbal's presence that troubled her later; that was one of the things that kept her interested in him. He had the ability to bring something out in her that was not entirely rational. An unknown quality that was equally scary and liberating. Here in one of the world's most charming cities, she was allowing herself to think, speak and act freely. With a man who was at once part of and disconnected from her reality.

'So, what's the verdict?' Iqbal said, pointing to Fiza's plate of half-eaten haggis.

'It's a bit like when Kavi – my friend Kavya – tried meat for the first time. It's fun right now. Not sure if it'll last,' she said, while sipping on her Guinness.

'That sounds deep and wise,' Iqbal replied, forehead rippling in agreement.

'You sound surprised.'

'I think that about a lot of things you say, actually,' Iqbal ventured.

'Really?' Fiza said, scouring the menu for dessert. 'Cranachan, please,' she said to the waitress.

'How do you know so much about the food here? I've been here dozens of times and I've never heard of this dish,' Iqbal said with genuine amazement.

'An outsider's perspective can be very useful.'

'See? There. You speak in … in aphorisms.'

'Hmm. Okay, I'll try similes instead.'

Iqbal dipped a finger on a water ring on the table where the Guinness had sat, and drew a shape. 'A simile face!' he said as a goofy smile formed on Fiza's lips, too. First Dhruv, and now Iqbal. She was beginning to wonder about her susceptibility to silliness.

When the cranachan arrived, Fiza dug her spoon into the glass, enjoying mouthfuls of the cream, raspberries and honey, leaving most of the oatmeal at the bottom.

'That's just stunning, the whisky twist,' Iqbal said, licking his spoon dry. 'Thank you. Will you be my Edinburgh guide?'

'Gladly. But some rest first?' Fiza said, suppressing a yawn.

'Sure. Shall we dump the bag at the Murphys', freshen up and head out again?'

'Sounds good.'

Iqbal gestured for the bill. 'I know you're a strong, confident woman standing on two very dependable feet, but please don't fight me on this. You've come to my favourite city and it's our first meal together. Anywhere.'

'I wasn't planning to. God, you make me sound like such a bore!' Fiza said, wiping the non-existent cream off her chin.

'Get this. If there's one person I regard as faultless, it is you.'

'Even my taste in jackets?' Fiza said, diluting the seriousness of the moment.

'Primark-ily because of your taste in jackets,' Iqbal replied, recovering quickly.

She laughed at the cheesy pun and polished off the last of the cranachan. Iqbal finished his second glass of Guinness and they were off.

Iqbal's friends' home wasn't far from the pub. After the sprawling geography of London, Edinburgh seemed like a town in a storybook, easily traversed on foot. Iqbal had a key to the place, which surprised Fiza.

'Shouldn't we ring the bell? What if we're disturbing them?'

'Oh. They're not here. Did I not make that clear? I'm sorry, I thought I did,' Iqbal replied with genuine surprise.

'Ah. No, you didn't say they were ... I just assumed ... It's nothing,' Fiza replied, appearing to be more comfortable than she was. Iqbal sensed her unease and offered, 'Look, if you're not comfortable staying here, we can book rooms at a hotel. It's just that this is ... home.'

'It's a matter of one night. I think we can stay out of each other's hair,' Fiza smiled.

'It would be tragic. But sure. Whatever you like,' Iqbal replied.

The main door opened into a large living room painted teal, with an old-fashioned fireplace and an open kitchen. Brass pots and pans hung cheerfully from a wall. The kitchen block had a bowl of fruit on it, in the manner of a still life painting. In a corner was a little piano with a sagging seat. It was a house out of a book, in a town out of a book, at a time out of a book. And everything smelt of apples.

'So, there's a room downstairs and one upstairs. You pick.'

'Anything's fine. I love the place. Your friends seem like ... very warm people.'

'That they are. When Sila and I broke up, I lived here for a few months. Wasn't the best company. Almost set the house on fire on two separate occasions. They're still okay having me over. I judge them, actually,' Iqbal joked.

Fiza peeped into the bedroom downstairs. She pulled the heavy drapes apart and wondered how far they were from Arthur's Seat, the famed extinct volcano, and beyond it, the North Sea. *How did this happen?* Fiza thought. She said to Iqbal: 'I haven't seen the upstairs room, but may I have this one, please? I love the back garden it opens out on to.'

'Of course. I'll be right back. There's a rose patch there that I've been working on. I'll be back to gloat in a minute.'

Iqbal ran up the wooden stairs, whistling Jethro Tull's '*Aqualung*' tune as Fiza opened the glass door. It was a band she had never warmed to, but she was careful not to bring up such things for fear of passionate defences from devout fans. Plus, it wasn't half as bad as Kavya disliking the Beatles, she consoled herself. She stepped out on the grass lawn with rows of winter blooms bordering it. Then she shut her eyes and pulled her jacket tight around her. As she took a deep breath, she found herself humming the '*Aqualung*' tune.

CHAPTER FIFTEEN

The evening unfolded gently, with Fiza and Iqbal floating above the chilly Edinburgh streets in a cloud of warmth and laughter. They stopped every few minutes to explore a passageway, drink in a sip of history, catch an iconic sight. In the courtyard of the Writers' Museum celebrating the big three of Scottish literature – Burns, Scott and Stevenson – Fiza stepped on a little flagstone that carried a commemorative quote: 'The transfiguration of the commonplace.'

'Look! Look!' she said, tugging sharply at Iqbal's sleeve.

'Muriel Spark. Yes. Okay.'

'Muriel SPARK! Only my favourite writer in the whole world! What are the chances of my stepping on a quote commemorating her?' Fiza gushed.

'At the Makars' Court in her birthplace, pretty big, I'd say,' Iqbal replied wryly.

'Yes, sure. But stepping on *this* particular quote, and noticing it. It's—'

'Transfiguring the commonplace fer ya?'

'Mock all you like, it's a moment,' Fiza said. '*The Prime of Miss Jean Brodie*. Have you read it? When we studied it in lit class with Frances, I was blown away. Creating such worlds with such ... economy.'

'Hmm. You're clearly having a moment. I'll just wait till it's passed, if you don't mind.'

'How not to? It's all Walter Scott this and Robert Burns that. This woman was so damn skilled. And weird. Have you ever read her?'

'No. But something tells me you're going to make me.'

'Oh, stop being such a boy. All those fellows in our class who'd go on about Jane Austen being tedious. Uff. Please don't turn out to be one of those. Are you?' Fiza said, frowning.

'One of whom?'

'Those *boys* who try to blow smoke rings like Gandalf and think you're illiterate if you haven't read Terry Pratchett.'

'Pratchett's okay. Tolkien – I had my phase in school. Austen – she's out of my league,' Iqbal said in defence.

'Try the film versions?' Fiza ribbed him.

'Certainly, my dear Miss Khalid,' he replied in his best Regency manner.

'I've never liked being called that. But it beats Miss Hepatitis, so...'

After completing the writers' pilgrimage, they walked on for a quarter of an hour, finally settling at a kerbside café.

'I know I'm supposed to have whisky and steak since we're in Scotland, but I'd really love some pizza and beer,' Fiza said, glancing at the menu.

'A contrarian in our midst. How refreshing.'

'It's too much pressure, being the perfect traveller.'

'But you are.'

Fiza looked away from Iqbal, trying hard to prevent an eye-roll. She had had a wonderful evening and was determined to keep things in an easy, friendly space with just the right amount of flirtiness. Somehow, the formula she had in mind required more balancing than she had imagined.

'Okay, so meat on your pizza?' Iqbal asked.

'Sure. But if they could add artichokes, that'd be great. I love 'em.'

Iqbal placed the order and the young waiter, dressed in a Jimi Hendrix T-shirt, served them their drinks.

'You know, on my first evening in London, I went to a bar that Jimi Hendrix used to visit,' she said, clinking her glass with Iqbal's.

'Yes, you'll find history everywhere you go. It'll find you, in fact. After a while you're just blind to it. It's quite sad, actually.'

'But how? It's so … *alive*.'

'Yes, but diminishing marginal utility and all that,' Iqbal said sagely.

'Hmm. That *is* sad. "People from a planet without flowers would think we must be mad with joy the whole time to have such things about us." Iris Murdoch,' Fiza said in the recitation voice picked up at her convent school.

'It is what it is.'

'Ah. Father Philosophy strikes,' she said, shaking a few grains of salt on to her palm and licking them off.

'It's a useful adage, actually.'

'Yes. Either madly profound or painfully banal, depending on what mood one's in. Okay. Non-sequitur alert. Do you know a Carole?'

'Er, I know plenty. You want me to sing one? "*Deck the halls*"?'

'Wise guy,' Fiza said, stifling a giggle. 'I mean Carole Higgins, the artist.'

'Ah. For a moment there, I thought this trip would have to be abandoned immediately on musical grounds. Yes, of course I know Carole Higgins. I love Carole Higgins. How do you know her?'

'I'm staying at her place in London. Thought you might have some "art" connection.'

'You're staying in her Chelsea flat? No way!' Iqbal replied enthusiastically. 'I only know her work. Everyone does. Big crush from my penniless artist days. Still might be. Fix up a meeting?'

'She's not here. But the flat is stunning. There are these birds, with the giant wings...'

'And the iron beak. Her most famous work. She's refused to sell it all these years.'

'But what does it mean?'

'It means you need to fly out of your safe zone. Was it not clear?' Iqbal said, looking expectantly at the server chatting with the French tourists at the next table.

'And what is it that I'm doing now?'

'Skipping along, twittering, maybe even preening. There's no flying. Yet.'

When dinner arrived, Fiza tore into it. All the walking and talking had made her ravenous. She had settled for a barbeque chicken pizza with a sprinkling of artichokes. The pizza was thin and biscuity – different from the thick crusts she enjoyed in Bombay. Iqbal's Aberdeen Angus steak looked almost alive, raw and juicy as he sliced it. Neither had room for dessert, and once they had wiped their plates clean, they ambled back to the Murphys' in a happy stupor.

'Right then, Fiza Sahiba. I'll climb my lonely tower in desperate need of rescuing. See ya,' Iqbal said, giving her a quick hug.

'You smell of ... steak,' Fiza said.

'Yes. I'm manly that way,' Iqbal replied, walking towards the wooden staircase.

'One moment,' Fiza said, stopping him along the way. She walked up to the bottom of the stairs, held his right hand and leaned in. He wasn't expecting to be kissed and she wasn't prepared for the stubble. Both withdrew after a few seconds, assessing next steps.

'Would you like to come in?' Fiza said after an eloquent pause.

'Are you sure?' Iqbal said softly.

'I'm not really into romance novels, but I'm pretty sure this is not how the dialogue progresses at this stage in the evening.'

'I think at this stage it's all Cathy's ghost beating Heathcliff's window,' Iqbal replied.

'Yes, far too much dialogue,' Fiza said, leading him to her bed. She flung her Daunt Books cloth bag on the bed, pulled the drapes shut and took off the green boots she had borrowed from Kavya. Iqbal sat at the edge of the bed, eyes crinkling into a smile.

'Decisive moves. How long have you been planning this elaborate seduction?' he said when she was done.

'Vaguely for months, I think. But quite resolutely since I saw you at the station today.' Another out-of-character declaration. Another chill down the spine.

'Good to know,' Iqbal said, grabbing Fiza by the waist and placing her in his lap. He moved her curls away from her face, loosened the muffler around her neck and got to work on her jacket.

'It's like excavating a mummy!' he said after the first few buttons.

'Thank you, Iqbal. That's what every woman wants to hear from her lover, who reeks of raw steak.'

'You're welcome to treat me like a piece of meat,' said Iqbal.

'Shh. The dialogue is getting you nowhere,' said Fiza, laying him down against the lavender sheets that smelt faintly of pine.

Fiza woke the next morning to an empty bed. She gathered her hair in a bun, reached for her phone and felt for the bunny slippers gifted by Marc before remembering they were in London. No sign of Iqbal in the living room either. When she parted the bedroom drapes, there he was, in a flood of light, digging in the garden with a set of tools about him. Fiza let out a yawn and stretched her arms. Then she got into the shower. She wasn't ready to greet him in her morning face just yet.

When she stepped out, Iqbal was busy making breakfast.

'I was hoping you'd put some coffee on,' she said, walking to the breakfast table.

'Scrambled eggs and toast on the way. With the best bacon you've eaten.'

'That's presumptuous. But you're probably right.'

Fiza took a long sip of her coffee. Iqbal walked over from the stove to her, running his hand through her hair.

'You wash your hair every day?'

'Only after sex.'

'Really?'

Fiza bit off the edge of her toast and nodded a no.

'That's a lot of hair washing in your future.'

'And past,' Fiza said with a smirk.

'Yes, yes, woman of the world. Did you sleep okay?'

'Dreamlessly. It was beautiful. What were you up to in the garden?'

'I like to earn my keep. It's easy with Daisy and Ian. Plant a seed and they're putty in your hands,' Iqbal replied.

'That's a good phrase for a sculptor.'

'Yes, it is. And here's your breakfast.'

'These eggs are so creamy!' Fiza said with her mouth full.

'Must be the cream.'

'And you were right. I'd give up religion for bacon reasons.'

'That's quite good. How many times have you used that before?'

'This is the first,' she lied.

'And have you? Given up religion?'

'Never really possessed it. Been raised pretty godless. Do biryani and qawwali count?'

'The very tenets of the faith,' Iqbal replied, serving Fiza the remnants of the eggs and the last lashings of bacon.

'Hmm. And you? I don't see a beard, prayer beads, or any attempt at abstinence.'

'Religion gave up on me,' he said facetiously. 'Heavy talk after the lovemaking...'

'Lovemaking. That's a big word. Fornication?'

'Are you editing my thoughts now?'

'Sorry. I'll stick to praising your cooking. Coffee?' Fiza poured them both their second mugs as they stepped out into the back garden. 'Is it actually warmer than yesterday or have I just acclimatized to the weather? And it's so bright outside.'

'You might want to run in to get your show-stopping jacket soon. It's still as cool.'

'Hmm. So what's the errand you needed to run here? The reason you came,' Fiza said while bending to pick up a fallen elm leaf.

'It's done.'

'Huh? When? What?'

Iqbal pointed to the rose bush he had been working on in the morning. 'These. I'd promised they'd be done before the Murphys' return. That's tomorrow. We catch the evening train as planned,' Iqbal said, sounding pleased with himself.

'You came all this way to … to plant a few roses? I'm sorry, I mean, that's really … sweet, but…'

'You sound surprised.'

'I don't *know* you, Iqbal. So everything's new and surprising.'

'Right. I'm going to jump in the shower. When you see me next, I'll be in my trench coat and hat, convening a meeting of the international Mafiosi in the living room.'

Before he could leave, Iqbal walked towards her and buried his face in her neck, smelling her freshly-washed curls.

'You smell of spring. I love that smell.'

'You smell of mud. I love that smell,' she reciprocated.

'A vast improvement on the steak,' Iqbal said, continuing to nuzzle her neck.

'Do you *have* to get into the shower now?'

'Looks like my rose ruse has worked. Muhahahah,' Iqbal said, pulling Fiza's arm and walking her indoors.

When they were back at the train station, the weather had turned for the worse. An insistent rain lashed the window as the two carried on an easy conversation fuelled by pints of wine from the refreshment counter. When they were almost in London, Fiza asked Iqbal, 'So where do you live here?'

'Notting Hill.'

'So posh,' Fiza teased.

'Occupational hazard. Artist's life and all that.'

'Will you be in Bombay soon?'

'No plans yet. But I can't stay away too long, I've noticed.'

'How's the … epilepsy.'

'Under control, for the most part. Nothing nearly as disturbing as that thirty-first night. Meds. Precautions. Luck. Will you come visit? It's nice. Good light. A garden. We can do the walk from the movie.'

'Definitely the walk from the movie,' Fiza replied.

'Ray's back soon. Can meet him, if you like. Or we can keep it unreal, too.'

'I'd love to meet him. I said that on the way here, didn't I?' Fiza said sincerely.

'Yes. That could have been out of politeness.'

'Nah. I mean it.'

The train had pulled in at St. Pancras. The London night was cool, but Fiza's new jacket was too warm for it. She was glad of the 'homecoming'. 'So this is where we switch lines,' she said, taking Iqbal's hand.

'Sure. Journeys end in lovers meeting/Every wise man's son doth know,' Iqbal whispered.

'Woh afsaana jise anjaam tak laana na ho mumkin…'

'Bohat khoob. I'd challenge the defeatism of the thought, but it's late and cold. Thanks, Fiza.'

'I'm glad you did this crazy thing,' Fiza said, embracing him.

In a moment, Iqbal began to walk towards the pink Hammersmith & City line, while Fiza made her way to the blue Victoria line, two travellers lost in a colourful maze of a million love stories going this way and that at that very moment.

Fiza had been sending Noor email updates every few days, but had left the Edinburgh part of her trip out. Too much to get into, she thought. The distance, the living on her own, was a charming new experience. The mother–daughter unit that she had always belonged to had its limitations. Everything was public, everything was shared, like her relationship with Dhruv. With Iqbal, she wanted it to be her own private affair, not a community holding.

This afternoon, while writing to Noor about the British Library, her thoughts returned to Paper Moon for the first time in any serious way since she had left Bombay. Life at the store came back to her in a big wave of emotion. When the thoughts she had been blocking proved too strong to ignore, she decided to walk down to the convenience store and use the pay phone; international roaming rates made her mobile phone impossible to consider. It would be close to sunset back home, and she wondered what the scene must be like.

'Hello, Sudhir?'

'Yes. Who is speaking, please?'

'It's me, Fiza.'

'Oh, ma'am. Sorry, ma'am, the line is not very clear, ma'am. How are you? Everything is fine here,' Sudhir blabbered.

'That's good. How's business been?'

'One big party had come. Bought many books for a new library. I wanted to approach you about discount, but then I referred Noor ma'am. We made over a lakh, ma'am.'

'That's lovely! I should be away more often,' Fiza said, feeling the familiar thrill of a big sale.

'No, ma'am. Everyone here is asking for you. We are all missing you also. When you'll be returning?'

'Soon, Sudhir. The London Book Fair will be on soon. I'll be back after. Keep up the good work. Give Rosy and Bharti Aunty my regards.'

'Ismail Anna is standing here, asking about you.'

'Please say hello. Tell him I'll bring him a T-shirt, like I said.'

'Okay, bye, ma'am. Good evening. Oh, good afternoon over there.'

Fiza put down the receiver with a smile. A few weeks ago, she had felt worlds away from the bookshop she had built. Now, standing in a corner shop thousands of miles away, having failed in the mission that had brought her there, she suddenly ached to be back.

The next day, around noon, just when Fiza was about to set out for the day, she received an SMS that planted her wandering mind firmly back in London.

'Hey. Are you still here and up for meeting? Vivek.'

Fiza read the short text a few times before replying: 'Yes ☺'. She wondered whether the smiley looked too desperate. Her thoughts were interrupted by a fresh beep.

'Okay. Free to meet for a coffee at Monmouth opposite Borough Market at noon? It's not half bad.'

Fiza had given up on the thread with Vivek after the difficult last conversation. Now here was this fresh opportunity, though she didn't want to raise her hopes too high. But even this reaching-out felt like a little victory.

It was a windy day, and although all covered up, Fiza was enjoying the chilly weather all the same. It hadn't snowed for a few weeks, but it was forecast for later in the day. Vivek met her at the entrance of the café, which was painted a forest green. She was glad she had been there on her own before; one less unfamiliar thing to negotiate. He had on a frayed leather jacket and a five o'clock shadow. Around his neck was a rainbow-coloured muffler. His jeans were torn at the knee. *Perfect casting for a struggling actor*, Fiza thought.

'Doesn't the cold get in there?' Fiza asked after they had shaken hands, pointing to the scruffy knee.

'Yes. It does. But it's too much trouble to get them fixed. Maybe it's time for another pair. Maybe.' The first words were tentative. But they had made a start.

'Coffee, then?' Vivek asked Fiza hopefully. 'I'm sorry, I just assumed you...'

'I'd love some. An Americano. Unless it's called something else here.'

'The same,' Vivek smiled.

'If you could just grab that table there, I'll get in the queue.'

Fiza noticed how the café was different from the ubiquitous Prets and Neros she had been to thus far. It even smelt different. A more grown-up clientele, apart from the harrowed crowd that came in to escape the hectic activity at the overpriced artisan stalls in Borough Market.

'So how's it been, your visit? Is it your first?'

'Yes,' Fiza replied brightly. 'First time overseas, in fact. It's been ... *wonderful.*' Adjectives eluded her. Somehow, there weren't any words to hide behind, so she held on to the warm cup of coffee for support. 'Smells beautiful.'

'Yes. It's an extravagance I allow myself. Better than any I've had in London,' Vivek replied.

So this was going to be the pace of things, Fiza thought. She decided to go with the flow rather than press the matter. 'I've been trying to do all the must-dos. I wonder what'll be left when I get all that stuff out of the way,' Fiza joked.

'I haven't managed to get it out of the way yet. And I've been here three years now. There's just so much. And you feel this sense of—'

'Duty?' Fiza offered.

'Yes, duty. To see the art. Visit the gardens. Eat the best steaks. I'm waiting for it to wear off. It's not "normal" yet, you know what I mean?'

'Yes, I feel that way about my bookshop. It's still not "normal". It feels unreal. Not like real life.'

The conversation had achieved a rhythm, and Fiza was mildly relieved.

'Real life,' he repeated softly. A stinging wind sneaked in through the open door, catching Vivek by surprise. He adjusted his muffler that had shifted to one side. 'I've heard a lot about your bookshop. Paper Moon?'

'Yes, that's the one,' Fiza said, rubbing her hands together and blowing into them.

'Do you get a lot of people comparing you to Meg Ryan?' he asked suddenly.

'Yes, I'm afraid so,' Fiza said, searching her half-brother for traces of herself, and of their father, while at the same time telling herself not to.

'Don't like her?' he asked with a smirk.

'No. It just kind of reinforces the "not real" business, I guess. I hadn't thought of it till I just said it. That's funny.'

'You know, it's nice and warm here, but do you feel you'd be up for a walk?' Vivek suggested. 'Once we're done with our coffees, of course.'

'Sure. I'd love that.' The fog of the phone chat seemed to have lifted. Here they were, having the meeting she had hoped for. Nothing extravagant. Just two strangers who had a lot in common spending an afternoon together.

'Too cold?' he asked, voice deep but warm, as they made their way towards the south bank of the Thames. 'Sorry, this is a bit of a meandering walk. Not very efficient from the sightseeing perspective.'

'I love the cold. Don't get any of it in Bombay,' she replied.

'Think about setting up a store in Bangalore, then. It's still got it,' he said while tying up a shoelace.

'Ah. Another store. That will need another – *me*.'

'What do you mean?'

'I find it takes a lot out of me,' Fiza replied vaguely.

'Hmm. You mean emotionally? Because of the whole thing with … history?'

So far the conversation had cruised. But now the first barrier had raised itself. The Great Barrier.

'Yes, I suppose. History,' she echoed, as the Tate Modern rose before them in its sombre beauty.

'I believe Dad named you Fiza,' Vivek said as they sat on the bench facing the stark brick building, formerly a power station. Fiza thought of the Picassos and Dalis hanging inside the galleries, hit again by that mix of awe and delight that a proximity to great art evokes. 'And I was given a hand-me-down. My grandfather was a great guy, but it really weighs you down, going about your life with a name that means "conscience".' The conversation had now taken on a life of its own, gaining cubist dimensions.

'Did you spend all your years in Bangalore before coming here?' Fiza asked, suddenly unnerved.

'Nope. I was in boarding school. Rishi Valley.'

'Ah. I've always envied that life. Sounds like a cool place to grow up in.'

'It was all right. Made some good friends. Crazy memories. You could say that about any school, I guess. Walk?'

'Sure,' she replied. 'But all that sense of space. And nature. All that other stuff.' Fiza's school years were unremarkable but for the fact that she had studied practically for free up to the tenth standard, thanks to a government provision that made girls' education free in the state. Boarding schools seemed terribly fancy in the middle-class world she inhabited.

'Yes, it had its cultural qualities,' Vivek said with a sardonic grin. 'I'd much rather have grown up in the real world, if you ask me. Saves you a lot of time as an adult.' They were now at the Millennium Bridge, where Vivek bought a bunch of cherries and held them out for Fiza.

'Mmmm,' she said, picking a few. 'They look as big as our plums back home!'

'Ha! When in doubt, blame Monsanto.'

They walked at a gentle pace as Vivek pointed to the various floors of the Southbank Centre.

'That's an interesting perspective about Rishi Valley,' Fiza said, returning to the earlier conversation. 'Kids go on and on about how they'd never trade their boarding school years for anything.'

An empty can clanged in a gust of wind on the pavement. The temperature seemed to be dropping by the minute.

'Are you sure you're good with all the walking? It's getting a bit chilly.'

'It's fun,' Fiza said, rubbing her hands together.

Vivek had stopped at a building that looked like so many of the Tudor structures Fiza had seen in period dramas. 'We're here,' he announced. 'Shakespeare's Globe.'

Fiza just stood there looking blank. She had pencilled in the pilgrimage, but hadn't expected to be accosted by the sight quite like this. 'Fancy a tour? Got some mates in there, so we might get to see more than the usual.'

And so it was Will Shakespeare who had steered yet another tentative scene to an area of ease, as if it were inevitable.

CHAPTER SIXTEEN

Fiza and Iqbal had decided to meet at the London Book Fair on the morning of its opening. He had friends in publishing, and was forever collaborating with artists on their books, so to him it was a familiar and happy place. To Fiza, it was wonderland. Her mind raced back to that first day at the book suppliers' in Bombay, when she had feverishly filled her cart with hundreds of titles. This was even more surreal. Publishers, authors and distributors milling about, glasses of wine and cackles of laughter punctuating business talk. Fiza wondered how she should go about it. She had carried just a few visiting cards from the store thinking she wouldn't really need them. In about forty-five minutes, she had run out of them. Everyone she spoke to was interested in her little store in distant Bombay. She first wondered whether it was the famous British politeness at work. Then she realized how every book publisher and distributor was looking at her as a representative of the Great Indian Book Market. It was far from accurate, this descriptor. She was hidden away in a suburb of the city, fussing over details like dusty bookshelves and unwashed cups. But here, in the literary capital of the world, she realized Paper Moon was part of a long and rich history that connected booksellers everywhere. She met owners of corner stores, on their yearly pilgrimage to the Mecca of books. She met representatives of Penguin and Vintage, Faber and HarperCollins – all names that she had grown up revering. Now they were striking up conversations about literary trends in urban India. Did e-books pose a big threat there as they did in London? Were footfalls decreasing? How many people just come in for the coffee? Are remaindered books a game changer for sellers?

When she was done for the day, Fiza's head was buzzing with ideas. She had allowed herself a single glass of wine, keen not to miss out on any of the goings-on. Now she found she wanted more. She headed out for some air, followed by Iqbal. They found themselves at Charing Cross, not too far, where second-hand bookstores had plied their musty trade for ages. After all the glossy new titles, and the fuss around publishing that animated the fair, Fiza was pleased to be surrounded by these unassuming books and their quiet guardians.

'Are you serious? *More* books?' Iqbal said in exasperation.

'But these are *old* books! If you don't mind, I'd just like to peep in at one or two of these stores.'

While Fiza picked up books, running her hand over crumbling spines and smelling yellowing pages, Iqbal walked up to her with a relatively new copy.

'Read this? Which is a foolish question, I know, since you seemed to know *all* the books at the fair today.'

'It's not like I had read them. It's what I do. I need to know things about books. But I know nothing about this one.'

'Hallelujah!'

Iqbal walked up to the counter, paid up and set about inscribing it.

For the Mallika-e-Kitaabistan,
With affection,
A lowly page

Fiza read the tribute as they walked out of the store.

'It's set in a bookshop here. I think that's where it used to be,' Iqbal said, pointing to one of the nondescript stores in the line. '84 Charing Cross Road. Remember the place. You'll want to, when you're done reading.'

'I'll remember,' Fiza replied while taking Iqbal's hand in hers. 'I've had *such* a great day. It's not just about the important people or famous authors or whatever. It was overwhelming at first, but then I felt ... like I belonged. I don't often feel that way. I know it's silly.'

Iqbal gave her hand a little squeeze and said, 'I feel *we* belong.'

Fiza instinctively moved her hand away. 'Let's go out and *do* things,' she said, waving her arm about in an extravagant gesture.

'Oh, it's funny. I thought we already were.'

'No. I mean things people do when they're celebrating. I know, I'm not being very articulate, but it's like I've had an epiphany.'

'Ah, I'm sorry, is that a condition like epilepsy? If it is, I know it well.'

Fiza groaned at Iqbal, who took her into his arms, kissing her on the lips.

Checking his impulsive gesture, he blabbered, 'I know you're not into PDA and you'd rather we stayed quiet about this thing and you don't like being taken by surprise, but—'

Fiza placed a hand on his mouth and kissed him back just as a row of streetlamps came on, casting a warm, yellow glow on the scene.

'Yes. The first world isn't exactly as it appears from the outside,' Vivek said, the wry smile returning to his lips as he sipped on his cappuccino at Monmouth. The first meeting had spilled over into the next, bubbling with easy conversation.

'Exactly! Just puts my so-called middle-class life in Bombay in perspective.'

Fiza and Vivek had been talking about the difference in lifestyles between their cities.

'For example, I'm just so used to having people take care of everything for me. Like in my store, Ismail looks after the maintenance. Sudhir and Rosy manage the sales. Bharti Aunty – a friend of my mother's – runs the café. If I had to run a bookshop here, I'd be doing everything myself,' Fiza said, a picture of her store appearing before her eyes in vivid detail.

'Yes, that's what I keep telling Pat. How laundry and cooking and washing are just not in my DNA. It makes me, with my brown skin and subaltern politics, sound like an entitled jerk to a white woman, which is really funny, but what can I say? Mea culpa.'

'Pat?' Fiza asked while taking a bite of her buttered bread.

'Sorry, my partner.'

'Ah. You live together, then?'

'Yes. In my apartment in Brixton, funded by the Holy Father. Would you ... er ... like to visit?' Vivek asked, as if unsure of her answer.

Fiza was immediately struck by the idea of Iqbal's division of property between his two children. A bookshop in Bombay for the daughter; a flat in London for the son. Clean, simple, generous. Made him sound like a stand-up dad. 'I'd love to,' she said, eager to keep up the rhythm of the conversation. 'And you guys should come over to where I'm staying. It's really fancy. And I'm allowed to have guests, I promise.'

'Ha. Sounds quite lovely. When I first got here, I stayed with two slam poets and an interpretative dancer in a hovel in Camden. We thought we were the stuff. Took me about three days to realize the difference between grotty and cool.'

The two sipped their coffees by the window, talking about everything and nothing. There would be a time, Fiza supposed, when the inevitable conversation about family history would come up. But neither was in any hurry to get there. There were gaps in their lives that could never be filled. Perspectives they would perhaps never share. But there was enough to salvage from the wreckage of the past, if these two charmed meetings were anything to go by. When they walked out into the afternoon, a light snow had begun to fall. Fiza felt the powdery flakes on her face like a special grace, making the special day unforgettable.

Sunday had begun promisingly with poached eggs and avocados, and Nina Simone on BBC radio. Fiza was upbeat about visiting Vivek and his partner, and once in Brixton, she began following the very specific directions he had texted her. When she reached a large market, with Caribbean music blaring out of old tape recorders, she knew she was close.

Walking through the gentrified covered market – hipster London reclaiming the immigrant settlements – she stopped at a barbershop as she had been instructed. There she saw the already familiar face in an old barber's chair, smiling at her from the mirror in front. The little stall was one of many establishments run by West Indians and Asians, selling goods and services that made migrants feel less homesick and locals more global.

Vivek often strolled the aisles, sometimes buying spices from Sri Lanka, and chatting with Raasta idlers on other occasions. 'You need something? A toilet mug? Tape recordings of Marley covers? A twee coaster from an artisanal stall?' he asked Fiza now.

'Actually, if you're going to take a bit longer, I'll just return in about ten.'

'Sure. Just stay away from that French store with the enamel mugs. Exorbitant.'

Fiza wasn't sure how Vivek was with people in general. All she knew was that she felt good around him.

Walking to the barbershop, Fiza had noticed a little hole in the wall where a young woman, presumably Indian, had set up a beautician's stall. She seated herself in the shaky plastic chair and bravely asked the woman to thread her eyebrows, stray strands from which were beginning to branch out into unexplored directions.

'Sure, madam. Come from India?'

'Yes. You?'

'Pakistan,' she replied, while unspooling a roll of thread and placing the free end between her lips. She continued to speak as she plucked.

'Ladies here do on their own. Tweezing and plucking. But we like this system, na?'

'Hmm,' Fiza said through pursed lips. Never one of her favourite activities, threading was at least less traumatic than waxing. She had decided to use her razor while on the trip; no point spending a London afternoon subjecting oneself to medieval tortures.

'Upper lips also?' the woman asked while running a finger over the area. 'Little little has come. Nikal jaayega.'

Fiza relented. She always felt helpless in situations where women with strong opinions on beauty wielded sharp instruments. Plus, the memory of the aggrieved lady at the salon in her building was still fresh.

When she was done, Fiza strolled back to the barbershop to find Vivek paying up.

'So wha'd'ya think?'

'It's … it is … What *is* it?' Fiza asked, scrunching up her face.

Vivek had had a radical transformation. The top half of his head seemed pretty much the same. Behind, his curly hair stood stiffly over a razed-off lower half.

'Hahah. I lost a bet to Pat. Else I'm not into statement hair.'

'Must've been some bet,' Fiza teased.

'It was silly. Too embarrassing to get into.'

'You already have *that* hair.'

'True. But still. Anyway. I'm going to keep it for a week, then shave it all off. Sorry you had to be here for this.'

'Don't mind me. Actually, when I look at you from the front and don't think about the rest, it's okay.'

'Whatever works.'

They arrived at the apartment, which was a mad whirl of books, plants and light. Nat King Cole tumbled out of a speaker. Two cats lay curled on a battered rug.

'How lovely!' Fiza said spontaneously. 'Finally, a home with people in it!'

'What do you mean? Pat? Patttttyy? I'm here. You can gloat.'

A petite young woman walked briskly down the short flight of stairs, carrying a bottle of rosé. She walked up to Fiza, placed the bottle on a water-ringed coffee table, and said, 'Okay. I can't look at it. Please tell me it's not ghastly. I've been ruing this bloody bet all morning. Has he actually gone and done it?'

'I'm afraid he has. But there are angles from which it's almost tolerable.'

'Thank goodness. I'm sorry, I'm not always this jittery. Welcome home. I'm Pat. It's great to meet you, Fiza.'

'Likewise. Thank you for having me over. I love your home.'

Vivek walked up to Pat and turned around to reveal the misdeed. 'Oh no oh no oh no!' she cried out. 'Okay, please get in there and shave it at once. It's like dating a delinquent.'

Vivek walked upstairs, agreeing that there was nothing to be done but to shave it all off. Pat poured Fiza some rosé, laid out an elaborate cheese platter and sat down on the couch beside her. She had on a faded grey T-shirt, almost the same shade as her eyes. She was ragged and beautiful, and had a lightness of touch that endeared her to Fiza almost instantly. Fiza felt a sudden surge of well-being sitting there in her brother's home, drinking wine in the afternoon, the day unfolding spontaneously, surprisingly, like jazz.

It was almost time to return and Fiza did not want to end the trip without keeping her word about Ray. One sunny March morning, Iqbal and his son waited for Fiza by the Peter Pan statue at Kensington Gardens. Fiza had fancied the spot as a place of assignation ever since she had read Iris Murdoch's *A Word Child*. Never had she imagined the assignation would involve not just a man she fancied, but also his son.

Ray – a boy with floppy hair and a furtive manner – had brought along his bicycle with training wheels, and was circling around his father. Iqbal was paying close attention to every move, without appearing too protective. When Fiza reached them, he asked Ray to step off the bike and greet the stranger.

'But why?' the child asked defiantly.

'Because we're nice to good people, and the lady here is very nice.'

'But why should I believe you?'

'Because I'm your father. And I can lift you off your bike if I wanted to.'

At this, Ray reluctantly got off his cycle, head bowed low.

'Hello, Ray. I'm Fiza. It's great to finally meet you.'

'Why finally?'

Fiza took a moment to process the question. Iqbal looked at her, bemused.

'Because your father has spoken about you.'

'Why?'

Fiza looked at Iqbal but found no assistance forthcoming.

'Because, because … he loves you.'

'Does he love you?'

'All right, R. Enough of the interrogation,' Iqbal said, sensing Fiza's discomfort.

'What's an intorregation?'

Iqbal lifted Ray's bike while the three walked over to the famous Round Pond. The two adults settled on a bench while the child busied himself with the ducks and geese in the water.

'He's a handful,' Iqbal volunteered.

'All kids are,' Fiza said, trying to be evasive.

'Oh, don't be so noble. He's very shaana.'

Fiza smiled at the Bambaiyya slang. 'What's it been like for him, with his mother and you...'

'Oh, Sila's been wonderful as far as that goes. She's actually not been sidestepping any of the serious questions, which is quite brave of her. I'm learning how to do that. But how do you tell a seven-year-old that the two people he feels safest around aren't going to be around him any longer? Together, I mean. Even without his condition it's impossible to address this in any useful way. At least for me. So I'm the parent who takes him to parks and birthdays and bookstores, while she tucks him in every night. It is what it is,' Iqbal said with unusual seriousness.

'It must be heartbreaking,' Fiza said, trying not to nod sympathetically.

'It's better than the alternative.'

'What happened there? With your wife?'

'Never trust these Pakis,' Iqbal said with a sneer.

'Huh?'

'Relax. Sila used to find it funny.'

'What changed?'

'She stopped finding a lot of things funny. Realized she's out of my league, I guess.'

'You're a young, good-looking artist who cooks well. And still?'

'That might perhaps be the first compliment I've received from you, Ms Khalid. I realize it's not fully earnest, but I'll take it anyway.'

'So go on. What happened?'

'Nothing. Something. Everything. We woke up one day – on different days – and realized we're each other's past. The routine scared us, I guess. It's a scary thought, when everything looks like it's been decided. Groundhog Day. Everything eternally on loop.'

'But … love?'

'It stopped being romantic a while ago.'

'Just like that?' she went on, thoughts from the end of her relationship with Dhruv returning unbidden. She hadn't yet found a way to explain why she had bolted from the situation.

'It's a fiddly emotion. Ray was my idea. She was never interested in kids. I'll give her that – this was something she did out of love.'

'You don't *gift* someone a child, do you?'

'You'd be surprised. Then in a reciprocal gesture of love, I decided to move to London. And then the England sky rained on our parade for a whole year. We're only just recovering from the horror.'

'Did it get ugly?' Fiza asked softly.

'No. Just sad. But then sad *is* ugly…'

Ray walked back to where the adults were sitting, throwing his bike down and slumping on the grass by his father's feet.

'I'm hungry,' he scowled.

'And what do we say when that happens?'

'I'm hungrrrrrryyyy,' he yelled.

'No, that's not what we discussed, Ray. Regulate yourself, yes?'

The little boy, getting more agitated with each passing second, began to pull out clumps of grass and drop them down his T-shirt.

'All right. This little idyll ends here, I'm afraid. I'd invite you to walk with us to the bus stop, but there might be words. And some scratching and spitting. Nothing to subject a lovely lady on holiday to,' Iqbal said while getting up.

'I'm happy to—'

'Nah, I'd rather not. See you before you leave?' Ray was now in the middle of a full-blown tantrum, attracting disapproving stares from people around. A little girl in overalls, quietly playing with her toys up until then, broke into a fit of wailing, inspired by Ray's outburst.

'Okay, this is getting to be dramatic. Bye, then. And sorry.'

Iqbal lifted Ray off the ground with one arm and his bicycle with the other. His reaction to the situation led Fiza to believe nothing extraordinary had happened. This was how it was with the little boy. She was beginning to grasp just how complicated things were for Iqbal, and the permanent nature of the struggle. The man who breezed in and out of her store – and life – had responsibilities and entanglements that she had never quite imagined. She had first thought of him as roguish and irreverent. But here he was in another mode altogether. The surrounding circumstances had always been smooth with Dhruv. Two people together, with the world conspiring to keep them that way. Here was the reverse. And she was beginning to worry that the difficulties were drawing her in deeper.

Back at her apartment, she kicked off her shoes and lay in bed, strangely exhausted. After all the breeziness of London and Edinburgh, that morning was a reality check. She decided to pull herself out of the gloom that was threatening to suck her in, spontaneously calling Vivek.

'Hey. So do you and Pat feel like doing something this evening?'

'I'd love to, but I'm down with a nasty cold. Poor Pat has cooked and cleaned and everything, and now she's at work. You can ask her, if you like. She deserves a night out. I've been a bit of a bore lately.'

'Oh, no. Can I bring you something? And of course I won't drag Pat away when you're feeling like that.'

'No, no, please do. If she returns home, I'll be cranky and say stupid things I don't mean. Please call her. She gets done by five today, I think,' Vivek insisted.

'Okay, if you're sure. I just have a couple of days left, and I realized I've spent most evenings indoors. So this is just a panic outing, really. I have nowhere to go.'

'Pat's your ticket. Ta, sis. See you before you leave.'

Vivek had dropped the 'sis' into the sentence casually, but to Fiza, it was a breakthrough. Her sagging spirits were reviving already. Her phone beeped. It was Vivek sending Pat's number. In another five minutes, the two had fixed up to meet at the Dominion Theatre on Tottenham Court Road. The outlandish musical *We Will Rock You* had launched the year before. And Pat had decided Fiza could not leave London without saying hello to Queen.

When Fiza got to the theatre, Pat had already got the tickets and refused to let Fiza pay her share. Fiza made some noises about the unfairness of the situation, but Pat calmed her down, saying, 'I'm the biggest fan of Queen in history.

And I haven't seen this yet, which is a most disappointing and glaring omission. It is my absolute honour and privilege, Mizz Khalid.'

'Okay, then. Thanks! Also, is there more to the name? Pat, I mean. There must be, I'm sorry.'

'Patricia Welles. Makes me sound like someone in one of those kitchen-sink comedies, endlessly tending to her geraniums. So I prefer to go by the diminutive.'

'Wise.'

'Is your name common where you live?' Pat asked while they made their way to the refreshment counter.

'Not very, I don't think. It was the name of a Bollywood movie a few years ago ...' Fiza trailed off.

In no time, the two were armed with glasses of cider, being ushered to their seats. The atmosphere was exuberant, with a few audience members dressed in Freddie Mercury regalia. The last-minute seats were close to the stage, and Fiza sank into her chair, ready to be rocked.

The day of her departure, Fiza was in high spirits. She woke up with a smile, bags packed, tasks checked off, mind clear. The previous evening, she had met Iqbal for a walk around the neighbourhood, ending in a drink at Chelsea Potter, the pub she had walked into on that first night in London. She introduced him to Midge, the cheerful bartender who had made her feel welcome in the new city, the new world. Fiza showed Iqbal the rock memorabilia, sharing stories from the pub's history.

'Sounds like you've lived here forever.'

'I'm a single pub kinda girl. I have one in Bombay, too. Never needed another.'

'That's heartening to know,' Iqbal said, lightly grazing Fiza's fingers across the table. 'Will you miss me?'

'You'll be in Bombay soon?' Fiza counter-asked.

'I'll miss you. And you haven't seen my home yet. I still can't believe you're here, which is weird, considering you leave tomorrow. Did you do what you came here to do? With the book fair?'

'Yes, I think so,' Fiza said, looking down her glass of wheat beer, still avoiding any mention of Vivek. It didn't feel like the right time to get into the unfolding story with Iqbal. Adding any more layers of intimacy seemed like a mistake, knowing what she did about Iqbal's life situation.

When Iqbal walked Fiza to Carole's apartment, she invited him in. Fiza sat down on the couch in the living room and flicked on the electric fire as Iqbal walked up to the bird sculpture. 'Just look at that slope,' he said caressing its back. 'They can't teach you that in art school. I should just retire.'

'Was art school useful? Is that where you learnt...'

'It felt terribly important at the time. Didn't help in the obvious ways, I guess,' Iqbal replied, walking from one piece to the other in a trance. 'In fact, Carole took a class one semester. I wasn't picked. Lifelong regret.'

'Somehow I've never got sculpture. I appreciate the form, but it doesn't grab me like painting does,' Fiza said, watching Iqbal take in the exhibits around the room.

'It's what speaks to me most. It's like you're doing what the material asks you to. Not making them follow your vision, like in other forms of art.'

Fiza nodded. She hadn't yet had a conversation like this with Iqbal. Talking about his craft, Iqbal was sincere and forthcoming, not facetious. She suddenly realized it was getting late, and wondered where Ray was. 'I'm sorry, I've been hogging your time. Is there someplace you need to be?'

'The one place I'm interested in being is the nape of your neck, if you could do me the courtesy of moving that cascade of curls, please,' Iqbal said sidling up to Fiza on the couch. Ray's au pair had called to say the evening had gone off relatively peacefully and he was now asleep, wearing a raincoat he refused to be separated from. At about midnight, when Iqbal finally made his way to the Tube station, Fiza decided to get her packing done. The parting had been quick and cheerful. She would delay the aftermath for as long as she could.

The next morning, on the way to the airport, she called Vivek as promised.

'So the conquering hero returns?'

'Pretty much. Cold better today?' she asked.

'Yes, just in time for a *Dr Who* audition. They're looking for a brown corpse. My big breakthrough. How're you doing for time?'

'Classic Indian early airport arrival. No problem there. Listen, I just wanted to say—'

'It's been so great to see you,' Vivek replied, pre-empting her words.

'Yes. It was … Maybe we could—'

'We have time.'

'Yes,' Fiza agreed. 'Thank you. And Pat. That show was such fun.'

'She loves you. I'll look up your store when I'm there next. Maybe get a summer internship?'

'Of course! Free meals even.'

'You take care, then. Hold the family nose up high.'

It was going to take time to make proper sense of their presence in each other's lives, something beyond the light-heartedness and bonhomie of that visit. But the trip was more than she had hoped for. As she walked past immigration and into the duty-free shops, Fiza was suddenly beset by the fear of returning home empty-handed. She used up all her remaining currency on liquor-filled chocolates, boxes of shortbread and a bottle of single malt that she knew would please Noor. Up in the air, she shut her eyes, happy at the thought of sleeping in pounds and waking in rupees.

CHAPTER SEVENTEEN

It had been a week since Fiza's return and she had just about caught up with what she had missed at Paper Moon. Rosy and Sudhir had both done a great job of not just keeping the place running but also devising new schemes and plans to bring more people in. Spikes in sales around events and exhibitions made up for the dispiriting days when the only people who walked in were either delivery boys or people asking for directions to Mount Mary's Church.

Back at home, Fiza had given Noor a general summary of her trip, without getting into any details. That would have meant introducing Iqbal to the scene, and she was not prepared for that, and not sure if she would ever be. For all the comfort of their time together there, there was the realization that they inhabited not just different time zones but different worlds altogether. Somehow, Fiza wasn't disheartened by this distance. It was easier, she told herself, that he was in another part of the world rather than in her everyday routine. London had, among other things, reminded her about what she needed to hold dear. The bookstore had been an unexpected gift, but she had come very close to sending it back unopened. The book fair was an eye-opener; a zooming out into the larger world, of which her bookshop was a tiny yet intrinsic part. No, she wouldn't let it all drift away.

'Madam, India will pakka win World Cup this time. Solid Sachin is batting. And fast bowling also is chakachak,' Ismail informed her. 'Only Australia we have to watch out for. That Ponting will never leave any chance.'

Fiza had kept up with match results, but hadn't managed to catch any games so far. London had effectively taken Sachin Tendulkar off her mind.

'How it is looking?' Ismail continued, pointing to the Big Ben T-shirt made, inevitably, in China, that Fiza had bought off an insistent Indian at a Trafalgar Square kiosk.

'It's great, Ismail! Do you like it?'

'It's my best shirt, madam. First time from abroad. So soft-soft,' Iqbal gloated.

Fiza had distributed gifts to everyone at the store. Sudhir had got a new wallet, with 007 inscribed on it. For Rosy, she had picked up a bandana with English roses. For Bharti Aunty, a pretty tin of teas from Fortnum & Mason in Piccadilly. And for her mother, old jazz records of her favourites from Camden, apart from chocolates, cheese and a bottle of single malt.

'So extravagant, Fizu? What's all this?!' Noor exclaimed when she saw the loot.

'It's nothing. Most of it is for the house.'

'Since when have you been interested in jazz and malt? Nonsense.'

Noor had been relieved to hear about Fiza's meeting with Vivek. The girl hadn't really shared too much information while she was away, and Noor was worried the well-intentioned trip had missed its mark. It made her think about her own prickly reaction to Gayatri at the store.

One evening, as Fiza absently watched *Remington Steele* reruns, Noor said suddenly, 'Don't think this Brosnan fellow ever did anything better.'

'He's a good Bond, I feel,' Fiza laughed.

'Fizu, do you think I should call Gayatri and apologize? Now that you and her son are...'

Fiza took a moment to figure out who her mother was referring to. 'You mean Vivek's mother? Apologize for what?'

'That day in the store was pretty ... awkward. And her boy was so good to you in London...'

Fiza took a moment to process the offer. 'Not at all. It was a shock, that's all.'

'But she was reaching out. Then I saw those earrings and I don't know what happened. I have to get over this sudden ... madness that comes over me when it comes to Iqbal. It's not ... healthy. I've been thinking a lot about it. Why I'm still so cut up about it all. Things have turned out okay for you, for us. They have, right?'

Fiza sat down on the bed beside Noor. She was learning not to dismiss her own feelings and say the first thing she could to placate Noor. She took a moment to think about what she had just heard, and what she truly felt about it. Then she looked straight at her mother and began to speak.

'You know, ever since Vivek's mother walked into the store, or even before, since this bookshop thing came up, I've struggled with the idea of my father. I'm calling him that now, but it's not how I grew up thinking of him,' Fiza began haltingly. 'He was this cold, selfish man who walked out on his family. Then, when I had any news about him, he was gone. And suddenly there was this store. It's been ... weird. And difficult. But meeting Vivek somehow made it all feel – less odd.'

Fiza was speaking calmly, aware of the fact that this was the first time she was sharing her thoughts about her father with Noor. There had never been a good time. And now, with all the events that had occurred since he died, it became impossible not to address this mass of feelings, still inchoate after all these years.

'I know we don't do this. These intense, meaningful chats,' Fiza went on, too deep into the conversation to pull herself out without getting to the bottom of it. 'I'm not even sure who does. It's been so dark and confusing, this history. But now there's Vivek. He lives in a lovely apartment in Brixton, with cats and books and a beautiful girl named Pat. That's not just reassuring, it … it makes me feel less incomplete, if that's even a thing. It sounds corny and sentimental—'

'Not at all!' Noor cut in affectionately, then reconsidered with a chuckle: 'Okay, only a little.'

Fiza smiled and exhaled. 'Chocolates?'

'Single malt?' Noor offered in return.

'Sure.'

Noor poured out the whisky, threw in a few cubes of ice, and clinked Fiza's glass saying 'Welcome back' as Laura Holt and Remington Steele ran down a green slope, escaping exploding bombs.

It was the hottest day in May and the AC in Fiza's office was acting up. She had recently bought herself a laptop and decided to work sitting in the café. Across from her, Bharti Aunty was busy with the next week's menu, drawing up lists of ingredients and squinting over handwritten recipes. The café menu, though small, was always a surprise, with new additions, seasonal favourites and chef's specials jazzing up the little glass display. The items were usually sold out by the evening. Whatever was left over, the staff either took home or got together and finished up at closing time. Of late, that had become a ritual; a catch-up on the day's events over an assortment of cakes, chops and cutlets. In the summer, sweaty college kids streamed in through the day to escape the punishing heat. And though few books were sold, the café always did good business. Today, too, there wasn't much to take back home at closing time. The staff were all at the store; a big consignment of books needed to be sorted and put on display.

At about nine, Sudhir came up to Fiza, saying, 'Ma'am, we'll leave?'

Fiza, caught up in her catalogues, hadn't noticed it had got that late. 'Yes, sure,' she said, flashing a look at the café. 'No leftovers, today. Again.'

'Yes, good no, ma'am. They loved the tarts,' Rosy added, knotting the rose-printed bandana behind her head.

'I'll make it a regular affair. I have this new recipe book by Nigella and I'm dying to try all the desserts. These kids can be my bakras,' Bharti Aunty said while collecting her things.

'Why don't we do something tonight?' Fiza suddenly perked up.

'Meaning?' Rosy asked, fastening an earring that had come loose.

'We've been working late these past few days. Let's do something different. Whatever everyone wants. You decide.'

Fiza called out to Ismail, who was putting things away for the night. 'Are you free tonight, Ismail?'

'Some work is there, madam? I'm free only, every night.'

'Not for work. We were all thinking of going out for dinner somewhere. Please come.'

Ismail broke into a coy smile, revealing jagged teeth. He pulled at one of his earlobes and bit his tongue in that familiar gesture that said: I wouldn't dare. 'How I'll come like that, madam? You all go and enjoy.'

'Everyone, are you in?' Fiza asked the rest.

The little group assembled around her nodded, bewildered at this sudden burst of enthusiasm. Something was up since London, they all thought. Something good.

'Fizu, I would love to, bachha, but Mahesh isn't well. He'll be watching his football, but I'll go and see he gets something warm to eat.'

'Bharti Aunty, come just for a bit. I want all of us together. Just for an evening. A drink. A bite. That's it. Let the microwave stand in for you at home?' she added cheekily.

Ismail had now fixed his gaze at a spot on the floor. 'Ismail Anna, aa jaao. Achha lagega hum sab ko,' Sudhir insisted.

Soon, Ismail pulled down the shutters and the bookshop bunch walked down the road, discussing restaurant options. When they had reached the Yacht corner on Hill Road, Fiza asked everyone where they would like to go. Bharti Aunty pointed to the permit room they were standing outside and suggested they go in. 'Mahesh and I used to hang out here after college. Do they still have that beef chilly fry? It was fantastic. And so cheap.'

'Yes. Yacht's still great. Is everyone okay with the place?'
Fiza asked hopefully. Everyone loved the place, she was
relieved to hear – they just hadn't ever been there together.

Since it was a weeknight, Fiza's favourite table by the
window was still available. The three women squeezed into
the maroon Rexine sofa on one side, while Sudhir and Ismail
took up the sofa across from them. A surly waiter appeared
instantly; hanging about without ordering food or drinks was
a strict no-no. Beer and beef chilly were ordered to begin
with, along with a bowl of masala peanuts.

Ismail asked for a Sprite; he wasn't a drinker, though he
had once been knocked out by some toddy he had unwittingly
had at a Kerala wedding. When everyone had a glass in their
hands, Fiza raised a toast. 'Thank you for taking such good
care of things while I was away. I'm lucky to be working with
you all, and I hope you enjoy it, too. To Paper Moon, and its
team of superstars!'

'Madam, superstar se yaad aaya, Armaan ...' Ismail began.

'Ismail, can we please talk about happier things today?'
Fiza requested.

'I told you not to bother ma'am with any more news. She
doesn't like Bhai,' Rosy interjected.

Fiza had many things to add to that claim, but she decided
to let it go. The plan was to spend a relaxed evening, but the
mugginess of May was making it impossible. On the table
next to theirs, a middle-aged man in an Arsenal T-shirt and a
French beard sat with a glass of gin and a plate of cheese cubes
in front of him. He was dissecting the cubes into triangular
pieces, smaller and smaller as he went along. *Gin, cheese cubes
and toothpicks: what some evenings are constructed of,* Fiza
thought with a hint of sadness.

By the second glass of beer, things were easing out, and there was a steady flow of laughter and conversation. The staff were filling Fiza in on the regulars and one-off visitors, sharing gossip only they would appreciate. At about 10 p.m., Bharti Aunty decided to head back home. 'Manchester United would have either won or lost by now, and my poor fellow will be screaming at the TV all alone. Bye, everyone. We must do this more often,' she said. Fiza walked her out; there was always a line of autos waiting outside Yacht. Bharti Aunty got into one, saying, 'Fizu, there's something different about you since you've returned from London. It makes everyone around you happy.' She placed a palm on Fiza's cheek, as she had done since Fiza was a little child, and sped away in the auto. Fiza had felt the change strongly too, and was reassured that it was visible to those around her. All the fiddly emotions that had begun to rearrange themselves internally were starting to show. *Was this too good to last?*

A round of noisy laughter brought her thoughts back to the present. With more space on the ladies' sofa, and a wall fan turned in their direction, the bookstore party found themselves getting comfortable. Bhurji-pao had been ordered and polished off within minutes. The gin drinker at the next table had ordered another plate of cheese cubes.

'Madam, how are bars and all over there? In London? Must be hi fi, no?' Sudhir asked.

'They're everywhere. And they let everyone in. Even dogs, most places. So that was a surprise. Here, there are so many rules. Don't do this, don't do that. There, it's more relaxed. Inside the pubs, it's nice and friendly; outside, it can get ugly. They travel together on the train later. It's noisy and a bit scary on the weekends,' Fiza replied, while ordering another beer, thoughts tumbling out freely.

'And the roads? And buildings? I heard everyone is always dressed in formal clothes,' Rosy asked.

'Depends on who you meet and where. There are a lot of people who struggle there. Fewer than here, but it's a big number. We don't hear about it much. The homeless. The jobless. The hungry.'

'*Hungry?* In *London*? And school-college?' Ismail asked incredulously.

'I mean, education and healthcare are provided for. But it's tough to survive there, Ismail.'

'But it's a rich country, no?'

'Yes, it is. If you have money,' Fiza said, recalling the ragged people in the streets and on the Tube, holding up signs for help. The buskers at busy squares and hobos in parks. The millions whitewashed out of the 'prosperous city' myth.

'This you have told me is very new. People are always running there and America and all for life improvement – they are poor there also?'

'It's complicated, Ismail.'

'My aunt in Australia is a housekeeper. She makes good money, but they don't let her eat with them,' Rosy said softly. 'She feels quite bad.'

Ismail looked uncomfortable all of a sudden. This was the first time he was sharing a table with an employer. He looked down at his plate, with a strained smile. Fiza caught the awkward gesture.

'Yes, we need to learn a lot as humans. Ismail, the next time we go out, you decide what kind of food we'll have. I've heard there's a great place for egg roast and parottas in Mahim.'

'Madina! You know Madina, madam?'

'Yes. I've heard about it. My friends from the college hostel used to go. We'll all go together one day. But you'll have to guide us.'

Ismail flashed a proud smile, and the conversation picked up the easy tone that it had begun with. A few minutes later, plates of greasy mutton biryani arrived and the table fell completely silent except for the smacking of lips and licking of fingers.

When the rains came, they made everything about themselves. This year, the pattern was unlike others. It poured madly for a few days, and stayed dry for the next, confusing the locals, who expected the unpredictable monsoon to nonetheless bring rain every day. Walk-ins at the store had decreased as expected, and Fiza was trying hard to make up for the slump by thinking up offers and services like rainy-day discounts and home deliveries. The Dial-a-Book service was catching on, and Ismail had become a familiar sight in and around Bandra, bravely motoring his way through potholes and puddles in his bright-red raincoat.

One such afternoon, he set out to make a delivery in Khar. This was traditionally the stronghold of Danai, the well-stocked neighbourhood bookshop owned by Mrs Mango, the Parsi bibliophile married to a Greek-origin diplomat. The customer, a senior manager at an FMCG company, had ordered a set of management and self-help bibles – from Richard Branson's mantras to *Who Moved My Cheese?*. Securing the books against the rain was a difficult task, but

Ismail had fastened a little box on to the back of his moped, like a pizza delivery guy.

On the way back to the store, Ismail was caught in a flash shower at Hill Road. The sudden squall made it difficult to see even a few feet ahead; it was like someone had thrown a shroud over the busy street. Before he could turn towards the pavement, his moped fell into a pothole near Bandra Medical Centre. He was moving relatively slowly, but a three-wheel goods carrier was hurtling towards him, swerving to avoid a child running across the street. The collision threw Ismail off his two-wheeler and onto the pavement outside St. Joseph's Convent, where he was unlucky to hit a streetlamp. He was picked up and packed into an auto immediately by passers-by, and taken to Holy Family Hospital a few hundred metres away. A cobbler left his little stall and took charge of Ismail's moped and helmet, following his auto to the hospital.

'Hello, Paper Moon, how may I help you? What! Where? How he is? I'm coming.'

Sudhir placed the receiver back on the hook and ran up to Fiza's office.

'Madam, Ismail Anna has had accident. He is bad. They took him to Holy Family. They got our number from moped. I am going.'

Fiza and Sudhir left the store in an instant, promising to call Rosy and Bharti Aunty with an update from the hospital. When they arrived, Ismail was in the casualty ward, being attended to by a team of doctors and nurses, with a curtain drawn around his bed. A few minutes later, he was wheeled to the lift, ready to be taken to the ICU. Fiza caught a fleeting glimpse of Ismail; he looked unconscious, blood smeared all over his shirt, a leg hanging limp. Sudhir was too squeamish to look. He held his face in his hands and looked worriedly at Fiza. She turned her face away from him and walked up to the doctor in charge of the emergency unit.

'You are his care of? He's your worker?' the man in the too-tight shirt asked casually, gold chain gleaming from his neck, a tilak on his forehead. A far cry from the resident doctor on the night she had been admitted to the same hospital.

'He works with us. We are his ... people. What do you know so far, doctor?'

'Please fill all these forms. And his scooter is lying in our parking. Please take it somewhere. It's not allowed,' the man continued, pushing a set of papers towards Fiza.

Just then, a young couple walked up to the desk, leading a little boy of about seven or eight. The boy was mumbling to his parents, holding an arm up.

'Can you please take a look?' the mother asked the doctor as her son continued to mumble.

The man in charge looked up at the parents and asked, 'He is normal or abnormal?'

Both were taken aback by the rudeness of the question.

'He always talks to himself? He fell down on head?' the man rattled on.

The father took a moment to compose himself and replied with all the patience he could muster: 'Yes, he's normal. He's hurt his arm. He fell while playing. Please get it X-rayed.'

Fiza recalled her previous experiences at the hospital and decided this doctor was an aberration. Then she tried to bring his attention back to Ismail.

'Excuse me, doctor, what is the status of my patient. The accident victim?'

'You saw status. Very bad. Call his real family,' he said, busying himself with papers and stamps.

Fiza completed the admission procedure and asked Sudhir to take the scooter back to the store and stay there till she had more information.

'Madam, I will park bike and return. Ismail Anna is ... I will do anything for him. I'm coming back. You please don't worry. We will all take care of everything together.'

When Sudhir returned, Fiza was with a Dr Allwyn Dias, who was tending to Ismail in the ICU. He wanted to have a word with the patient's family.

'I'm his guardian, doctor. Please tell me. I will take the decisions that need to be taken.'

'Can you call your parents, madam?'

Fiza flashed an impatient look and said, 'Doctor, please tell me.'

Dr Dias, who was trying to protect Fiza from the gravity of the situation, finally relented.

'Pulmonary laceration. Left leg broken. Heavy loss of blood. Injury to neck and possibly spine. We'll start the transfusion once we've stabilized him ... if we stabilize him. It's not looking good. Multiple surgeries will be required.'

Fiza felt numb against the torrent of bad news. 'But, doctor, no head injury?' she asked weakly, looking for some possibility of hope.

'No, the helmet was on. But there is a lot of damage. We'll know in time...'

'Okay, doctor. I'm here. Whatever needs to be done – procedures, requisitions, anything. It's a complete go-ahead from me. I'll sign everything you need. He's very important to us,' Fiza said plaintively.

The doctor put his mask back on and returned to the OT, neither giving nor taking away hope.

Fiza and Sudhir kept watch at the hospital through the troubled night. At about 1 a.m., the pulmonary intensivist called for Fiza.

'A lot of fluid has collected in the lung. We have to go in to drain it. There are other complications already, but we can't wait. Do you want us to continue?'

'What's the risk percentage, doctor?' Fiza asked anxiously. 'What is Dr Dias saying?'

'I can't give you a number. No doctor can. But it can be fatal. All I can say is if we don't go in now, it *will* be fatal.'

'Then go ahead, doctor. I'll sign the...'

'Caregiver consent.'

'Yes. I am willing.'

'I'll send the nurse out. We'll begin the procedure. The transfusion is still on. We have not begun treating the leg. The vitals need to start looking up first.'

A nurse followed soon after the doctor, asking Fiza to sign the documents. Sudhir went to the chemist on the ground floor to replace the medicines and surgical supplies. The bills were mounting, and he had to head back to the store to bring whatever cash remained there. Fiza requested him to bring her chequebook from her office; a big withdrawal would have to be made the next day.

In the waiting room outside the ICU, there were a few others spending a difficult night. A frail old lady by the window had just drifted off to sleep, prayer beads still in hand.

An athletic young man in a football jersey was looking vacantly at the wall facing him. On it was a picture of Christ with the bleeding heart. Under it, the words: I died for you. Fiza shut her eyes, willing herself away from the dark place and its desperate inhabitants.

A couple of hours had lapsed by the time Sudhir returned. There was still no word from the doctors. Fiza peeped into the ICU, trying to see if she could catch a few moments with a nurse. But the room was quiet, with no sound other than the hum of the machines attached to sleeping patients. Her thoughts moved anxiously to a possible time in the future when she herself would be attached to these life-prolonging devices in a freezing room that smelt of ether and death. Ismail must still be in the OT, she imagined.

Sudhir interrupted her troubled thoughts with news from the outside world. 'Madam, I finished the work at the shop and then went to your building. I met his friend, the watchman of next building, Padam Singh. They all know Anna. I told them about accident. All want to come and meet and stay. I told them to wait till tomorrow and I will give update. They asked if they should tell his family – I didn't know what to say.'

Fiza nodded. 'Yes, of course. Thank you, Sudhir. I hadn't thought of his – his people. We have to call his family. But let's wait until the morning. Whatever the news is, we will share it. And whoever wants to come and see him should come soon. We don't know what's going to happen.'

The rest of the night passed without any information from the ICU. At about five in the morning, Fiza, who was dreaming of a drowning man speaking incoherent words from underwater, was woken by a nurse.

'Patient is stable.'

'Huh?' Fiza replied, dazed.

'Patient is stable. He is in ICU only. Heart rate has come back to normal. We removed water from lung. Dr Dias will meet you when he comes back.'

Sudhir, who had sprung up on hearing the nurse's first words, clasped his hands together and began reciting the Hanuman Chalisa under his breath. 'Madam, whole night I was praying, non-stop. Anna can't go like that. He is fighter. He is superstar, bigger than Bhai.'

Fiza's eyes had filled with tears. She shut them tight and summoned a weak voice. 'Please inform his friends. And his family needs to be informed, too. They should come here. Let's not waste any more time. Please go home and get some rest. I'll go, too. We'll meet here around noon. We'll get him out of here in good shape, however long it takes,' she said, patting Sudhir on his shoulder.

'Yes, madam. I am ready. I will pack all my things and come, no problem. You please don't take tension. Now everything will become okay.'

The nurse's update and Sudhir's support made Fiza believe everything would, in fact, be okay. Just then she noticed the boy in the football jersey was missing from his night-time station. On her way out, she asked the nurse if everything was okay with his patient. She replied that his brother, who had been admitted with a head injury, hadn't made it through the night.

CHAPTER EIGHTEEN

The next couple of weeks went by in a blur. Sudhir, Fiza and Rosy would take turns at the hospital during the day, while Ismail's friends from the neighbourhood insisted on spending the nights. When Ismail had finally gained consciousness, and an awareness of the situation, he had insisted that his family desist from visiting, and stay put in Kanyakumari. It would worry rather than calm him to have them around. He didn't want his son, studying in the tenth standard, to miss school. And his wife Zulekha had never been out of their small town. He spoke to them over the phone and reassured them that he was taken care of. He had no recollection of what happened once he hit the pothole on the day of the accident, but was eager to know all the details. Once he had gathered all the information about the accident and the treatment, he turned to Fiza.

'Madam, all this you are doing, I will pay back. I promise. And who is taking care of store? I am very sorry, madam.' Ismail was a proud man, and struggled with this changed equation with his employer and colleagues.

'Ismail, *we* are sorry. You were on the job when this happened. The naariyal van that supplies your coconuts has been informed about your condition. They are worried about you, too. Don't worry about the accounts with them – we've sorted it out. Everyone wants to contribute to your recovery. And that will happen very soon. That's all you need to worry about.'

'Don't call that bai from next building, madam. She doesn't clean properly,' Ismail said unexpectedly. 'I know because I do delivery there and watchman tells me. You can get maid from building next to Little Flower – Kanaiyya, third floor. She will be good. She cleans clinic. Very proper. Give my reference. She will come as badli.'

Fiza couldn't help but laugh at his manner. 'Give my reference' was such an Ismail thing to say, even as he recovered from a near-fatal accident, still incapacitated. She promised him she would seek out the help he recommended. Walking back to the store from the hospital, she walked past Yacht and realized how things had changed since the night of the celebration, which now seemed so long ago. And things were already looking like they would get back to how they once were, as if the big jolt of the previous fortnight was yet another occurrence one took in one's stride. Ismail's leg injury, which doctors had placed at the bottom of their list of worries on the day of the accident, was the thing that was keeping him in hospital. It would take at least two months before he could properly walk again. And Fiza thought it best that he spend that time in the hospital ward. The accident also made her realize how she had been remiss in not insuring her staff. It wasn't what small businesses did, she had been advised by D.K. at the start. But the situation with Ismail had been a rude awakening. There had to be a better plan for contingencies.

When Ismail was finally discharged, a scar on his face and a slight limp were the only outward signs of the accident. The doctors were surprised at how plucky the patient was. When he returned to the store, it was with a renewed commitment. He knew he couldn't pay back the money anytime soon, but he would double his efforts at Paper Moon. He arrived even earlier than before every morning, and left later than usual. Dusting, cleaning, sorting, neatening – there was never a moment that found Ismail idling. He had had his moped fixed; the brunt of the accident had been borne by him and not his vehicle. Though Fiza had suggested he stay off the road for a while, Ismail assured her he'd be careful as always.

'Why to be scared of work, madam? That day, I never did anything wrong. And now also I won't. All is in *His* hands, no?' Ismail said, rolling his good eye skywards. Fiza had long since realized never to stand in the way of someone and their faith, even though – and perhaps because – she never had any to tide her through times of terror and anguish.

It was getting close to Diwali, and Paper Moon had begun to receive bulk orders from offices looking to give their employees meaningful presents to go with the silver-topped mithais and assorted dried fruits on decorative trays. The store had put together customized gift packages to please different kinds of companies. For the media houses, there were smartly designed books featuring pop culture and fine art. For the MNCs who wished to entertain and also edify, there was a mix of Robin Sharma and Dilbert, Osho and the inescapable Chetan Bhagat. For the kids, there was a mix of comics, general knowledge and puzzle books. After much deliberation about the cost, Paper Moon now had its own signature paper bag, featuring a crescent moon in blue, followed by the words 'Bandra, Bombay'. Despite the extra cost, Fiza had insisted on bags made of recycled newspaper. The store had grown into a well-loved Bandra hub – a happy retreat not just for book lovers, but for anyone looking for a quiet, reflective moment in an increasingly difficult city. That, and some top-notch snacks.

Lending the staff a hand with the gift packages, Fiza remembered she had to have the music system fixed. She stepped into her office to call the repairman, but had trouble finding his number. In no time, her desk and the floor around were a melee of papers and stationery, a mess she promised herself she would clear by the end of the day. When she finally found the number on a visiting card buried under the debris, Rosy was at her door, smiling her happy-news smile. 'Ma'am, two people have come to meet you. They had come when you were in London also. And then once when you were in hospital for Ismail Anna. They always come and take notes and all. I feel they will place one big order. All the best, ma'am.'

Fiza was doubly disappointed the music wasn't playing. Now she had new and potentially big customers to cater to without the assistance of Joni Mitchell or Lou Reed.

'Hello, I'm Fiza. Is there something I can help you with?' she said, leading them to the café.

A middle-aged Sikh man in a well-cut grey suit and a pink tie introduced himself as Manmeet Singh, and his colleague as Sanjana Mistry. She looked younger than him by a few years, and was wearing a beautiful green silk sari, pallu pinned neatly at the shoulder. 'We're setting up a new hotel in Colaba.

Do you have some time to chat?' the lady asked affably, the beautiful lines around her eyes deepening as she smiled.

'We're eco-friendly, fair practices, future ready, the works,' her colleague continued cheerfully, offering her his visiting card, made of handmade paper. 'Everything is handcrafted, from the linen to the experiences.'

Fiza quickly signalled to Bharti Aunty to send refreshments to their table. There was no way to explain away the mess in her office; so she decided to carry on the discussion right there.

'That sounds great,' she replied, anticipating a big corporate order. Perhaps her store could afford a new music system after all.

'We heard about you and your store way back in December last year. Do you remember an Australian family from New Year's Eve? You fixed them sandwiches,' Manmeet said, forehead creasing as he tried to jog her memory.

Fiza said she remembered clearly. 'I was so nervous, I don't know what I served them. It's really not my department, but they were so sweet about it.'

'They were floored by you, really,' the lady assured her. 'They're investors in the new project. In fact, it's Steve's baby. He's set one up in Melbourne. And now here we are, preparing for a Christmas launch. We really should have met you earlier, but there just hasn't been a moment.'

'That's ... really exciting,' Fiza said with expectations mounting. She had even begun to imagine the new music system: six speakers and a remote. Bharti Aunty served the coffees and croquettes, and though the guests said they would not eat, both were curious to try the snack and even requested another round when they were done.

'So, Fiza, to make the purpose of our visit clear,' Manmeet said in his business voice, 'we want Paper Moon there.'

'Ah. That's great. We've had some exhibitions before. Do you want to time it with the launch or a little later in the new year?' Fiza replied enthusiastically.

'Actually, we want Paper Moon there permanently,' he continued. 'We're looking to partner with people who share our sensibility. Handpicked products and thoughtful service. And a sense of community. Yes, we cater to a high-end clientele, but it's not a space for snobs. We see ourselves as a cultural hub in the making. Somewhat like Prithvi Theatre in Juhu? We have a small auditorium, too. Paper Moon is a community space here, from everything we've seen, heard and read. We loved the *Mumbai Review* piece in particular.'

Mumbai Review, the popular entertainment magazine, had featured the store prominently in a recent issue. Fiza had been interviewed, and much to her embarrassment, they had used a full-length picture of her, where she was pretend-reading Albert Camus's *The Stranger*. The shoot had happened in Ismail's absence, and Fiza had spent most of the evening getting the store to look photogenic. When it was time to take the pictures, her clothes, hair and mind were in disarray. She was thankful that pictures didn't capture smell. The offer from these well-turned-out visitors was a complete bolt from the blue. Much like everything in her life the past few years.

'That's ... that's really kind of you to say,' Fiza found herself struggling for words, trying not to sound overwhelmed. Bookshop entrepreneur. That's what she was turning into, she thought. In her head, the phrase sounded half-funny and half-scary.

'So what do you feel about it? We're good people to work with, I promise,' Sanjana said, the evocative lines returning to her face. 'And these things are divine,' she muttered, finishing off the last croquette.

'Thanks! And it's a great offer. But I'll have to consult my team. And other people who have been important to the store from the start. Can we meet again in some time?'

'Of course,' Manmeet said, finishing his coffee. 'And can we do something with the café, too?'

Bharti Aunty was glad she had her back to the group. She had just broken into the widest and silliest grin.

'So you're going to have a book empire!' Noor said with unabashed pride. 'Fizu, this is just terrific! And that too in Colaba. I can easily visit from office in Churchgate.'

'Yes, it's pretty exciting. But are we ready?' Fiza said cautiously.

'You will be. It sounds like a cliché, but it's true what they say about opportunity.'

'I think I should consult D.K. about this.'

'Haan, you can, but I hope you know you don't need to,' Noor shot back impulsively. Then, organizing her thoughts for a moment, she continued. 'The first store, yes. It was a gift. This new one is all your doing. Blessings and support are always welcome, but you don't need anyone's approval.'

Before she had said yes to the original bookshop project, she had found strength in Frances's words; this time, she found her mother's belief to be reassuring. There was no reason why she couldn't do this. Paper Moon was looking after itself and more. And now this new space – without having to worry about real estate or logistics – was a great reward. She would have to get into building mode, but now she knew how it was done. Marc would take care of the design. She knew which distributors to reach out to, and for what. And her A-team would train the new crop with ease. They could do this.

Later that night, Fiza found herself reaching out to Iqbal.

'Paper Moon 2 coming up. In distant Colaba. And speaking of distant...'

'Not too shabby, literary proprietress. Big hug. When's the London launch?'

'Find me an offer. All well with you?'

'Missing Bombay. Pining for it, actually.'

Fiza typed out a suitably teasing reply, but erased it before hitting send. This dance of intimacy and distance was beginning to wear her out.

Fiza didn't wait long to call back the hoteliers. They were delighted to hear from her. 'We were worried we would have to reach out to a big bad retail chain!' Manmeet joked. 'Honestly, we hadn't really prepared for rejection!' he admitted.

'I hadn't really considered it either,' Fiza laughed.

The big concern was whether Paper Moon would be ready to launch along with the hotel, and Fiza assured them she had it under control. It was time for another war plan – General Fiza surrounded by her trusty lieutenants. She had taken the staff into confidence, telling them the outpost could only work well if the headquarters were fully powered. All in all, there was great excitement over the new branch. Beyond balance sheets and people's responses, here was undeniable proof of the success of the original.

Marc began devising little reading nooks and lamps, revolving racks and wall décor. The new store would look like an extension of the charming old one, but it also had to fit in with the contemporary, near minimalist vibe of the hotel. The layout of the store was beautiful; it even had a lovely balcony with iron railings. Marc had already begun sourcing plant holders and pots; bougainvillea and frangipani would be just the thing. Natural light would stream in from west-facing windows. He spent hours working out plans and measurements, cheering Fiza up with his banter whenever her spirits flagged. In a couple of weeks, the bookracks were delivered. And soon, it was time to return to the trusty old book distributors to select books, the ingénue of a few years ago replaced by a sure-footed professional.

Heading back home after a long day with publishers and suppliers, Fiza got a call from Kavya. Fiza hadn't had the energy to hop on a train and had allowed herself a cab ride home for her efforts.

'Where have you been, Kavi? I thought you'd come take a look at the new space, see how it's shaping up. Been busy with a new film?'

'Yes, always busy with that. I hope everything's coming together well,' Kavya replied.

Fiza sensed that something was amiss. Kavya had always been the least tactful person she had known, incapable of subterfuge.

'What's up, Kavi? All okay?'

'Yes, yes. I know it's a bit last minute, but do you feel like a drink?'

Fiza was knackered. Apart from the book-buying, she had accompanied Marc to Princess Street near Crawford Market to source track lights for the ceiling of the new store. But she sensed there was something up with Kavya. 'I can go there straight. I'm just hitting Dadar Bridge. Traffic willing, another forty minutes.'

'Okay, super. See you.'

They didn't need to say where. In about forty-five minutes, they were seated at their table at Toto's, draught beer in front of them, sausages and fried onions on their way.

'How's it going? You've got the bandwidth to deal with it all? But what a great opportunity,' Kavya began, gulping her beer quicker than usual.

'Yes, it seems to be under control. Today's what? 16 November? Five weeks to go. The new staff will be the challenge. The rest we can manage.'

'Ya. It was a task the first time too, I remember.'

'I think I'm going to have to ask Ma to fill in for a bit if I don't find the right person. Then there's the matter of shifts. We can potentially keep the store open twenty-four hours since it's a hotel, but it doesn't seem wise. They have a coffee shop anyway, plus a lobby; so it's unrealistic to expect people who're not looking to buy books to come and hang out. But then they're keen on us curating other experiences too: performances, readings, things like that,' Fiza rattled on, trying to provide Kavya an in. But with every passing minute, Fiza could see her getting more awkward. She was now fiddling with her charm bracelet, drawing patterns out of the water rings on the table. 'All that trouble they take over coasters ...' Fiza said, pushing one towards her.

It was that time of the evening when REM's '*Losing my religion*' came on. The young man on the next table began mouthing the lyrics with eyes shut, head bobbing to the beat. His date drained her glass of wine, picked up the pint bottle from the ice bucket placed between them and refilled her glass wanly.

'Okay, before AC/DC comes on and we can't hear each other at all, can you tell me what's going on? Are you in trouble of some kind?' Fiza didn't want to push Kavya, but there was clearly something she needed to talk about. 'All okay with your health? You really have me worried now.'

'No, no, please don't worry. I'm completely okay. Well, I'm fine, health-wise,' Kavya replied quickly.

'Okay, that's a relief. So then? What's the problem?'

'Fizu, it's about Dhruv.'

This Fiza was not expecting. 'What's wrong with Dhruv? What's happened? Kavi?'

'He's fine too, don't worry. When you guys broke up, he and I somehow became ... friendlier. It wasn't a conscious move at all. I've known him as long as you have, but you know how that was. It was always you and him, and you and me. Never...'

Fiza was beginning to get a sense of where this was going, and she found her face tensing with a combination of unspecified emotions.

'When he was here around New Year's ...' Kavi continued with trepidation.

'Yes?' Fiza cut in, with mounting agitation.

'He was very cut up about the whole new year's thing with you. I'm sorry, he told me about it...'

Fiza found herself blinking rapidly. Her throat had gone completely dry and she took a big sip out of her glass. Kavya said some more things, but Fiza just stared at her blankly, as if she had never seen her before. She tried to focus on the news her friend was delivering to her, but, instead, her mind was flooded with images of Dhruv and herself over the years, like in one of those cheesy movies.

'We've been speaking all year round. He made a trip a couple of months ago...'

'Dhruv was here?' Fiza snapped, as if possessed by some primitive instinct she had no control over.

'Yes, he was. And we've decided to get engaged this December.' Kavya exhaled exhaustedly after her last words, as if she had crossed the finishing line of a marathon.

Fiza, meanwhile, was watching herself react to this new and painful situation from a distance. Her best friend, and her first love, were to be engaged. If there was some dignified way for her to express her emotions, she hadn't found it yet.

'Okay. Congrats, I guess,' Fiza pulled out the words at last.

'Fizu, I'm really sorry! But this has nothing to do with us. I hope you'll see that in time. Dhruv and I have been friends for years. And you've made it clear you want nothing to do with him.'

Everything Kavya was saying was true and rational. There was nothing deceitful about her relationship with Dhruv. They hadn't shared the news with her before, but that was understandable; things take the time they take. What was crushing Fiza at the moment was the fact that Dhruv was still part of her DNA, and would perhaps always be. She had chosen not to be with him. Now he was choosing someone else. It shouldn't matter who it was. But to her great anguish, it *did* matter. She wasn't one for drama, but right then, it felt like she was at the unhappy end of a classic betrayal.

'I'm sorry, I really need to get home. I've had a long day and...'

'I understand, Fizu. You take your time.'

'Take my time over what? You want my blessing? You want me to be your bridesmaid? What do you want from me, Kavi?'

'I want you to understand,' Kavya said weakly.

'You want too much,' Fiza replied, placing a 500-rupee note on the table before storming off. The walking off was warranted; the money was cruelty.

CHAPTER NINETEEN

Dear Reader,

The past few years, we've been delighted to connect you with the books that you love. Paper Moon, Bandra, will always remain your neighbourhood bookshop. A place for stories, friends and coffee.

Three years since we first opened our doors, we're thrilled to announce the launch of our new store this Christmas, in Colaba. The bookshop is part of an eco-friendly hotel called Sol, which promises to be a hub for art, music, and other cultural and community activities. Do drop by between 10 a.m. and 10 p.m. on 25 December. We'd love to share a glass of mulled wine, a slice of plum cake and a tale or two with you.

Warmly,
The Paper Moon Team

A pretty e-invite had been attached to the mail and Rosy had just sent it off to the database. Responses had already started to come in, making Rosy worry about the quantities of mulled wine that would have to be prepared.

'Relax, Rosy. It's a *proper* hotel. The kitchen will take care of it,' Fiza assured her.

Hill Road was decked up in its holiday best, tinsel in shop windows, giant stars perched high up above the traffic, family reunions and shopping sprees keeping Chapel Road and Waroda Road, St. Leo Road and St. Cyril Road busy. Down at Paper Moon, business was good. Locals dropped by with friends and relatives visiting from around the world, proudly introducing them to their little Bandra hideout. Rosy had even set up a Christmas crib near the old books, complete with sand, straw and little figurines. She had especially created little replicas of books, which the three wise men carried as an offering to the baby Jesus instead of gold, frankincense and myrrh. Paper Moon's own version of the nativity scene.

Weeks had passed since Fiza had walked out on Kavya at the pub, but she still hadn't been able to dislodge the block that had wedged itself into her mind that evening. She had thought it best to block thoughts of Dhruv and Kavya altogether, and focus on the launch of the new store. Things had never been better at work, or with her mother. With Iqbal, it was status quo. He responded warmly whenever she texted, but it had been months since he had visited. It irked Fiza that love was the big question mark hovering over her head at the moment. It isn't meant to be like that, she worried. After all, she wasn't the sentimental sort; she was the head-on-her-shoulders kind of person. She had never been able to settle on what exactly it was that made her end things with Dhruv, a boy she had loved dearly. Perhaps something about him being so single-minded, so sure about things at a time when she was only beginning to form her own ideas about the world and her place in it. That was the best she had arrived at. And now she was second-guessing everything that had happened with Iqbal.

Troubled by this train of thought, she decided to leave the Bandra store for the Colaba one earlier than planned. Just as she reached the door, she was stopped by two figures walking in.

'Noooooo!' Fiza yelled, surprising the few people browsing books in the store.

'Yesssss!' came the equally enthusiastic reply and, in a moment, Fiza had been lifted off the ground by a gangly man with a nose remarkably similar to hers.

'I'm sorry to break up the little family scene, but this *is* a bookshop and let there not be any yelling,' the young woman with the tall man said with mock seriousness.

'I cannot believe this! It's just ... fantastic!' Fiza said, hugging Pat tight.

'This *place* is fantastic! *You* did this? Seriously?' Vivek said, walking inside, drinking it all in.

'Come, let me show you everything. But how long are you here for? And you're staying with me, no question about it. You have to stay for the store launch. And I have to take you to Toto's and ...' Fiza blabbered away while the other two stood in stunned silence.

'Calm down, calm down. It's like someone spiked Popeye's spinach!' Vivek laughed. 'We really weren't expecting such a rousing welcome! We'll have to go back to the drawing board now, Pat. Also, where were you escaping to? A bit early to call it a day, no?'

'I was heading to the new store,' Fiza said, catching her breath.

'Okay. How many stores *do* you run?'

'I was going to tell you about it when it launched. Sort of like a surprise. And here you are!'

'He's acting cool and composed now, but he's been so excited, all he spoke about on the flight was about walking into your store and giving you a fright. I'm so glad it's over, honestly. But Fiza, this is just gorgeous. It's way cooler than I imagined. You're quite the star,' Pat said fondly.

Once Fiza had given them a tour of the place, they ended up in her little office. 'That nose!' Vivek said, pointing to the picture frame with Iqbal and Fiza.

'Just what your mother said,' Fiza smiled.

'Yes. She was so impressed by you and your work.'

'I'm actually a bit ashamed about how that day went. I hope to meet her again. I'll create a better impression, I promise. How is she?' Getting the elephant out of the room early on was a good way to go, Fiza was learning. Especially parent-shaped elephants.

'Doing great. Pat just met her for the first time, so she's thrilled. Her poor little Indian son isn't cold and forlorn in London any more.'

'She's a lovely lady,' Pat said nobly.

'You must meet my mother, too. At last count, these are the only consorts our father had.'

The three laughed as only they would. From knowing virtually nothing about her father, Fiza was now making wicked jokes about him. It somehow felt natural, taking such liberties. This fleeting sense of kinship had arrived in the most convoluted way possible, but it was something. A phone call interrupted the trio's chatter. It was Marc and it was urgent.

The books had arrived, and cheques and signatures were needed. Fiza had to rush to Colaba right away.

'So you don't have any plans for the afternoon, do you?' she asked hopefully. 'Maybe you can come with me and we could have a bite in town once I get the urgent stuff out of the way. By town, I mean the old side of town. Bandra is a western suburb,' she said, addressing Pat.

'We're staying at the Yacht Club, also in Colaba. Shamelessly using mom's reciprocal membership with Bangalore Club. So we're all yours,' Vivek shrugged.

In a flash, Fiza recalled Noor's story about her first meeting with Iqbal, at Yacht Club, but she stopped herself from saying anything. These ghosts from the past had to be treated with caution. They were still powerful enough to haunt her.

'That's perfect. We're a stone's throw away from there,' Fiza beamed. Vivek's curly mop of hair, that lopsided smile, the easy manner – it was just the pick-me-up Fiza needed.

When the three were in a cab, Fiza turned into their local Bombay guide, pointing out to little stores and big billboards, fishing villages and landmark buildings along the way. 'That's St. Michael's Church. Known for their Wednesday novena. And don't miss the thought for the day. "Hang out with Jesus. He hung out for you." That's my all-time favourite by far.' 'That's Haji Ali, older than the Taj Mahal. We must do the walk when the tide is low.' 'Oh, look! Bombay University. My convocation happened there. I faked a coughing fit to escape.'

Suddenly, in the company of two people she had grown very fond of, the road ahead didn't seem daunting. It was a pleasant December afternoon, light filtering through almond leaves and glinting off bus windows. The air carried the smell of fish, salt and smoke. But above all, it smelt of hope. That tantalizing smell that keeps people glued to big bad Bombay despite all the grief and grime it tirelessly peddles.

At the Colaba store, things were manageably chaotic. Fiza had sourced dozens of coffee-table books. The hotel expected international travellers and well-heeled Indians; so she had picked everything from Raja Ravi Varma's prints to Bob Dylan's lyrics. Since these were costly books, Paper Moon would only pay for them if they were sold. Fiza had earned enough goodwill in the business to get books on better terms than when she had first started out. And a new bookshop was a reason for celebration for all the suppliers in the business. The young woman who had emerged out of nowhere was growing the business for everyone.

The next few days, Fiza would begin the day early, wrap up work at the Bandra store, and head to Colaba, where Vivek and Pat would be helping out in whatever way they could. Marc would be steering operations, commanding his team of carpenters and fabricators, yelling out instructions in his broken, Bengali-inflected Hindi. 'Yeh kya kaam kar raha hai? Iktu dhyaan do, baba.' Pat had taken over shelf management, arranging the books subject- and author-wise once they had been accounted for in the software. At about two, they would all break for lunch, Fiza suggesting one neighbourhood restaurant after another. Pat was sold on the berry pulao at Britannia, and voted for returning there every day. Vivek, meanwhile, was keen to try out a different place for every meal. The Irani cafés were his favourite, whether it was the keema pao at Kyani or mutton cutlets at Sassanian. Most of all, he adored Kamling, a restaurant rich with the history of India's dwindling Chinese community. Then it was back to work till the evening, at which point the trio left for drinks and dinner.

Sitting at the rooftop bar of the Godwin Hotel in a leafy lane off Colaba Causeway, iconic buildings in the southern tip of the city piercing the sky, Vivek asked Fiza what her evenings were usually like.

'That's a difficult question. I'm usually quite tired after work; so it's back home. Unless Kavi ...' She had succeeded in driving her friend out of her mind for days, but an innocent question had suddenly brought her back. 'Unless I'm out with friends. Which would mean drinks and dinner, just like we're doing now. It's been ages since I've gone out for a film or a play. I'm hoping that changes now with the Colaba store. Get back to doing some of the things we did in college.'

'So there's no lucky fellow – or lady – who gets to spend their evenings with you, then,' Pat prodded with twinkling eyes.

'No, not at the moment. I was dating for many years, but now he's marrying my best friend,' Fiza said, tongue loosened by the rum and the company.

'Ouch!' said Vivek. 'And moving swiftly on to the next topic...'

'No, it's okay. I've looked away from it long enough, I suppose. I haven't spoken to either of them since I heard. And that's a bit ... harsh, I guess. It's not what I want to do, but it's just too difficult.'

Another round of drinks had been served. Pat tossed a few cheeselings into her mouth. Fiza had ordered mixed pakodas, out of which she was picking the onion ones and dipping into the mint chutney. 'There's this other guy...'

'A-ha! I knew it. You cannot be running two bookshops in this city and not be courted by at least a dozen literary men. It speaks terribly of the culture of a place,' Vivek declaimed.

'Perhaps it speaks terribly of me.'

Pat scrunched up her face in a sympathetic expression and held Fiza's hand. 'Not a chance. What's up with this second guy?'

'You know what, I don't know. He seems – *right*. He's clever and funny and sweet. And not bad to look at,' she said.

'If you're not having him, may I have his number, please?' Pat joked.

'Me too,' Vivek added.

'He's far away. He's in the middle of a divorce. And his little son needs him. Plus, he's an artist,' Fiza said, rolling her eyes. 'I don't know where I fit in, or if I fit in at all.'

'Honey, you don't strike me as a fitting-in kinda girl. If this faraway guy wants this, he'll have to turn the world around to have it. There's no other way. Don't settle,' Pat said, assuming an exaggeratedly American 'You go, girl!' manner.

'Where is he? How far?' Vivek asked.

Fiza looked at him sheepishly.

'I knew it! There was a fellow in London right under our noses and we didn't smell it. Give me his address and I'll sort him out,' he said, rolling up imaginary sleeves.

'That's very reassuring, but I don't think this requires a Sunny Corleone-style intervention. Or maybe it does, I don't know. It seems like he wants me to wait, till things get fixed in his life. But that could be a long wait. And meanwhile, life is happening to me, too,' Fiza said, thoughts spilling out half-formed.

'So call him and have it out,' Pat said, waving a fist in the air.

'I should call Kavi,' Fiza replied decisively. 'I've been a jerk to her. I've made it all about me. It's like I want Dhruv to be hanging on while I do whatever I want with my life. That's just – *twisted*.'

'You sure you're over this Dhruv bloke?' Vivek asked, sensing the significance of the switch in Fiza's thoughts.

'I don't know,' said Fiza, reaching for another pakoda. 'I don't know.'

It was Christmas Eve and Fiza was racing against time, frenziedly interviewing applicants for the role of bookshop manager, with no success. She was coming around to digesting the fact that she would have to manage the first few weeks herself, assisted by Noor.

'How's it going?' came a booming voice from the door, as Fiza was trying out the bill printer. It was Steve, the gregarious Australian whose family she had served at the Bandra café almost a year earlier. 'I believe things are going swimmingly. I've been here a few times, but it seems we've just missed each other,' he said, approaching her with a big smile.

Steve was thrilled to see the bookshop take shape. It was just how he had imagined it to be – bright, warm, welcoming. He was keen on displaying *Shantaram* – a bestseller about the life of an Australian convict in Bombay – prominently. Gregory David Roberts was a friend of his, and he had even invited him over for a book signing in January. 'We can do the *Shantaram* tour for our guests: Leopold Café, prison, et al. Run a contest or something,' he said, excited at the prospect. Fiza agreed grudgingly. She had never been able to get through the book. She had been spoilt by the Bandra store, where she could do as she pleased, but as the business was growing, she realized there were compromises to be made. Like when she had first let Feng Shui books and tarot card packs into her store. The fact still bothered her, but she was learning to make her peace. This wasn't Frances's lit class, she kept reminding herself.

At about four in the evening, just as Fiza was walking into the hotel coffee shop, her phone beeped: Merry Christmas. I'm in Bombay and was wondering if we could meet.

Dhruv had finally reached out, and though Fiza was not sure how she felt about the situation, they fixed up to meet at the rooftop bar of the nearby Strand Hotel. It was a windy evening and Fiza had wrapped herself in a handwoven old shawl; she remembered later that it had belonged to Dhruv's nani and been gifted to her by his mother.

'Congratulations,' Fiza said straightaway, not wanting to skirt the issue.

'That's kind. It must have come as a surprise,' Dhruv said leaning in, equally eager to get to the point.

'Yes, pretty much,' Fiza replied curtly, wrapping the shawl tighter around herself.

'I'm sorry, Fizz.'

'It's not about me, Dhruv. Why're you apologizing?' she said, reading the menu intently, so as to avoid eye contact with Dhruv.

'Don't be like this.'

'I'm actually completely clueless about how I *should* be.'

'You didn't want to be with me, remember?' he said, clutching a butter knife for support.

'Actually, *you* popped a wedding proposal like it was something I had waited for all my life. *You* decided it was either marriage or nothing. So let's not confuse the facts.'

'Fizz, there's still time.'

'Time? For what?' Fiza said, looking at Dhruv incredulously. A waiter approached Fiza, but his experience rightly told him he should back off.

'If you give us a chance...'

Fiza took a moment to understand what Dhruv was offering her.

'Is this some kind of silly game, huh? Some kind of sick prank? What's wrong with you, Dhruv? Kavi said you're getting engaged.'

'Yes. But we're not engaged *yet*. That's two steps away from being married. Which is why, there's still time. I was fine until I landed here and it became ... anyway. All that doesn't matter. A couple of years ago, I was proposing to you around this time. And if I could help it, I'd be doing it all over again,' he said in a soft but determined voice.

Fiza took her face in her hands and held it tight. 'What are you doing, Dhruv?' she mumbled. 'Kavi must be getting her lehenga stitched and you're sitting here and ... What kind of two-faced behaviour is this?'

'I've grown close to Kav. She's a wonderful person, we both know that. And she's so right for me, in so many ways. But it's not fair to her, or me, or you, if I'm still so hung up on *us*,' Dhruv continued.

Fiza was shaking her head in disbelief. 'Why did you have to take things so far with her if you were so confused?'

'I wasn't confused until I saw your damn email in my inbox, inviting me to have cake and wine at your new bookshop. I don't know what happened. It was like the best of you, speaking to the best of me. It just ruined everything.'

'Mark me as spam! I send those mails to the whole city!'

'Fizz, I'm serious here. Do you still have feelings for me? I'm not asking for a commitment. I'm okay with a maybe.'

'Dhruv, you need to be with someone who's more than "maybe" interested in being with you. It could be Kavya. Or someone else. But it's not me. We have a hell of a lot of history, but I'm still hovering over "maybe". Even after I heard about you two. There's something in me that says no every time the idea of you comes up.'

'Funny, because for me it's always a yes. Always a yes when it comes to you,' Dhruv took a pause, allowing the meaning of Fiza's words to sink in. Fiza hadn't intended to hurt Dhruv, but this was the best she could do – be brutally honest about where she stood. 'It'll take a lot of work, but I'll get to where you are,' Dhruv said, recovering himself. 'Comfortably alone in your "maybe" world. I'll be off, Fizz. I'm making a habit of these rejections. If you could do me a favour and not let Kav know about this?'

'I'll do it for her, Dhruv. *Just* for her.'

Fiza walked out a few minutes after Dhruv had left, making sure she didn't run into him on the pavement outside. She was struck by how he had assumed she was alone. He hadn't even bothered to ask.

CHAPTER TWENTY

I n keeping with the Paper Moon tradition, Frances D'Monte had been invited to launch the new store. It was a simple ceremony, with Frances signing her latest book of poetry and displaying it on the window. She arrived in a stunning mustard sari, gentle waves of greying hair falling to her shoulders.

'When I returned from the first bookshop launch, I was happy. Now I'm happy, and a bit suspicious,' she said, wine glass in hand, drawing giggles from the crowd. 'We need more spaces for books in the city. And spaces for people to come together. A place where socialites and socialists can judge each other at close quarters.' Then, turning to Fiza, she added, 'I hope you'll allow penniless students and teachers to have the books they want without going all Shylock on them, Fiza. And control the urge to have a poetry slam, oh, they're insufferable. Cheers, everyone. Now where's the smoking area?' The amused crowd clinked their glasses and continued their conversations.

Staff from the restaurant wove its way around the guests, serving mulled wine and plum cake, cucumber sandwiches and Bharti Aunty's famous croquettes. Marc's gramophone player had been summoned once again, and Fiza had brought over all the records she had gifted her mother from London. The glass doors of the bookshop opened and shut through the day, letting in and out poets in white kurtas, hipsters in linen shirts, students in faded denims and pretty people in pearls and cufflinks. It seemed a world away from the quaint Bandra corner they had started out with. This was Paper Moon's foray into the city's arts and business centre. Who knew what worlds would open up from here?

The days between Christmas and New Year's Eve rang out like musical notes. The Colaba store had a steady stream of visitors right from the launch, thanks to the location and reputation of the hotel. As expected, the floating population of year-end visitors checked into the jasmine-scented rooms, or stopped by for a bite at the fusion restaurant, drifting into the bookstore. Noor spent her afternoons there, before heading to the AIR office for her evening show. She had meals with Manmeet and Sanjana, slipping into a comfortable work routine that never felt like work. Fiza left the Bandra store in the evening, closing the day at Colaba. Vivek and Pat were to leave soon, catching up with family and friends in Bangalore before New Year's Eve.

On the night before their departure, Noor invited them over for dinner. Maria had laid out an extravagant Goan feast, featuring her legendary mutton pan rolls, prawn cutlets, pork vindaloo and chicken cafreal. A side of spinach had been laid out to placate everyone's conscience, and it did its job well. The palak was the first dish to disappear.

'You remind me of your father. Witty, disarming,' Noor said while serving everyone more pan rolls. Maria had got the mince stuffing just right, and the casing had been fried to perfection, with the breadcrumbs turning crispy. Noor had decided against bringing up any difficult family history, but it was impossible to do that, after having heard Vivek speak. Fiza looked at her mother warmly, assuring her it was okay.

'Thank you, ma'am. That's good to know. I hope there's a lot else, besides,' he laughed. The tension had dissipated and Noor thought it safe to carry on.

'Were you two very close? I'm so sorry for your loss.'

'Thanks. I'm not sure,' Vivek replied in his usual forthright manner. He had arrived at the dinner expecting – even hoping for – some mention of things that mattered. Enough time had been wasted, he believed. No more, if he could help it. 'You could never really tell with him,' he continued. 'Mom and I had our own world, and he'd just peep in every now and then. He wrote me good letters. But when we were together, just us, there was hardly any serious talk. I think the only time I saw him get emotional was with music. Jazz. Or even Hindustani classical. Mom and I joked it was what light was to a vampire; it broke the defences. We played it at his memorial, which he had categorically told us he didn't want. But aren't these things supposed to be for those left behind? We played John Coltrane and Kishori Amonkar.'

Noor excused herself and went into the kitchen to refill the cafreal. She didn't want the evening to turn maudlin, but Vivek's words had hit her hard. She had introduced Iqbal to both artistes.

Fiza turned the subject to New Year's Eve in Bangalore. Pat, picking up the distress signal, replied energetically. Before leaving, Vivek held out a jute bag he had carried with him. In it was a photo album, and an old box. 'Mom sent this for you, ma'am,' he said to Noor. 'She apologized for taking the liberty, but she said it would mean a lot to her – *and* my father – if you had this. I tried to explain to her how death works, but ...' Vivek trailed off, shrugging his shoulders.

When Vivek and Pat had left, and the dinner things had been put away, Fiza and Noor finally sat down in the living room.

'Shall I?' Fiza asked, pointing to the bag. Noor nodded hesitantly. It was a new photo album, with black-and-white pictures. All from the days of Iqbal and Noor, and a few of Fiza. It also contained an envelope, out of which came a few crushed old petals, brown and brittle, and a letter. Noor's name was on the envelope, so Fiza handed it to her while hungrily going through the photographs. Noor put on her glasses and took a deep breath.

Dear Noor,

It is not my place to write to you, but a lot has happened in the last year, and I'm happy to find that our children are getting to know each other, making sense of a difficult past.

Iqbal was a troubled man with many sides to him. One of these sides he kept hidden away in a box. I found it after he was gone. And also these petals that I know nothing about, except that they smell of you.

I cannot rewrite the past for him, but I know that he suffered for what he did. But let there be no suffering now.

Gayatri

Noor took a couple of the petals in her hand and closed her eyes. She went back to her wedding night, remembering how she had put her soul into her singing, Iqbal sitting nearby, a string of jasmines around his wrist. It was a joke at the time, recreating the look of a Hindi film villain. Now all these years later, enclosed in an envelope along with a letter from the woman who took her place, the crushed flowers reminded her of something beautiful about the painful past.

Before the year could end, Fiza had exchanged some friendly texts with Kavya. Any more contact and Fiza was sure she would blurt out the truth about her unsettling meeting. She was cut up about keeping her best friend in the dark, but in the end, she decided against adding to the drama. Not only would it break Kavya's heart, it was also sure to ruin their friendship. There was nothing left to do but to wait it out. Meanwhile, the engagement, celebrated at the Alibaug home of the Banerjees, was a lavish affair. Fiza had been invited, but she politely declined, using the new store as an excuse.

On the last morning of the year, a strong breeze blowing in from the sea, Fiza made her way to the Bandra store wearing the red scarf that Pat and Vivek had gifted her for Christmas. As she opened the door, its dangling tassels got caught in the brass door handle. As she disentangled the strings gently, making sure the scarf didn't rip, she caught sight of a bunch of flowers on the checkout counter. A dozen white tiger lilies, filling the room with their fragrance. Fiza smiled as she entered the store, not bothering to look for a note. *So it's the flower thing all over again*, she thought. Things moving in a loop that she didn't know how to get out of.

Climbing up the stairs to her office, she caught a figure at
the bay window, looking out onto the ocean.

'So you've progressed to delivering the flowers yourself?'
Fiza asked nonchalantly. 'Also, in this dream world that you
live in, is there any concept of arranging to meet people? Or
is it just this floating in and out of the frame, leaving everyone
guessing?'

'Says the person who appeared in London like some
kind of vision and then drifted away, too far to reach,' Iqbal
said, turning towards Fiza. 'Even the *Sunflowers* have lost
their colour, aching for you. By the way, I'm so glad you left
this window intact. It's always been my favourite part of
the building. I'd wait for my mother to get back from work
standing here. Look out for my father's green Ambassador in
the distance and clear up whatever mess I had made. Watch
the church burials with morbid interest.'

This was how it always was with Iqbal, Fiza thought – a
rambling conversation followed by a long silence, and so on.
After London, she realized how unreal the template was.
Some kind of start and stop emotional pattern.

'Can I interest you in a bike ride? Some Chinese food? A
play, perhaps,' Iqbal went on.

Fiza was afraid of speaking her mind just then, standing in
the middle of the bookshop, but she knew that it was important
to address this thing with Iqbal. She was thrilled to see him –
there was that. It would have been easy if she wasn't. But she
didn't want this to turn into yet another reunion followed by a
long absence. There was nothing wrong with the idea, except
that it just wasn't enough for her.

'I have lots to do today, year-end and everything.'

'Yes, of course. How about after work?'

'I'll be ending the day in Colaba. At the new bookshop.'

'I'd love to come visit. You've turned into a real kitaab khaanabadosh.'

'Iqbal, I'll text when I'm free. I'm not sure today's a good idea,' she said, studiously ignoring the pun.

'You seem unhappy. Is it something I didn't say?'

Fiza's face crinkled into a smile despite herself. 'I think it's things *I* haven't said. We'll speak soon, yes? Unless you fly out in an hour to some undisclosed location, in which case, Happy New Year.'

'Ooh. *Definitely* something I didn't say. I'll wait by the phone. Be nice to a poor boy on the last day of the year. Okay, I'll be off. Have some other bookshop owners to stalk.'

Fiza saw him walk out with that familiar sinking feeling. *Stop it, Fiza*, she told herself. Then she headed downstairs, made herself a coffee, and joined Ismail in arranging the second-hand books on the cart outside.

By noon, she was on a Churchgate-bound train, keen on finishing her Muriel Spark novel before the train hit the last stop. She was rereading *The Prime of Miss Jean Brodie*, and it was even more delicious than when she had first read it in college.

One's prime is elusive. You little girls, when you grow up, must be on the alert to recognise your prime at whatever time of your life it may occur. You must then live it to the full.

The words leapt out of the page this time around. Was this her prime? These days of miracle and wonder, of family lost and found, love chased and escaped. She had never been a curious child, never an explorer. She was too scared to dream and she hadn't even known it. But, of late, the world had opened up to her inquiring mind. It had offered her a glimpse and she was hooked. There was no turning back. She was moulding life into the pattern it was dictating – like Iqbal had said about sculpture that day in Carole's apartment. Even the past was offering itself up to be reshaped, redescribed.

When she walked into the Colaba store, Noor was busy chatting with Manmeet. Something about her mother's laughter made her look twice. She had been spending a lot of time with the friendly hotelier, but Fiza hadn't given it any special thought. *Did my mother just blush seeing me walk in?* Fiza thought. Noor had, in fact, turned a shade redder. She also had her lipstick and kajal on, which made Fiza doubly curious.

'Fizu, you're here early,' said Noor too breezily. 'Mr Brar and I were just discussing New Year's Eve at the hotel. I was due to go to Alibaug with Bharti and Mahesh as usual, but he thinks I'd enjoy the music here.'

'There's an exquisite pianist here from Sydney. I think he and your mom can work magic.'

'You're going to sing?' said Fiza, her voice rising a few octaves higher.

'I thought why not give it a try? I *have* sung before...'

'Wow. *Really?* Tonight? Just like that?' Fiza went on, with growing excitement.

'Okay, ladies. I'll get going. Noor Sahiba, sound-check whenever you're ready. And Fiza, I suggest we shut the store early tonight. Don't want the party spilling into the store, quite literally, with all the liquor we're going to be laying out.'

As if on cue, the piano downstairs broke into a tentative melody. The pianist had begun preparing for the evening, testing the instrument with a jazz tune. Noor found herself humming along to the notes as she looked over the bills from the past week. She was smiling to herself, and Fiza didn't want to interrupt. She pretended to busy herself with the books in the biography section, trying to assess the probability of her mother being in love. All she knew about Manmeet was that he was a genial, well-read man, a widower with two children who lived abroad. In Fiza's memory, Noor had never had a romantic interest, and this was a monumental step. Books, music and romance – she couldn't think of how the moment could get any better. Ironically, it was her mother who was at the centre of it all, while she was still muddling her way through things.

When Noor had stepped downstairs, Fiza walked over to the landing and looked down at the ground floor, where the piano sat in the lobby. The vast hall was decorated with recycled materials: a Christmas tree made out of old green bottles, bunting out of painted paper plates, cane armchairs strewn around, and old tyres holding up glass tabletops. A team of designers had made sure every nook and corner was perfectly decorated, a stunning display of installation art bedecking each of the six floors. Paper Moon straddled the fifth and sixth floors, connected by a staircase much wider than the one in the Bandra store. Leaning over the iron railing, Fiza took in the scene below.

As Noor and the pianist discussed the evening's music schedule, Fiza began replying to the messages that had piled up in her phone since the morning. Early new year wishes from book suppliers, customers and other acquaintances. And a reminder from Marc about his poolside party, which she had completely forgotten about, as usual. Nothing from Iqbal. She wondered if she'd been too cold when they had met that morning. She wondered if she wondered too much when it came to him. There had been no promises. No admissions of undying love. What bothered her was the distance, which could not be helped. So what was the way forward?

'Relationships aren't public transport. They don't have to go anywhere,' Marc declared, digging into a profiterole at the hotel patisserie. 'I'm sure I heard that somewhere. Oh, didn't you once quote it to me? Anyway, it's true!' He had come in to set up the magazine display, his last task at the new store, after which he had walked down to the pastry shop with Fiza. There was something about the moment, the last day of the year, Noor's husky voice rising over the soothing notes of the piano, that made her open up about Iqbal.

'I noticed him at the launch. You never introduced us. I'm glad there's someone who's good enough for Queen Fiza. I went to the engagement party of the season, by the way, and ... oh, boy, what *was* that?' said Marc animatedly.

'What? Why?' Fiza asked with unabashed interest.

'It was like you were the neon sign of doom looming over the happy occasion. Wasn't she your best friend?'

'She is,' Fiza said, protective of Kavya even though their friendship had changed forever.

'About this artist fellow – Fizzy, my love, please stop searching for absolute and complete meaning. You can't impose something like that on people, like a plaque that explains a work of art in a museum.'

'I'm not trying to force any meaning into it,' Fiza replied. 'All I'm saying is, I care too much and have too little of him. But I'm not sure it's fair to ask for more.'

'Good grief. Find yourself a real problem, kitten. I have to get going. See you at ten. Bring the boy. Now go sell some Hugh Prather and Richard Bach to people doing some last-minute soul-shopping. Oh, but this is Colaba. So Gibran and Gurdjieff.'

Fiza stayed back at the table, listening to the music streaming out of the lobby. Noor was now singing '*Paper Moon*' with a rapt quality Fiza hadn't heard in her voice in years.

At about six in the evening, Fiza decided to head back home. She finished the last few pages of the book on the train and called in to check how things were going at the Bandra store. Rosy said it had been a slow day, but people had started streaming in all of a sudden. Fiza decided to head back to her apartment. As usual, she would get in to work early on the first of January. The others could take the morning off.

It had been an eventful year, packing in everything from a foreign trip to a family reunion, an unexpected engagement to even a new store springing up. Fiza suddenly felt exhausted going over it all in her mind. A few years ago, she was like a bit player in her own life. Things had changed dramatically. There was always something on, something that needed *her* attention, *her* involvement. But for the moment, she didn't have the energy to take a single new step. It was New Year's

Eve, and the night demanded celebration. But Fiza, snuggled up in bed with a cup of chai and a book of poems, had called it a day. This was how she would end the year, with her favourite things about her, drifting away well before midnight.

When she woke up the next morning, it was not yet six. Noor hadn't yet returned, and Fiza found she had received a couple of missed calls from her around midnight. Marc had called a few times, too. Still nothing from Iqbal.

It was January 2004. The street outside was desolate. Stray vehicles were making their groggy way back home. Fiza realized she was starving. The last thing she had eaten were a couple of profiteroles with Marc at the pastry shop. She went into the kitchen and put the electric kettle on for some tea, but it seemed like too much work. She changed into a white T-shirt and an old pair of jeans, slipped into her kolhapuris and got into an auto. At that early hour, on the formless first day of the new year, the rickshaw hurtled away, leaving Linking Road, crossing the Bandra post office, turning onto Hill Road, making its way past Elco Arcade, speeding past her school. Then, turning left at the church, it flew past Khoja Florist, past her bookshop, past Mehboob Studio. Then, making a U-turn at the traffic island, it stopped abruptly, just ahead of the bus stop.

Fiza walked into Café Good Luck and sat at a table that looked out onto the street. She asked for a chai, a fried egg and a plate of keema. In a few minutes, the sun burst out of the sky, like the egg yolk on her chipped china plate. The resident tabby cat curled up by her left foot.

An old man in thick glasses hobbled in, newspaper in hand, commenting on the state of the world that morning. 'Musharraf will win confidence vote today. Just see,' he said, referring to the friendly neighbourhood army general-turned-president. 'Kya rakha hai news mein, chacha?' the owner replied genially from the till. 'Aap bun maska enjoy karo.'

Fiza took a long sip of oversweet chai out of the glass and signalled to the waiter for another. Then she picked up her phone and began typing out a message with a faint smile.

ACKNOWLEDGEMENTS

It takes a village to raise a book, so here goes. Thanks are due to my mother, the feisty Nasreen. To my sisters, Kausar and Mariam, the world's greatest support system for everything from heartache to manuscripts. To Balki, Aditi and Deepak, for early encouragement. To Akshay and Sanchia, for invaluable help with the proofs. To Appu, for making the writing of this book a joy. To the generous Khera family and their idyllic mountain home. To Bonita Vaz-Shimray, who lit the spark that became this book, and for her efforts and encouragement at every stage. To Udayan Mitra, for believing in the book and for backing it whole-heartedly. To Prema Govindan, for meticulously – and cheerfully – working on the edits. To Hafiz Uncle, who gave me the chance to run a bookstore all those years ago – the real-life inspiration behind the Paper Moon bookshop. To Ismail, the spirited coconut seller, who allowed me to weave stories around him. And finally, to my niece, Sophie, whose fondness for the book is my biggest reward.

ABOUT THE AUTHOR

Rehana Munir ran a bookshop in Bombay in the mid 2000s, a few years after graduating with top honours in English literature from St. Xavier's College. An independent writer on culture and lifestyle, she has a weekly humour column in *HT Brunch*, and a cinema column in *Arts Illustrated* magazine. She is also an occasional copywriter. Rehana lives in Bombay among food-obsessed family and friends. She is a local expert on migraines, 1990s nostalgia and Old Monk.